Life
in the
Cul-de-Sac

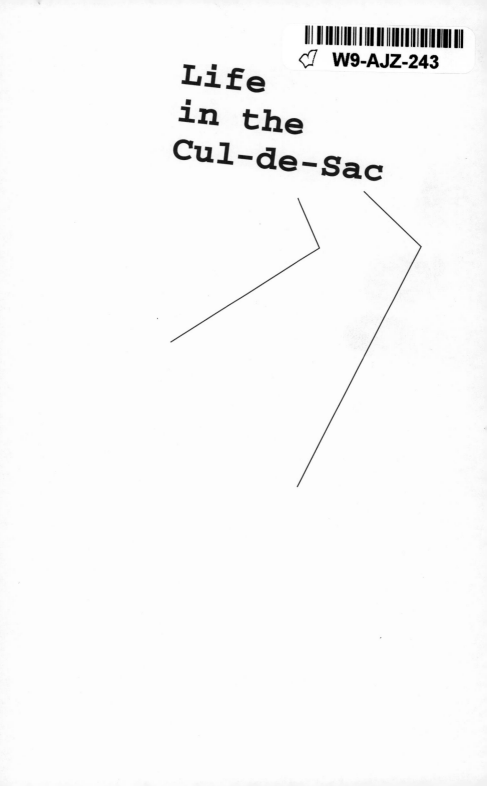

THE ROCK SPRING COLLECTION
OF JAPANESE LITERATURE

Life in the Cul-de-Sac

Senji Kuroi

Translated from
the Japanese by
Philip Gabriel

Stone Bridge Press • *Berkeley, California*

Published by
Stone Bridge Press, P.O. Box 8208, Berkeley, CA 94707
TEL 510-524-8732 • FAX 510-524-8711 • E-MAIL sbp@stonebridge.com

For correspondence, updates, and further information about this
and other Stone Bridge Press books, visit Stone Bridge Press
online at **www.stonebridge.com**.

*Except on the cover, title page, and this copyright page, names of Japanese
persons throughout this work appear according to Japanese convention,
that is, family name first.*

Publication of this translation was assisted by a grant
from the Association for 100 Japanese Books.

Originally published in Japan as *Gunsei* by Senji Kuroi. © 1984 Senji
Kuroi. Original Japanese edition published by Kodansha Co., Ltd.
English translation rights arranged with Senji Kuroi through Japan
Foreign-Rights Centre.

English translation and text © 2001 Philip Gabriel.

Printed in the United States of America.

10 9 8 7 6 5 4 3 2 1   2005 2004 2003 2002 2001

LIBRARY OF CONGRESS CATALOGING-IN-PUBLICATION DATA
Kuroi, Senji, 1932–.
    [Gunsei, English]
    Life in the cul-de-sac / Senji Kuroi; translated from the
Japanese by Philip Gabriel.
        p.   cm.
    ISBN 1-880656-57-4
    I. Gabriel, Philip. II. Title.

PL855.U697 G8613 2001
895.6′35—dc21

                                        2001018396

contents

acknowledgments

I wish to express my gratitude to Mr. Kuroi Senji for allowing me to translate this novel and for answering the many questions I put to him over the course of the translation. Ms. Kurita Akiko helped to arrange translation rights, as well as a subvention from the Association for 100 Japanese Books, for which I am most grateful. My heartfelt thanks go to Mr. Peter Goodman of Stone Bridge Press for recognizing the value of this novel and for his tireless efforts to shepherd the translation into print. Finally, my thanks go to Prof. Kageyama Tsuneo, who introduced me to Kuroi's work, and to whom I dedicate this translation.

P. G.

Life
in the
Cul-de-Sac

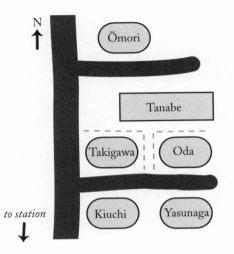

A single road runs north and south, straight through the neighborhood. People walking from the station, which is to the south, might notice a narrow little cul-de-sac off to the right as they pass by.

On its near corner stands the Kiuchi house, with the Takigawas' on the corner opposite. Further back, next to the Kiuchis, is the Yasunagas' residence; next to the Takigawas is the Odas' home.

At the entrance to the cul-de-sac, the Kiuchis and the Takigawas face one another; further in, you find the Yasunagas and the Odas opposite.

Set in the far back, behind the Odas, are the Tanabes.

Within this little neighborhood of families, the story begins with the Oda house, the second one from the corner on the left.

Oda Family
Fusao (husband)
Kiyoko (wife)
Kōichi (son)
Mayu (daughter)

Tanabe Family
Mr. Tanabe
Mrs. Tanabe

Takigawa Family
Takahiko (husband)
Shizuko (wife)

Yasunaga Family
Yūzo (husband)
Masayo (wife)
Tsutomu (son)
Tōru (son)
Yoshiko (Yūzo's mother)

Kiuchi Family
Masaki (husband)
Michiko (wife)

Ōmori Family

the toy room

Silently, the clock struck 7:00.

Choking back a sound, a presence just behind the pendulum moved quietly, but that was all.

They'd replaced the batteries, even hit the side of the encasement, but to no avail. The clock had lost its voice for good.

The sun was supposed to have set at 6:57, but outside it was dark and raining.

In the room, the fluorescent light shone down on the food laid out and lit up the three family members sitting around the dining table.

Fusao was the only one eating the miso-grilled eggplant. The two children wouldn't touch it, claiming the taste made their tongues itch. Miso soup with onion, rice, hamburger steaks with ketchup, and a large bowl of lettuce, tomato, and green asparagus salad rounded out the meal. A plastic bottle of mayonnaise, red capped, stood stolidly next to the salad. The kids just sipped at their water.

Without thinking, Mayu had set out her mother's chopsticks on the table; they lay untouched at one end. The window was slightly open and the sound of a television from the house in back filtered in through the rain.

"They said the rotation of the earth is speeding up." Kōichi put his greasy lips to his cup and swallowed more water.

That cup would have to be scrubbed well when it came time to do the dishes.

"And the rotation speed of the earth is getting slower."

"I don't get it. Which is it?" Sounding as if he didn't care one way or the other, Fusao popped another piece of the miso-coated eggplant into his mouth.

"The earth's rotation was slowing down," Kōichi continued, "but then speeded up. I read about it—the American Naval Observatory discovered it."

"Why the Navy?"

"'Cause its getting slower does something to the moon's gravitational pull on the ocean. Since it has to do with the ocean, the Navy found out."

"Is the gravitational pull getting weaker, then?" Fusao asked.

"No. The rotation speed of the outside of the earth is slower than the inside. But the inside suddenly started moving faster, so the rotation speed is getting faster. Get it?"

"I don't. So, is it getting faster—or slower?" Fusao felt irritated, unable to grasp the logic.

"Faster."

"It's speeding up more than it's slowing down?"

"I guess so." Kōichi twirled the tips of his chopsticks around, then stabbed a slice of tomato.

"What happens if it gets faster?" Mayu set down her rice bowl to grasp her cup with both hands, looking at her brother.

"It'll be night sooner."

Still holding her cup, Mayu glanced uneasily out the window.

"Sooner doesn't mean that much, just a second or so a year," Fusao explained, his tone of voice different, talking to his daughter, than to his son.

"It'd be nice if it got sooner," Mayu answered, but as if rebuffing her father's words. "Then, Mommy would come home sooner."

"That's right," Fusao agreed, swallowing back the spiteful words he wanted to add: *as long as she doesn't catch on.* The earth might very well be speeding up, but if Kiyoko heard about this, you can bet she'd use it to stay out even later.

"D'you know that the cherry tree in Mr. Tanabe's yard is gone?" Kōichi blurted, slurping down more water.

"That's right," Mayu chimed in. "When I got back from school, there was a man, smoking a cigarette, up on a ladder, cutting the tree."

"Dummy. When I got back from school, it was just a stump, and pieces this big were stacked up outside the gate."

"You mean the cherry tree beside his front entrance?" Fusao asked.

"Yes!" the children chorused, looking proudly at their father.

Fusao peered outside through the narrow crack of the open window, checking out the darkened backyard of the house behind them.

"That tree's older than I am," he said. "When I was even smaller than Mayu, it was already blooming."

The Tanabe family's cherry tree blossomed this year, too. And all the feelings Fusao had had as a child came rushing back: the sight of the flowers in full bloom, the cool touch of the white petals he would scoop up from the roadside.

"Why did they have to cut it down?" he asked sharply.

"I don't know. It's their business."

"There's no reason to cut it down, is there? Everything I grew up with is disappearing."

"Daddy, when you were a little kid, did you live in this house?"

Fusao had to smile wryly at the note of sympathy in Kōichi's voice.

"This house was built just before you were born, Kōichi. But when I was a child, I lived on this very spot." Fusao stabbed a finger to the floor. His finger seemed to reach down underneath the floor to the moldy soil below.

"What about Mommy?" Mayu squeezed in.

"I didn't know Mom back then. Mom lived in her house in Setagaya."

"So, what kind of place was this?" Kōichi asked, ignoring his sister.

"It was a big, old house," Fusao replied.

"What happened to it?"

"We tore it down."

"Because it was old and falling apart?"

"No, the house was still fine. The people who lived in it were gone."

"But why tear it down, then?" Kōichi asked. "It's such a waste."

Fusao thought, really, it was too hard to explain to his son all the comings and goings in his father's generation, his grandparents' deaths, and the parceling out of land to the heirs—complicated matters you couldn't expect a child to understand. Instead of answering Kōichi, Fusao looked around from where he sat. The air around him seemed to stir.

"Right here is where the living room of the old house used to be. . . . We had a toy room, too."

Attracted by the drafts crawling along the floor, Fusao's eyes were drawn to the half-opened door leading to the foyer and outside.

"Were there lots of toys?" Pulled in by her father's eyes, Mayu squirmed around.

"Yes, there were. It was a six-mat room, and the whole right side was wooden shelves with my toys and those of your uncle who went to England. It wasn't the children's room, though. . . ."

On the south side, a large bay window had looked out on the lawn, no, not a bay window, really, but a sort of narrow wooden shelf with a handrail running along the edge. A black Singer sewing machine stood in front of the window. Was it his mother's room? But the image that came to Fusao was not his mother's but his grandmother's back as she pedaled the sewing machine treadle while she sewed up white cloth. Maybe it was his grandmother's room? Outside the window stood a persimmon tree; its trunk grew slanted and invited easy climbing. In the fall, sweet red fruit clustered at the tips of the branches.

"That's it. Where the front door is now. That's where the toy room used to be."

Fusao's voice grew louder. He turned in his chair to face the entrance. In his mind's eye, he could see in the dark shadows beyond the open, living-room door, another room with a wonderful view of the world outside, brimming with the light reflected from the persimmon tree's pale green leaves.

"You want to go?" Abruptly, Fusao put down his chopsticks and stood up. Mayu scrambled down from her chair and grasped her father's hand.

"Where?" Kōichi, his mouth full of the last bit of hamburger, looked up at his father.

"To the toy room." Mayu answered firmly in her father's stead. Her hand clasped his with uncommon strength. Still chewing, Kōichi got up to join them.

Only one remnant remained from the old house—the square stepping-stones half hidden in the dirt running along the north wall, separating their house from the Tanabes'. Not fancy enough to be called flagstones, the stepping-stones had lined the corridor connecting the rear entrance and the backdoor of the kitchen. People living in the house usually left the kitchen by going around to the south side, over the lawn, which made the corridor seldom used. But when Fusao's friends or cousins came over, that was where they often played. The stones jutted further up from the ground then. Fusao remembered tripping in his geta once and falling against the edge of another stone, badly gashing his lip. And when he was scolded for unlatching the kitchen door from its thick nail hook and leaving the door open, he'd scamper down the back corridor.

Even after the old home had been torn down and the empty lot became overgrown with weeds, the stones stayed. A few more years passed, and Fusao's family built a small house on one portion of the property. Even after all this time, the square stones still lay in place; using them as a guide, he could figure out the layout of the old house. Fusao had understood this for a long time and wondered why it was only now that he felt so determined to work out how all the old rooms had been arranged.

Fusao imagined the stepping-stones back then, wet now in the rain. Revived, his vision urged him on. He could sense the dark corridor on the north side of the old house, the damp bathroom, the strange-smelling storeroom. The memories all reappeared and seemed to begin to move about from beneath the house. Under the dining room-kitchen area, where the table was now, lay the old sitting room with its sunken hibachi. Indeed, the toy room—to the southeast of the sitting room, which extended out a bit into the garden—must be where their present foyer is. Much smaller than the toy room, the foyer occupied only the front part of the old toy room.

"Straight ahead, there was a shoji screen, 'cause it was a corridor with a southern exposure." Fusao walked slowly into the living room, pointing with his right hand, the one Mayu wasn't holding. Her eyes wide open, Mayu nodded.

"You didn't go out into the corridor but through the door here. . . . Hold on a sec. . . ."

Fusao walked to the center of the living room, right below the fluorescent light, deliberately turning ninety degrees to the left and halted. Kōichi tiptoed closer.

"There was a glass door, I think, separating it right about here. That would make the toy room just about . . ."

But the old sitting room, of course, had been a tatami room, so there wouldn't have been a glass door between it and the toy room. For a second, Fusao was surprised at the momentary illusion. Underneath the south-facing window of the toy room was a small, varnished, Western-style section of floor. That was where the sewing machine had been. That spot must have been the brightest in the house.

"I'm so stupid. This had to have been a shoji screen."

The thin, tall frame of a shoji, not a glass door, stood before him. For some reason, the doors and shoji of the old house were shut tight.

With his slippered foot, Fusao pushed the door leading from the living room to the foyer, then gently slid open the invisible shoji. A large, unexpected object lay at his feet; neither lying down nor crouching, it lay prostrate on the floor, strangely contorted.

"This is the spot where Grandfather collapsed. . . ."

Grandfather, dressed in khaki trousers and a white, collarless, long-sleeve shirt—his usual attire when he worked in the garden—lay there, trying feebly to raise himself.

"What's the matter?"

Fusao had stopped suddenly, and Mayu tugged at his arm.

"Grandfather died in the toy room," Fusao said.

"He died here?"

Kōichi reached out from behind to grab Fusao's other arm.

Why was Grandfather trying to go into the toy room? Grandmother, a pretty stylish lady, Fusao realized only years later, often sat in the toy room at her sewing machine, but Grandfather hardly ever went in there. If Grandmother had been sewing, she would have noticed him right away; the room must have been empty. Maybe Grandfather wanted to play there all by himself.

The corpse was laid out on a futon in the toy room for the wake. Grandfather's head was near the window, so it was facing the wrong way, south, not north as custom dictated. If you were to spread out a futon here now, half of it would cover the concrete floor of the foyer.

"Turn on the light! Now!" Mayu yelled, clinging to Fusao's arm. The murky light from the living room threw an indistinct shadow of the three of them onto the floor.

"Wait a second. It's OK."

Fusao pushed his arm down, restraining his daughter. If the light were turned on now, the toy room would vanish into thin air, leaving behind only a foyer with children's shoes scattered about.

I spent the night with Grandpa, to say good-bye to him.

His grandmother's words the next day stayed with Fusao. He found it strange that she didn't feel creepy lying next to Grandfather, the roof of his palate showing through his wide-open mouth.

From outside, the streetlights shone in through the aventurine window glass casting a heavy shadow of the leaves of the rain-dappled plum tree inside the front room.

"So, whenever we come into our house or go out," Fusao said, "we're passing through the toy room."

"And right next to Grandpa." Stepping as if to avoid something, Mayu grabbed Fusao's arm and twisted away.

"No, he was *my* grandfather; he was your *great*-grandfather, whom you never knew."

"Was he sick?" Kōichi's voice asked boyishly as he let go of Fusao's hand.

"It must have been a stroke." Mother had told him to run to the neighborhood clinic for a doctor. He was about as old as Kōichi was now.

"Let's go." Mayu tugged her father's hand to get him to go back to the living room.

"If you go this way, there's a long hallway."

"No, there isn't. There's nothing there," Mayu shot back, dead earnest, but even so she looked around to check. The white wall of the living room stood, blocking the way.

"The hallway ran all the way to Mr. Takigawa's house on the corner."

"Must have been pretty big." Kōichi stared beyond the wall. His eyes seemed to be imagining how he could, if he wanted, saunter right into their neighbor's house. Fusao watched his son, thinking he'd have to warn him if he started to run down the hallway, past the drawing room, the guest bathroom, to the end where the sitting room used to be.

The latch on the gate outside clicked quietly open.

"It's Mommy!" She looked up wonderingly at Fusao, who slowly shook his head. "Well, then, who?" Mayu asked her father, who stood listening carefully. She dug her fingernails into his palm.

Piercingly, the door chime rang in the empty kitchen.

"Don't open it yet," Kōichi whispered to his father.

Fusao fumbled for the switch, stepping down into a pair of sandals in the entrance.

"Who is it?"

"Sorry to bother you so late. It's Tanabe from the house in back."

On the other side of the wooden door, Fusao could feel him fidgeting. He unlatched the chain to open the door. A small, old man stood there, folding up an umbrella, a bunch of white hydrangeas hanging down in one hand.

"I meant to come over earlier, but now look at the time," he apologized. The old man thrust the flowers forward, just cut from his garden, he explained. Raindrops on the blossoms caught the light and sparkled luminously.

"I'm rebuilding my house," Mr. Tanabe said, one hand behind him still clutching the doorknob. "If the weather clears up, the workmen will be over tomorrow to start work; I know it'll be inconvenient for all of you; I thought I'd better come over tonight to let you know." He spoke in a rush of words, punctuated by an occasional sniff and snort, deep in his throat.

"So, is that why you cut down the cherry tree?" Fusao inquired.

"I'm thinking of making some rooms on the second floor that I can rent out to young people."

"The flowers on it were gorgeous. It's a real shame."

"Yes, but it had worms, you know. The tree and the house were getting too old. The people who live there, as well." The old man sniffed again.

"Your house is the only one left on the street from when I was a kid. The last of the quiet, old homes."

A feeling of helplessness swept over Fusao as if the Tanabes' house, just discernible through the leaves to the north of their house, had already vanished, leaving behind only the night.

"That's right," Mr. Tanabe replied. "My house was built

around the same time as your original home. Nearly sixty years ago. But, of course, yours was much bigger and grander than mine."

The old man pointed a stubby index finger upward, moving it from right to left as if tracing the shadow of a form.

"'Cause the east side of your house was just in front of where the wall is now, wasn't it?"

Pushing open the door suddenly, the old man tipped the point of his umbrella at the cinder-block wall, palely visible in the gloom. "Wait a second," he muttered, stepping back, his eyes searching out a memory. "No, that's not right. The gate to your old house was right about where the Kiuchis have their garage. . . ."

He tottered out into the rain. A small sound clicked near his hand, and, swiftly, black wings spread over him. He skipped a few steps out into the rain, whose streaks showed clearly against the porch light. He held the umbrella up high, muttering beneath it.

"Here it is. You remember, don't you?"

The old man's sharp voice reached Fusao, who stood there, vaguely, watching him.

"Come on out! It's your house I'm talking about!"

Propelled by the sudden change in the old man's voice, Fusao stepped out into the rain in his sandals. He gestured to the children to stay inside because they'd get wet, but they hurriedly searched for their shoes anyway.

"From my verandah, you could see the lights of your guest house. Come on, stand right here."

Craning to see the lights of his own home, the old man took Fusao's hand and led him to the hedge. His palm felt rough and dry but strangely warm. Fusao noticed for the first time that the old man had on rubber boots. It was this way, he insisted, childishly pointing, stretching one hand out in front of him from where he had made Fusao stand. Mr. Tanabe started walking off, but before he did, he shoved the umbrella at Fusao. Its smooth handle felt faintly warm, as if it were alive.

"If this was the hallway that ran north and south, then you

turn there and end up where the guest house was, right over here."

The rain fell even harder, pelting the old man. Immediately in front of the concrete wall, he stomped the ground with the heel of his boot.

"It sure made a loud sound. A very loud sound."

As if to rise above the sound resounding in the darkness, the old man's phlegmy voice rose a notch. With nothing to reverberate against it, his voice echoed here and there in the dark garden.

"Your Grandma was trying to put up the sliding shutters in the guest house when she had a seizure and fell down, into the garden, shutters and all."

The old man lifted up his hands to send the grandmother crashing to the ground. The rain, starting to puddle, made the depression where she'd fallen glimmer.

"It was a quiet night. Later on, we talked about how maybe her husband had called her from the other side."

The old man's voice weakened. Fusao approached, proffering the umbrella. From the front door, two shadows watched them, unmoving.

"There was a well just over there."

Fusao was about to go back to where the children were when the old man grabbed at his sleeve. He trotted off toward the back of the house. Fusao motioned to Kōichi and Mayu to go inside, then set off after him. The old man was squatting down below the frosted pane of glass at the top of the door to the kitchen, a cluster of strongly fragrant, white perennials surrounding him.

Slowly, as if he were hugging a huge tree, the old man brought his arms together in a circle and linked his fingers together. He looked momentarily confused about where to place the heavy circle that appeared before him. Positioning it from one side to the other, he let the circle drop for a while, resting it above the wet ground, next to the flowers. Finally, full of confidence now, he raised his arms, lifting as if to push forcefully through the kitchen door.

"You built your house on top of the well."

Rebuffed by the door, the old man, still half crouching, turned, looking up at Fusao, surprised. Diagonally behind him, the square stepping-stones peeked out from the surface of the ground.

"Hmm . . . you could be right," Fusao said. "I seem to remember the carpenter saying he wanted to keep the well hole to convert it into a sewage drain."

"Yep. This is right over the well. What a shame."

Giving a throaty snort and a disgusted look, the old man stood up. Lightly, he let the circle of his arms fall apart and wiped the mud off his hands. Fusao thought he heard a far-off, deep echo underground.

He'd completely forgotten about the well. Next to the pump, there'd been a weathered grey board covering it up; naturally, he never gave much thought to the idea that a deep hole dug out of the earth was there. In the summer whenever they had bought a watermelon and wanted to chill it, they'd remove the wooden cover and lower the watermelon down in a bucket attached to a long rope. Just a rough board and a little roof. Fusao was always amazed that a deep hole was hidden there.

"How are your parents doing?" The old man suddenly spoke and reached out for the umbrella Fusao was holding.

"They're fine, thanks. Sometimes, I ask them if they'd like to live with us, but they seem to be comfortable where they are."

"It's wonderful they can still manage on their own. Anyway, tell them I said hello."

That said, he quickly turned and hurried away.

Fusao leaped back under the eaves of the front door where the children stood; they seemed about to speak up but he held his hand out to stop them, listening carefully. Beyond the rain, he could hear the wet squeak of the lattice door shutting in the house behind theirs.

"He's gone. . . ." Fusao said quietly and urged the children inside. Undaunted by the goings on about the layout of the old house, the kids scampered off as fast as two little animals, straight to the living room.

When the sound of their TV filled his ears, Fusao closed his eyes. The toy room—a bright room where his son, daughter, and wife were absent—steadily took shape around him. He squatted down on the tatami, breathing lightly, as a child does. Fusao was the one who always got scolded because his shelf space was a mess. His brother's little treasures stayed neatly lined up in their boxes and cans, all arranged by size. But on Fusao's shelf, his little tin cars stuck their rear ends out; blocks were piled up haphazardly, ready to fall off at any moment; his game boxes and picture books were all shoved together. Rarely could he find a toy he was looking for the first time. Whenever he tugged his cloth gloves out from where they lay in the back of the shelf, toys would tumble, the lid would fly off his can of marbles, and they'd all roll around the tatami. Impatiently, Fusao would pick them up, heedlessly cramming them back in.

Searching for where the bottom of the shelf had been, his hand touched—not finely woven tatami—but rough concrete. His fingertips brushed against the canvas shoes Kōichi had thrown aside, sending a bicycle pump clattering to the floor.

"What's going on?" Kōichi yelled out.

Fusao stood up, closed the shoji heavily, and left the toy room.

There's a well underneath the kitchen. He couldn't shake Mr. Tanabe's words. He put on the rubber kitchen gloves, hating how they felt, as if he were sticking his fingers inside someone else's hands, and began washing up the dishes. Still, he couldn't get the kitchen door, which normally remained unused and locked, out of his mind. Underneath the plywood parquet floor, softly shining in the fluorescent light, was a hole, a very deep hole. He remembered thinking that the idea of converting the well, which hadn't been used for a long time and had dried up, into a sewage drain had made a lot of sense. But because he hadn't seen the actual construction himself, he didn't know what condition the old well was left in. Until the old man mentioned it, he'd never thought about the well that lay under their kitchen floor.

Fusao finished the dishes and crouched down again on the floor beside the pillar where he'd hung up the dish cloth. Before him, the kitchen door, thin with its long, narrow pane of frosted glass on top, was shut. Even now, he sensed the old man outside, moving around, his heavy arms in a circle. If the door hadn't gotten in the way, Mr. Tanabe might well have placed his circle right here on the floor. Or perhaps most of it, with just a small portion sticking outside.

Fusao made a fist, lightly tapping the floor. The plywood parquet gave off a slightly different sound, depending on where it was knocked. A hard dry sound meant it was solid underneath; a soft echo meant a cavity. But this only showed where the joists were, not whether a hole was there or not. Still, Fusao couldn't keep from tapping the floorboards. Now hard, now softly, listening carefully to the different sounds, he marked out invisible signs with the invisible chalk in his hand. Finally, the marks took on a vague outline; the more he tapped, the more the dots connected into a smooth curve, with a clear, white circle forming just above the kitchen floor. . . .

"What are you doing?"

A tiny, pink slipper approached the edge of his white circle.

"Watch out! Step back!" Fusao shouted, his fingertips grazing the tips of Mayu's feet. Then the floorboards gave way in the shape of the white outline and, with a hearty laugh, fell into the dark depths. First, a sharp clang as if metal sheets were banging together echoed in the deep, then he heard water splashing, as if the sides of the walls had followed and plunged down the well.

A black hole gaped in one corner of the kitchen. Drawing his face close, he could feel the slightly moist air quietly rising up from the deep underground. Fusao grasped the glass toothpick holder from the top of the table, held it out right over the hole, and let go. *One, two, three*, he counted, the time it took to be sucked up by the hole and the splash of water to come back, the same sound he used to hear when, making sure no one was watching, he and his older brother lifted off the discolored board covering the well and dropped in pebbles. His brother taught him that the time between the release of the pebble and the splash told you how deep the well was. Fusao felt distinctly that a weird creature, colorless and shapeless, lived in the well and swallowed the pebbles.

He was seized by a strong desire to throw everything into the hole—cups, knives, rice bowls, vegetables, pans, bottles—anything he could lay his hands on. He raised his body.

"There's a well here. It's a deep hole with water in the bottom. If you fell in, you'd be a goner, so be careful."

Mayu, leaning against the refrigerator, nodded incredulously. "Where? Here?"

Bending forward but away from the edge, fearfully she slid one pink-slippered foot forward.

"Not there. It's a round hole, right in front of the door."

Kneeling on the floor, Fusao slowly traced the well hole.

"Kōichi!" Mayu suddenly shouted toward the living room. "There's a deep hole here!"

"It's OK here, right? And here, too?" Mayu asked, easing sideways around the lip of the well, dragging one slipper, then the other.

"There isn't much space near the door," Fusao warned. Then he saw that it was too dangerous to go any further and held her back.

"How do you know it's here?" Kōichi asked, one hand resting on the table. He leaned forward a little and gazed at the spot next to Mayu's feet.

"Old Mr. Tanabe told me. I'm checking it out."

"How deep is it?"

"About as much as the two-story house next door."

"So, two stories underground, then," Kōichi figured, and returned to the living room to watch TV.

Mayu completed about one circuit of the hole, ending up back in front of the door. *Wow!* she sighed. *That's deep!*

* * * * *

With the kids asleep, the house was still. Tucked into the beds along with the children were the spaces they had occupied while awake: gaps opened up here and there in the rooms. Seeking to fill those gaps was another house, slowly seeping up through the floorboards.

Fusao stood beside the refrigerator, grasping its long, shiny, metal handle. The pump beside the well hole began to move in time to the motion of his arm. He pushed down hard on the handle, which came up above eye level. His arm felt the handle's resistance, and the water trapped by the bulb tumbled out of the mouth of the pump. So the kitchen floor wouldn't get wet, Fusao hurriedly raised the lever at the base of the pipe attached to the body of the pump. Now the water didn't come out of the pump mouth but ran along the pipe into the tank, set near the ceiling. Each time he pumped to draw up water, a moment later he heard water gushing into the tank. On bath days, pumping all the necessary water was quite a job. Turning the faucet on above the old-fashioned metal bathtub in the dark bathroom, then facing the bath furnace, which was out of sight, they had had to pump and pump the water from the well. At first the job was his mother's, then his brother's, and finally his. Fun, at first, the chore soon turned monotonous. The only small comfort was the sound of the water filling up the tub. The pump in his hand grew hot, and his arm and shoulder warmed. But still the bathtub was only half full. Gazing steadily at the black knobs on the gas range next to the refrigerator, Fusao pumped the well harder. As he did, the well handle grew longer, his exertions more pronounced. Blood coursed through his out-of-shape body, he panted, and exhaustion overtook him.

A wavering light coming in through the frosted window above the kitchen sink brought Fusao's movements to a halt. The light was weaker than usual from the house in back. Shoulders heaving, Fusao leaned forward, toward the window. The light brushed in again and slipped sideways, disappearing then re-appearing. Twigs crunched in the quietly falling rain, and the light—a flashlight, he realized—flickered through the trees in the Tanabes' garden. Fusao slowly eased the window open and gazed outside into the rain. *So it's about here. Turn a bit to the north . . .* The voice of old Mr. Tanabe could be heard. *Can't you do it tomorrow? It's raining . . . ,* a woman called out from far away. No answer, just the sound of footsteps on the ground, turning to the right. *So it was about six meters from the fence . . .* The incomprehensible muttering continued for a while, with the sound of someone walking around. Finally, the light from in-between the bushes disappeared, leaving only the sound of the rain.

The old man had finally given up and gone inside, Fusao concluded, drawing back from the window. But then the light beamed in full on the glass in front of him, slowly climbing up to the roof.

You've got your wood, your mortar, your fireproofing . . . The old man's singsong voice suddenly boomed near Fusao. Mr. Tanabe was shining his flashlight from between the old hedge. Feeling as if he'd been caught red-handed, Fusao slunk down below the sink. He could feel the vibrations of the old man's footsteps through the floorboards; soon, they faded. His footsteps were hesitant, unlike when he had shined the light on the house.

* * * * *

Soundlessly, the clock struck 11:00; a key slipped quietly into the front door. The chain on the door rattled impudently. The key turned pointlessly in the lock.

Fusao unfastened the chain, and outside stood Kiyoko, her whole body glistening with raindrops.

"You should have called. I could have taken an umbrella to the station," Fusao said, glancing over at the invisible guesthouse around which the old man's boots had left their mark. The rain water was beginning to form streamlets on the ground. He couldn't quite make out the depression where his grandmother had fallen.

"I went out on my own. I couldn't make you do that." Kiyoko and the moist night air came in together. She closed the door, looking up, shaking out her wet hair.

"Was dinner all right?" she asked.

"Yes, it was really good."

"Did Mayu go to sleep on time?"

"Yeah. Oh, I showed her around the old house that used to be here."

"The old house?"

Kiyoko looked up at the clock on the wall, then eyed her husband dubiously.

"The old house that was here before we built this one."

"I don't know anything about that," Kiyoko said from inside her black dress as she slipped it off, sounding as if she didn't want to know, either.

"That's why I wanted to tell the kids about it. Like, for instance, the sitting room that used to be here—"

"Where did these flowers come from?" Kiyoko interrupted, spying the white hydrangeas lying tossed in a plastic tub in the sink. Fusao turned his gaze from the black borders of the tatami in the old sitting room, the one with the long hibachi, to his wife.

"Old Mr. Tanabe brought them over. He dropped by to tell us about the rebuilding he's going to do."

"Rebuilding? The house behind us? That's going to be pretty noisy, with trucks coming and going."

"It means that the last old house on the block will be gone."

Kiyoko was down to her blouse and slip. She sat down at her dressing mirror, before her was her row of cosmetics. Kiyoko examined the label of a large jar of cleansing cream and sighed. "They're going to build a new house, but I wonder how many more years Mr. and Mrs. Tanabe think they're going to live."

"Kōichi said the earth's revolution is speeding up."

"Well, that means they'll have even less time, doesn't it,"

Kiyoko said, striding over to the bathroom sink. Fusao was about to tell her what Mayu had said during dinner when they discussed this but kept quiet.

"Maybe we should think about building an addition to our house," Kiyoko blurted, while she splashed water on her face.

"Where?"

"If we extended the house to the outside wall of the foyer, even to the front door, we could fit in another room."

In Fusao's mind, he saw the black ground the old man had stomped his heel on. That's the guest house. To go from the toy room to the guest house, you turned at the L-shaped hallway on the east side. . . .

"Pretty soon, we'll need an extra room for the children," Kiyoko said. Her back, and the white blouse, leaned toward the sink, shaking slightly as she washed up.

"I have a feeling they'll be around for awhile," Fusao murmured, half to himself.

"They say it's a good idea for boys and girls to have separate rooms." From behind her towel, makeup gone, Kiyoko's new face emerged.

passersby

Turn the corner, and there's a line of streetlights.

Like thin, infant arms reaching out, angled high up in the poles, the lights gave off a pallid light. The poles lined up neatly, running at regular intervals, along one side of the deserted street. As one lamp begins to fade, falling, the next one rushes over to lift its companion from the ground. Seen from a distance, gloom seems to float up in the valley between the lights; but close up, the darkness, heavy enough to conceal a person, visibly recedes.

"I knew we should have gone in there," Hiroshi muttered, the words peeling off one by one from his parched throat. "Hello! . . . I am speaking here, you know."

Mariko walked on, obliviously. She halted suddenly right beneath the lights, now so bright that she could read a paperback book.

"Everywhere you go in Japan, it's streetlights," Hiroshi said.

"Listen—can you hear it?"

"You keep standing there, you're going to get a sunburn."

"It's moaning." Mariko patted the thick thigh of the light pole.

"'Cause electricity's flowing through it."

"Inside the pole?"

"Hey, don't look at me."

"*Let me out . . . let me out . . .*" Mariko dangled her largish, wet tongue out of her mouth, its tip, thick and pointed. Hiroshi's fingers darted out to make a grab for it.

"Idiot."

"But it's mine."

Hiroshi loudly tried to suck her tongue into his mouth. Mariko broke free and walked on. The whites of her eyes shone.

"If I gave it to you," she said, "then I wouldn't be able to talk."

"I'd still understand you."

"But I couldn't eat."

"I'd eat for you."

"____"

Slowly, they crossed over from the edge of one light to the next.

"Those yellow letters on the roof bothered me," she said.

"You're not supposed to look at neon signs."

"I felt like it was staring at me."

"Then, you should just ignore it."

"I just—hate that kind of place."

"I bet you wouldn't mind if you were with someone you liked more than me." Hiroshi spoke drily and grabbed Mariko's hand. Her palm felt damp, as if everything inside her were concentrated in it. Mariko spread her fingers, intertwining hers with his.

The next streetlight loomed above them. A clump of dead insects at the armpit of the stretched-out infant's arm looked like a child's underarm hair.

In the quiet road, water gurgled faintly below them.

"Someone's going to the bathroom," Hiroshi said.

A manhole cover lay under the dim shadow that the two of them cast. Small, yet under the lid the rush of water could be heard running ceaselessly beneath.

"Now, that's what I'd call a major leak."

Leaning forward, Hiroshi playfully pretended to pull an invisible chain at shoulder height. Mariko wrinkled up her nose, laughing soundlessly. Her white sandals trod on the sound of the water and walked over the iron cover.

"In the bath, use Bath Clean!"

"What?"

"Over there." At the corner, an ad for a bubble-bath liquid was draped around the neck of a red fire hydrant.

"Oh, so that was *Bath Clean* flowing under there."

"Or Emeron Shampoo."

"I go for Tonic Shampoo myself, the heavy-duty kind." Hiroshi's voice had lost its rough edge.

"Do you have a bath in your dorm?" Mariko asked.

"'Til 10:00 P.M."

"So, it's too late."

"I can always take a shower."

They passed the brightly lit corner and continued down the deserted block, where the lights—those peevish, shiny children's arms—again lined one side of the road. The houses were different here, with hedges and cinder-block walls stretching out on both sides. Under the street lamps, the overgrown cedar hedges, dyed a thick green, were undulating in thick, enticing shadows.

"What a lot of big houses," Mariko's voice said, low and indistinctly.

"Not really," Hiroshi challenged her, pointing at three or four small, neat homes crowded together where the long wall ended.

"Well, what d'you know—Mr. Kiuchi."

"Who?"

"My math teacher in high school had the same name," Mariko explained.

"Why'd you bring that up?"

"That nameplate over there."

At the end of the hedge was a low cinder-block wall; above the mailbox was an inlaid, ceramic nameplate.

"He got married to one of his students, a year older than us."

"Takes all kinds," Hiroshi said.

"He used to drive a sports coupe."

Behind a small black gate, a cream-colored car crouched, as if blocking the front door.

"Oh, look at this. This one's my section chief," Mariko said.

"You're kidding."

"See, it says Takigawa."

"Must be a real pain."

"Every time he phones his wife, you wouldn't believe how polite he is."

"Henpecked, for sure."

"Makes you wonder who he's talking to."

"Does he have any kids?" Hiroshi asked.

"A bunch. Four."

"A real tiger, eh?" An affected laugh rolled around in Hiroshi's throat.

"He sure is," Mariko's voice answered; suddenly, she strode away. "What's going on here?" she asked.

Seemingly, a dark pond had opened up between the houses. An empty space, bereft of trees, lay sunken behind a hedge. To one side was the frame of a house with only the roof completed.

"Looks like they're building a house," Hiroshi muttered disinterestedly.

"It's big. Must be 300 square meters at least."

The hedge over here was not the cedar variety they'd just passed. Mariko pinched a hard, pointed leaf between her fingers and tiptoed up to peer over.

"Dummy," Hiroshi said. "It's at least 900 square meters. Maybe up to 1,200."

"Must be pretty rich."

"Gotta be some wrinkled old geezer. They're the only ones who can afford this much land and build a huge two-story house on it."

Hiroshi started off, pulling Mariko by the hand, but she resisted, staying rooted to the spot. She craned her neck up over the hedge, as if to breathe in as much as she could of the clear air that gathered over the dark and silent vacant lot.

"If they told you, you could have this house, what would you do?" Mariko peeked inside, her voice moist in the evening air.

"I'd sell it right away and open up a little snack bar somewhere."

"But wouldn't it be nice to live here for three or four days?"

"_____"

"Sleeping on a big sofa and everything?"

Hiroshi gave up urging her to move on; suddenly, he was pulled himself toward the hedge. Standing next to Mariko, he stared fixedly at the half-built house.

"You want to go in?" Hot, heavy words escaped his throat.

"Where?"

"Come on."

Hiroshi yanked Mariko's hand, and they walked alongside the hedge. Two stone pillars stood in place, nearly covered by the broad leaves of the hedge. Two ropes stretched across, between the pillars, and several sheets of plywood leaned on them, blocking the opening.

"Good evening, Mr. Tanabe." Glancing at the nameplate on the pillar, Hiroshi addressed the crack between the plywood sheets.

"You're going inside?" Mariko sounded frightened.

"It says here that all deliveries should be taken to the Odas' house. Must get a lot of presents."

The note was written in felt pen on a piece of cardboard that dangled from a string just below the nameplate; Hiroshi's voice was droll as he read the words in the light of the street lamp.

"But what if someone's inside?"

"Good evening!" Ignoring her question, Hiroshi did a karate chop in the direction of the rope and carefully slid a sheet of plywood off to one side.

"Well, it's been a long time. Sorry I haven't gotten in touch. Let me introduce . . . Mariko. Go ahead, say hello."

Hiroshi lifted the plywood board above the ropes and to one side. He turned to Mariko.

"We could get in trouble," she said, "going in without permission."

"That's why I said to hurry up and say hello."

"But I don't think we . . ." Hesitating, Mariko twisted her neck as if she were a little kid looking in the street, then nodded, tentatively, a greeting to the gloom that lay behind where the board had been. Hiroshi stuck one foot between the ropes, bent down, and slipped through, then lifted up the top one and beckoned to Mariko. She clutched her shoulder bag to her side, nervously slipped in headfirst between the ropes, and found herself standing in a garden. Hiroshi quickly slid the plywood back in place to cover up the opening.

"But we're not going to stay very long. . . ."

"Make sure you close the door behind you—old Mr. Tanabe's pretty particular about that."

Hiroshi rubbed the dirt off his palms, gazing up at the half-built, two-story house to his left. Once inside the hedge, the house—only pillars and a roof, basically—towered against the night sky. In the wide space opposite the frame, a tarp covered what looked to be a pile of lumber. Beyond the dark hedge lay the exposed side of the roof of the house they'd just passed. From the road you couldn't tell, but inside, now, he could see that there were two houses lined up along the hedge. The house on the corner facing the road was the Takigawas', so perhaps the one further along in the alley was the Odas', the name mentioned on the piece of cardboard.

"This is nice—it's so spacious." Mariko stood on the bare, flat ground, about to glance skyward when her hand was roughly pulled.

"Where are you going?" she asked.

"To the Tanabes'."

Hiroshi strode toward the house, its perimeter surrounded by metal-pipe scaffolding. Below the large roof appeared a smaller, separate one. When he reached the protruding cement foundation, he stopped.

"Good evenin' . . . ," Hiroshi called out into the house, his voice husky again, its sound crawling along the bottom of the frame with its pillars and open ceiling rising upward.

"Aren't they going to say we're trespassing?"

"Who?"

"Well, Mr. Tanabe for one."

"We gave a proper greeting, didn't we? Look—here's old Mr. Tanabe now."

Hiroshi ducked under the scaffolding pipes to stand astride the foundation framing under the roof.

"Looks like it's going to be a wonderful house. Mind if we take a look?"

The dimly lit pillars listened in silence.

"Uh, no slippers for us, thanks. We'll keep our shoes on. I promise we won't get anything dirty."

Paper wrapped around one of the inside pillars was ripped off from the top and hung down.

"Sorry to bother you so late. We were going to another place tonight, but things didn't work out . . ."

Beams firmly gouging the pillars cut across the open space above. "Hey, look." Hiroshi motioned to Mariko, who still stood outside. Timidly, she extended her hand to him and he yanked her closer. Her denim skirt spread wide as she stepped over the foundation frame. A manly arm encircled her waist. Unexpectedly, the wind did not flow in freely from the outdoors; once inside, under the roof, a homey darkness, redolent of wood, settled over them.

"He told us to come all the way in."

Tugging at his partner's waist, Hiroshi straddled the lumber bolted down on the concrete that formed a partition and moved further inside. He slipped, encountering an obstruction at his feet, and lurched off balance. A faint metallic noise emanated from what looked like a wooden box. A large, squarish-shaped room lay in front of them. On the floor, flat square sections of concrete lay at regular intervals. Passing over the edge of these slabs of concrete stepping-stones, Hiroshi and Mariko again stepped over the frame surrounding the foundation to enter an adjoining room, which was long and narrow. The ground here seemed a bit more finished. Adjacent was a larger room, depressed in one corner. To the left was a tiny unpartitioned space that might be a hallway and at its end was a smaller room. Here, well within the house, which up 'til then had had only pillars but no walls, suddenly appeared a three-sided pile of blocks rising from the foundation to about eye level.

"Hey, this is the bedroom," Hiroshi said. Standing before the partition, he nodded in satisfaction.

"Isn't it the bath?" Mariko whispered breathlessly.

"It's OK. That's what Mr. Tanabe told me."

"It's so dark."

"Bedrooms are better that way."

So saying, Hiroshi climbed up lightly on the room divider, poised to leap outside the house. Flustered, wondering where he could be going, Mariko was about to follow, when his shadowy figure motioned her to stay put. In a moment, Hiroshi soon returned from the back of the house, lugging a sheet of plywood, nimbly passing it under the scaffolding, slipping past the pillars, and arriving back in the room.

"What're you going to do with the board?" Mariko asked uneasily.

"The bed's arrived. Step aside for a second, OK?"

In the small room, Hiroshi fumbled at the bits of wood and pieces of roof tile on the ground, throwing them aside; after diligently smoothing the ground, he carefully set the plywood board down.

"You want to do it here?" Mariko asked.

"There's no yellow neon sign on the roof, right?"

Faintly, in the darkness, she could see a white cloth wiping the board.

"Yes, but—"

Cut short, her words stopped as her lips were sucked in by another pair. For an instant, the darkness of the bedroom swelled up. Only their breathing seemed alive.

"Take off your shoes," Hiroshi told her.

Their stocking feet on the board-cum-bed padded about, quietly, gently rippling over the entire board and out into the darkness.

"I wonder if Mr. Tanabe can see us."

"He's asleep already."

Their voices, blending with the odor of their bodies, floated up in the darkened room, hovering. On one side, where there had been nothing, bit by bit, a new, heated wall formed. Its surface grew slippery with the sweat seeping out, glistening like wet ceramic. Hiroshi's fingers fumbled over Mariko. A warmth and dampness new to the half-built house responded to his touch. The thick tongue he'd been unable to grab on the night road before now filled his mouth. Hiroshi's belt buckle jangled slightly under Mariko's fingers, and he could feel cotton cloth being pulled down along his slightly rough skin.

"What do you think you're doing there?"

From above the block wall, suddenly, a voice fell on the tangled bodies of the two lovers. Hiroshi had just entered Mariko, and she clung to him. Hiroshi leaned up on one elbow on their bed, flustered, groping for his clothes in the dark. His hand touched only their exposed, helpless skin.

"What's wrong, Tatchan? Come here."

A sugary, high-pitched voice filtered in between the pillars into the house. The air shivered in confusion, finally releasing its breath silently. Hiroshi's hand finally came upon the cotton material at his feet.

"Come on, Tatchan. I'm going to close the door. Time for beddy-bye."

The sticky voice belonged to an unseen figure of an old woman, who moved behind the wall. A dry cry followed her.

"A cat . . . ," the odor that was Mariko said. From somewhere, a loud rattle of a glass door banging shut could be heard.

"Damn it. Scaring us like that." Hiroshi pushed the clothes he'd been clutching back down near his feet. "I wonder where it was. . . ." The words escaped his lips in snatches. "Not up on the wall, I hope. . . ." he gasped.

"Cats can see in the dark, you know."

"Coming in, uninvited like that—stupid, Peeping Tom."

Moving away, Hiroshi slowly raised his head up along the top of the wall, peering over the blocks, at the house in back. Closer than expected, the light of the neighbor's house shone through the hedge.

As if nothing had happened, evening stillness returned to the house.

"I guess this kind of place isn't so . . ." Uneasy, Mariko's hesitation hovered as she took in the sheet of plywood lying on top of the dirt. Hiroshi's failing vigor quickly pushed against and enveloped her doubt, trying to slip inside. Mariko struggled against the force from above. *It's OK. It's gone. I refuse to lose to some silly cat.* Hiroshi poured out a stream of whispers, almost muffling the protests below him.

Inside, within their now barely restored hidden room, their heat of a few moments before returned. Mariko's body melted, her warmth fragrant, reaching Hiroshi. *Even so,* she blurted, *are you sure it's all right? No one's watching?* as Hiroshi repeated under his quickening breath, *It's OK. They're gone.* The flow of time in the hidden room did not last long. The glistening wall finally shrank back, its heat dissipating into the night.

". . . The ceiling is so high . . . ," Mariko said in a fresh voice, as if she'd just broken the surface of water. Her white arm languidly pointed at the bottom of the roof showing through the interlacing of beams above. A little apart from Mariko, Hiroshi lay face up, half off the plywood board, one hand touching the gritty dirt.

"When the house is finished, this will be under the floor." A sense of ease crept into his voice.

"We're the very first people to live here."

"If the carpenters came and built the house without noticing us, we wouldn't be able to get out."

"We'd live underground," Mariko said.

"And spend the whole day sleeping."

"Not me. The house is so big, I'd want to walk around in it."

"Don't be silly. Your head would get stuck and you wouldn't be able to stand up." Mariko reached out to brush Hiroshi's tousled hair, giggling. Leisurely, her fingers stroked his forehead, and the word *forehead* slipped out in a whisper. Her finger traced the bridge of his nose. *Nose*, she whispered, then slid her finger along the upper lip of his open mouth. *Mouth*, she recited child-ishly. Her finger traced his mouth, then, very naturally, was sucked inside, welcomed into the spot where, a few moments ago, her tongue had been. Hiroshi's tongue wrapped around her fin-ger. Instead of whispering *tongue*, Mariko said, *bite it*. The after-glow of their heated embrace continued for a while, then silence descended.

". . . You know . . . I wonder . . ."

Mariko slowly put an idea into words, as Hiroshi nestled closer.

"Ummm . . ."

"I was thinking. Maybe 'Tatchan' was actually Mr. Tanabe."

"Since when do cats build houses?" Hiroshi asked.

"That's what I mean. Maybe, he came to check out his house. Gives me the creeps."

"But when we came in, we said hello, all proper."

"Let's get out of here." Mariko sat up with a jerk.

"But it's such a nice house. Nice enough to stay over in." But Hiroshi's tone of voice was compliant.

"Let's leave something behind, to mark the occasion," Mariko said, pulled along by Hiroshi's words.

"But I don't have anything," he muttered.

"How about taking off one of your shirt buttons? The middle one seems kind of loose."

Just as she had said, the button on his polo shirt, hanging loosely from its threads, popped right off. Mariko reached into her shoulder bag for her rail-pass holder and tore off the little bell hanging down. It jingled a few times in her sweaty hands, then stopped.

"Where is it?" she asked.

The button and the bell in her palm touched, and she shook them. She began to scratch out a hole in the dry dirt beside their bed. The little Mariko and little Hiroshi in her hand were carefully moved over to the hole, and Mariko packed the dirt down on top firmly.

"Where are they?" Hiroshi now asked. She placed his large, hot hand on top of the dirt.

"Like kids playing a prank," he said. "What kind of bud do you think will sprout?"

"A house bud, don't you think? If you take good care of it, it might grow into a three-story house."

"Mr. Tanabe won't like it, but then it'll be our house."

"A house within a house."

"And the people who live in one house can't see the people who live in the other."

"If that's true, then maybe someone's living here already. . . . I really want to go." Mariko shook Hiroshi and began to dress hurriedly.

"What should we do with the board?" Mariko, finished first, quietly wiped the dirt off her skirt. "Should we leave it where it is?"

Fanned against the darkness, their bed stood leaning up against the concrete wall. Mariko was just slipping out toward the front door when Hiroshi held her back, grabbing her by the shoulder. With a swiftness that made her forget where she'd been heading, she found herself in his arms. Labored breathing spilled from their clinging shadows. Finally, slowly, they parted again and made their way past the pillars.

Good night. Mariko had stepped outside the foundation frame. Looking back up at the roof, her voice was gentle as she directed it toward the house.

"Wait," Hiroshi called out.

Mariko, waving her hand in tiny gestures, was yanked back into the shadows of the pillars. A strong white light rushed in, piercing through the leaves of the hedge. Light spilled over and grazed the dirt in the garden. An engine roared and a car sped by.

Tiptoeing toward the entrance, the two slipped between the

lean-to boards to emerge on the road, where they breathed sighs of relief. Outside, there was the line of streetlights and no sign of anyone else. Trying to quickly assume the appearance of pedestrians on a walk through the neighborhood, their pace was unnaturally slow.

"Think the trains are still running?" Mariko took Hiroshi's arm and looked at his heavy-set watch.

"If there aren't any, we can take a cab. Thanks to that house, we didn't have to spend any money."

"We'll have to thank them, won't we?"

Mariko gently rested her head on Hiroshi's shoulder. His strong arm encircled her supple waist and pulled her closer. In a while, they looked like ordinary passersby walking down the road again, albeit a bit entangled. The windows of all the houses behind the hedges were dark; only the white myrtle that hung trailing out over the road was up at that night hour.

Under a bright light standing to one side of the intersection, a figure tottered forward from a side street. A small man carrying a paper sack in both hands appeared. He stood in the middle of the intersection, motionless, looking around him. Finally, he looked up, lost in thought.

"Wonder what's the matter with him." Mariko raised her head from Hiroshi's shoulder and whispered. Hiroshi gazed at the figure without comment. The man's features grew more distinct as they approached. He was a small, old man, wearing an open-necked white shirt.

"Oh, excuse me . . ."

When the two had gotten close enough to hear, the old man, face still gazing upward, turned casually in their direction as if he'd been waiting to talk with them.

"I wonder if you would happen to know a Mr. Tanabe who lives around here?"

"Mr Tanabe? . . ." For an instant, Hiroshi was taken aback.

"I'm sure it's around here. It's so late, there's no one to ask."

"Is it a big house?" Hiroshi asked.

"Well, by today's standards, I guess it is."

"Then you'll see it on the right as you go down this street."

"Oh—this street. Thanks so much. You're young but you're quite on the ball, aren't you?"

"Are you stopping by there?" Hiroshi asked.

"Look at the time. Thank you again."

The old man bustled about, lifting the paper sack halfway up, turning to go back down the street from where Hiroshi and Mariko had just come.

"But—" Hiroshi began, and Mariko grabbed his arm. The old man's steps petered out and he came to a halt. "—that house isn't there anymore."

"Isn't there?"

"What I mean is, it's there, but it's still being built, so no one lives there."

"Are you an acquaintance of Mr. Tanabe's?" A lively expression sprung to life around the old man's mouth.

"No, not exactly. We just happened to be walking by that house."

"But you seem to know so much about it."

The old man gazed at Hiroshi and took a couple of steps back toward him.

". . . No, I just thought, what a big house they're building."

Mariko shook Hiroshi's arm a little, signaling him to say good-bye.

"I'm sure the house is there. Thank you for your concern." The old man turned with short steps down the road lit with the single row of streetlights.

"Something's strange about that man." Mariko, unable to wait until he was out of earshot, whispered into Hiroshi's ear.

"Maybe, we should check it out," he replied.

Mariko tried to hurry them off to the station, but Hiroshi hushed her, staring fixedly at the retreating figure. The old man passed several stripes of light from the streetlights, but as he neared the house under construction, his white-shirted back vanished.

"Should we go see?" Hiroshi asked.

"No way. Forget it."

"Maybe he'll be surprised and come back again."

"I doubt it."

"OK, so what's he doing in there?"

"How should I know?" Mariko said.

"But he came to visit that house, didn't he?"

Mariko didn't answer but just looked back to where the streetlights faded off into the distance.

"What if . . . what if that man turned out to be Mr. Tanabe?"

Hiroshi didn't reply.

The two started off quickly toward the station, both glancing back a few times. The street was still and silent.

the door across the street

When she opened the door, there stood her husband.

He was home a little later than usual. A tall, cardboard box hung down to his knees. Greeting him, Shizuko reached out to take it.

"Be careful. It's fragile." Takahiko carefully passed her the box, its light-blue handle tied on with string.

"Better close the door. It's cold."

"But be *careful* with it," Takahiko again cautioned. The box was light for its size but heavy for what was supposed to be so breakable.

"What is it? A present from someone?"

"No, I bought it myself."

"What a surprise!"

Box in hand, Shizuko went into the living room first. She put it down next to the *kotatsu* foot-warmer table she'd only just set out.

"Oh—you put out the *kotatsu*. Great!" Takahiko said. He stuck his feet under the warm quilt without changing his clothes. He pulled the box over and began untying the string.

Shizuko remembered how her husband used to like shopping and would often buy a trinket or other on the way home to enjoy seeing the children clamor over it. But somewhere along the line, his enthusiasm for shopping had died. It might have been just around the time *that* happened, Shizuko thought, pierced by a feeling as if she'd stepped on a sopping-wet cloth.

"Hold on a sec," Takahiko called out to his wife, who was halfway to the kitchen. "Try to guess what's inside."

"I've got something on the stove that's going to burn."

"It's a little on the expensive side."

"Not something strange, I hope," Shizuko said.

"What do you mean, strange?"

"You know, like that claw on the end of a pole you bought. So you could reach everything even when you're sitting down."

"That was ages ago. You have a good memory. I'd completely forgotten."

"I remember everything," Shizuko said.

"There's a light inside."

"A light?"

"Light is spilling out of the box. Why don't you take a look?"

Takahiko carefully removed the tape holding the box and cover together and pulled out pieces of white Styrofoam packing. Slowly, he put his hand into the tall box, almost as if he were trying to grab hold of a small animal inside, one that could easily escape his grasp.

What emerged was a thin, brass-colored desk lamp. Its top half was tightly packed, the lower half exposed. Around the single, slender pole of the lamp wound a stem. Takahiko's studied care was not necessary, as the whole lamp slid easily from its container. No doubt, the store had given him just an old box that had been lying around. Shizuko guessed the lamp to be imported and felt vaguely empty, seeing the box and its contents.

"Pretty unusual, don't you think?"

Takahiko grasped the pole, a candle-holder type, which rose straight up from a solid-looking base, and placed it proudly on top of the *kotatsu*. The stem, the same thickness as the pole, wrapped itself around the pole in a reverse S curve; at its tip rested a translucent hood made from a pile of white flower petals. But the bottom end of the fancy stem curved straight up in the air, so that the overall impression was less of flowers than of a swan hanging with its head down.

"It seems a little top heavy," Shizuko said. The stem was so slim the flowers looked out of proportion.

"It's only forty watts, but bright enough to read by."

"Would you call it an antique, I wonder. Pretty popular these days, aren't they?"

"I was out for a walk during my lunch break when I found it," Takahiko said. "It was just sort of slapped down in a show window of foreign accessories, and I thought it was kind of cute. I kept turning it on and off and before I knew it there I was, buying it."

"It might be just right on the writing desk," Shizuko said.

"No, let's just enjoy it here, or in the sitting room. Like in that poem, remember? Where the person's walking down some dark street he's never been on before on a cold night, and he sees a warm light in a window. Just seeing that makes him feel like the people there have befriended him. That's the kind of color this lamp has."

"I remember when you told me that poem. But didn't the people in the house notice the man outside and quickly shut their blinds?"

"Did they? . . ."

"You told me that was the main point."

"Looks like I've forgotten the most important part."

"You told me about that poem at that place in Shinjuku, at the *Vienna*. On a cold night."

"What a mess! That's the opposite of what I meant." With a sudden sheepish look on his face, Takahiko stroked the lamp's flower petals from below.

Shizuko found she could say no more. Takahiko always got depressed whenever she became caught up in memories of their younger days. Pointing out how inaccurate his recollections were only caused her to say more than she should.

"So, what do you think? Pretty nice, no matter how expensive it was, right?" Takahiko's voice, lively once more, followed Shizuko as she headed again for the kitchen.

"It's hard to find a Japanese-made lamp that's any good," she said. "It must have cost a lot. Over ¥50,000, I imagine."

"No way. I don't have that kind of money." Takahiko's good-humored voice rose up. He paused, then proudly announced: "It was ¥27,000."

"That would be about right, I suppose. Is it French?"

"Italian."

Takahiko let slide her inconsistent remarks about the price, concentrating instead on fitting a tiny bulb into the lamp from below.

Shizuko, standing in front of the gas range, turned to look at him. To her, it seemed as if a huge creature was playing with a lovely waterfowl there.

* * * * *

During dinner, Takahiko didn't switch on the TV as usual. He kept flicking the lamp on the *kotatsu* on and off. "Food looks different in this light," he said, holding pieces of boiled tofu and pickled cabbage in his chopsticks for Shizuko to see. It was true. The fluorescent light on the ceiling made food look sunken in coldness, but the gentle glow of the small lamp gave the surface of the food a certain luster and warmth.

"I like the base the best," Shizuko said quietly, as they sipped their after-dinner tea. A leaf decorating the squared base spread out above it; on top the base tapered off into three layers with the round pole rising straight up. The base reminded Shizuko of the sheen of the silver candlestick her father kept on his bookshelf when she was a child. Reading *Les Misérables* then and coming across the part where Jean Valjean stole a candlestick, mentally her image of it was of her father's candlestick. His, however, was not shaped as a series of flat boxes but more as a single piece, a sort of hollowed-out pyramid. Compared to it, the lamp Takahiko bought looked a little unsteady. The body of the lamp with its stem winding around was a bit overdone—which made one notice all the more how pleasant-looking the base was.

"The light is alive—look at the way it's all lit up."

Takahiko's voice sounded damp and muffled. As if hearing through a mist, barely registering his voice, Shizuko vaguely wondered what had happened to her father's silver candlestick after he died—that thick cylindrical base with its sharply etched vertical grooves around it. Suddenly, Shizuko felt a ground-shaking shudder in the pit of her stomach. The dry scrape of a metal gate roughly opening followed right after. Her face met her husband's, both illuminated by the lamp.

"It's the Kiuchis' car," Takahiko said. "Haven't heard it in quite some time."

"She goes out more often than you think. Seems that whenever you come home late, she's already sped off somewhere." Just like usual though, she knew Takahiko would be convinced that only what he actually saw with his own eyes really took place. What a happy-go-lucky man. Shizuko gave a small sigh.

"It's gotten cold, so it's not good to rev the engine that way," Takahiko said.

"I think the car is the least of her worries—when she runs out like that."

"Is she just running out? Seems more like she's abandoning her home."

"Yes, but she's always back by dawn. Every morning when I open the window, the car's there."

"If she comes back, then she's not necessarily running away."

"If she's abandoning her home, then she wouldn't come back, would she?" Shizuko asked.

"Sometimes people abandon something but find they can't go through with it and come back. That might be what's going on here."

"If she really wanted to abandon her home, then she wouldn't come back."

"Yes, but flying out the door like that—it seems less running away than throwing up a sort of challenge," Takahiko said.

As if underscoring his point, the car revved loudly and roared off into the night.

"I think Mrs. Kiuchi must be around thirty," Shizuko said, "but lately she looks much older."

"And they don't have any children, which doesn't help the situation."

The Kiuchis' gate shut with a small, timid click.

"I wonder if her husband sees her off each time," Shizuko said.

"Why don't you take a look next time?"

"No thanks. Like this is my little amusement or something. But you know—I never hear their voices when she drives off."

"See—you *are* enjoying it."

"Somehow, though, I feel I understand."

"What do you mean?" Takahiko asked.

"Flying out the door like that."

"Running out?"

"No. Abandoning everything." Shizuko said, the words intentionally crisp.

"In the end, maybe they're both the same—running out or abandoning everything."

Takahiko lit a cigarette. Shizuko reached for the ashtray on top of the low cupboard.

"They can't be the same. Not that I ever did either one," she said. *I just couldn't do it*, she said to herself.

Takahiko, his eyes smarting from the smoke, perhaps, raised his glasses, rubbing his eyes with the back of his hand.

"Running away, I might have been able to do."

Takahiko switched off the lamp.

"Why did you turn it off?" Shizuko nearly shouted, not reproachfully but more startled, as a child would.

Silently, Takahiko turned the light back on. It was off for only a moment but in that short interval, Shizuko felt the lamp twist, its shape changing. Dark shadows formed around the thin pole rising up from the squared base; the brass-colored stem winding around seemed suddenly more pliant, as if it were hanging languidly among the heavy flowers. The rounded stem, lit by its own light, gave off a thick, almost oily luster, and lay motionless, nestling close to the pole.

"Little by little, everyone runs away, and abandons something."

Seized by a sudden desire to smash the gently lit table lamp, Shizuko's words were the opposite of how she felt.

"So, you just grin and bear it," Takahiko said.

"I wonder. Maybe you put up with it so much you have to run away for a while, and then things are OK again."

"I don't know . . ."

"Instead of always putting up with things," she said, "maybe it's smarter to discover room to maneuver. Mrs. Oda, next door, for instance. Her youngest child's still pretty small, yet she gets dressed up and goes out by herself."

"I wonder where she goes."

"I have no idea," Shizuko said. "It's not my business. When Kimiko was about to go to elementary school, I never would have been able to do that."

"And I'm glad you didn't."

"Yes, but sometimes I wonder . . ."

"No, it's good. That's why Kimiko has turned out so well. 'Course she puts her own little one in day care. But I guess times have changed."

Now, it was Shizuko who switched off the lamp. The color of the room grew chill. The switch on the cord connected to the lamp was a throwaway design—not at all in keeping with the elaborate decoration of the stand. When she pushed the button, precious little resistance met her fingertips, an uneasy feeling. Its grey plastic handle made Shizuko feel as if she'd touched the head of some large, slow-witted woman.

"Let's leave it like this for a while longer," she said.

Takahiko, reaching out with a practiced hand, grabbed the switch and turned the lamp back on. The light escaping from between the heavy petals reminded Shizuko of eye mucus.

Shizuko, reading along in the evening paper through her

slightly weak bifocals, sensed a shadow pass over the room, as if a candle had flickered. She looked up. It took her a while to realize that she was hearing Takahiko's voice.

"Huh?" She looked at her husband.

"I talked with Mr. Imamura today," Takahiko repeated, his expression unchanged. Strands of smoke from yet another cigarette curled upward around his face irritatedly.

"Mr. Imamura from the head office?"

"Considering the future direction of the company, he said it'll be either in Hokkaido or Akita." Takahiko let out a thin breath of smoke.

"Why just cold places?" Shizuko asked.

"It can't be helped. That's where our subsidiaries are."

"We'll be far from the children."

"When they come for New Year's, though, the grandkids will love the snow."

"You still have more than a year to go, right?"

"But if we go, and end up leaving before then, they'll let me retire a little early." As if to warm himself, Takahiko turned his outstretched hands over the reddish glow of the lamp.

"We don't have to decide right away, but Mr. Imamura said since it's either Yamashita or myself, he'd talk to me about it first."

"He might have said the same thing to Mr. Yamashita."

"I doubt it," Takahiko said.

"We'd have to find some place to live."

"There's a company house vacant in Kushiro."

"But if we move, what'll we do with this one?"

"The head office is thinking of renting it out as company housing."

"I don't like this, one little bit," Shizuko said. "It sounds like everything's decided already."

"Today's the first time Mr. Imamura talked with me about it. I had a lot of questions, and the personnel and welfare section chiefs helped answer them. Can't make any decision until I find out what's what, right?"

"I think you're already more than half set on this. And that's why you bought the new lamp."

"That has nothing to do with it. I just thought . . ."

"This is important," Shizuko said. "Why couldn't you have told me sooner?" She and Takahiko had been looking at the same lamp but seeing something completely different, she realized. Feeling deceived, her anger deepened with the thought that he'd just used the talk about the lamp as a pretext to sound out her reaction.

"I've been waiting to find a time we could sit down and talk about it, but—"

"You're smoking too much," she said. "It's too smoky in here."

Waving her hand exaggeratedly in front of her, Shizuko stood up to move the curtain aside and was about to open the south-facing window. Across the road, the black front door of the Kiuchis' house was wide open. A man rushed out onto the cement carport in front of the entrance that, with the car gone, seemed somehow larger than usual. Not realizing the door he'd shut behind him had opened again, he struggled with one bare foot to slip on one of his shoes that had fallen off; finally getting it on, he ran out to the road in front. All the while, broken bits of pain came out of his mouth, sounding like words caught between a moan and a prayer.

"What's the matter with him, I wonder? . . ." Her face exposed to the cold air of the open window, Shizuko listened to the sounds as the man moved further away. A shout could be heard, mixed in with the clatter of footsteps.

"Something wrong?" Takahiko must have sensed something out of the ordinary was taking place across the street, too, because he stood up from the *kotatsu* to come behind Shizuko to peer outside.

"Look, he just ran out without even closing the front door."

From out of the half-opened door that Shizuko indicated, a reddish-brown light from inside shone out, as if exposing the house's innards.

"I wonder if something's happened to his wife, the one with the car."

"Maybe I should go over and close the door for them—just to be on the safe side."

"Don't do that," Takahiko said. "Someone there will notice and close it."

"But it's just the two of them. It's like they're inviting a burglar to come in."

"Maybe someone visited and they had a fight."

"I'm going to go take a look," Shizuko said.

"Don't go sticking your nose in where it doesn't belong. They're adults, so no matter what happens, it's their responsibility."

"But the way he dashed off like that—something's just not right. At least it looks that way to me." Brushing past Takahiko, Shizuko walked to their foyer to slip on her sandals.

The metal gate of the Kiuchis' was open as well, and Shizuko managed to squeeze past it without touching.

"Good evening, Mr. Kiuchi," she called out hesitantly.

Light spilled out of the entrance. The muffled sound of a TV, or maybe a radio, drifted out from inside. She glanced back at the window of her own house. Takahiko's dark shadow stood between the curtains.

"Mr. Kiuchi, are you at home?"

Shizuko clutched the doorknob and gazed inside. Among the shoes scattered about just inside the entrance was a single, felt slipper, still new and stiff, flipped upside down. On the step leading up to the main level, a man's overcoat, arms flung wide, lay tossed aside. Other than this, just bare walls.

"This is Mrs. Takigawa from across the street. I saw your door was open, and I thought I'd better close it for you."

There was no response. Shizuko called out one more time, then started to withdraw, closing the door. The light fixture dangling down from the ceiling with its stained-glass shade cover caught her eye. It was dark red. Suddenly, she was startled by a ringing nearby. For a second, she thought she'd set off an alarm, then realized it was a phone. Her head throbbed as she counted the number of rings. Three. Four. She was seized by a desire to pick it up. She counted ten rings, then moved back and shut the black door. It closed with a satisfying click; the door should stay shut. The phone rang on insistently, muffled behind the door. Shizuko tiptoed away, closed the iron gate, then went out into the road, glancing to both sides. The road, with its line of pale streetlights running off into the distance, was silently sunk into the depths of night. Not a soul could be seen.

Takahiko motioned to her to come back, his shadowy figure at the window beyond the low cement-block wall.

"There wasn't anyone there after all."

Shizuko stood behind her husband, who was carefully closing the curtains. She was out of breath.

"I was about to close the door and come home," she continued, "when the phone started ringing. Like an emergency call of some kind."

"How could you possibly know that?"

"This time of night, ringing over twenty times? Most people would hang up before that. I really thought I should answer it myself."

"Don't joke around. That would be trespassing or invasion of privacy at least."

"But this is a special case."

"You think so," Takahiko said, "but maybe it's not."

"No, you should have seen the way the entrance looked. Something's not right."

"The husband works somewhere, doesn't he?"

"I don't know. He seems to be at home a lot during the day, so maybe he quit his job."

"Quit his job, huh? Wonder how he makes a living."

"The entrance didn't have any flowers or plants. Just bare walls." Shizuko switched the *kotatsu* heater to high. Being outdoors had chilled her and she couldn't get warm. She pulled the gas space heater closer, behind her, and turned it on.

"It feels like the dead of winter," she said.

"Well, it is winter. We're not used to it yet, so it's the time of year when you feel the cold the most."

She still heard the phone ringing in her ears. If she'd picked it up, who would she have heard? The police? A hospital? Maybe a relative with an emergency? She shuddered to imagine if she had gone inside and right then someone had come back home. The word *trespassing* Takahiko had used now hit home with a different, more graphic meaning. How would it feel if a stranger was in *their* house on the phone? If her husband was transferred to Kushiro or Akita, that might very well happen. That's trespassing, she thought, that's what that is.

Suddenly a woman she'd never seen before picked up the phone lying beside the television and, as if she owned the place, began an endless conversation—completely oblivious to the fact that her child was banging his toy car against one of the pillars. Soot from a kerosene stove formed a chain of dirt hanging down from the ceiling. And as soon as she hung up, the woman rushed into the bathroom where she plopped her oversized behind on the toilet, which had some cheesy-looking, light-blue seat cover, and started peeing loudly.

"Ahh—" Shizuko, lost in this imagined scene, spat out the word, causing Takahiko, about to light a cigarette, to pause.

"That's trespassing, and I won't stand for it," she said.

"What are you talking about?" Unlit cigarette dangling from his mouth, Takahiko's face paled.

"I'm not moving from here. If you want to go to Hokkaido or Akita or wherever, fine, go ahead. But do it by yourself. The kids might come back to Tokyo, and there's no way I'm going to rent this house out to someone else."

"We don't have to decide right away," Takahiko said. "I'm just passing along what Mr. Imamura told me today."

"This is the house Tomohiko and Kimiko grew up in. If they see someone else going in and out of here, they'll feel like they don't have a place to come home to." She could still sense strange shadows of people crawling busily back and forth. The dim, red glow of the lamp Takahiko had brought home made them loom even more weirdly.

"I hope everything's OK with them," Takahiko said, finally lighting his cigarette.

"What do you mean?"

"With the Kiuchis."

Shizuko nodded vaguely, feeling he'd sidestepped the subject.

"Funerals in winter are too cold," he said.

"I don't like this, having to decide everything like this," Shizuko replied, still full of confused emotions.

"But if something happened to the wife there," Takahiko said, "and the husband followed, there'd be no one living in that house anymore."

"But then that might mean a new wife would come along?"

"That wouldn't be so bad."

"Wouldn't it?" Shizuko asked.

"Maybe wife number two was standing nearby, under the shadows of a streetlight."

"So when the husband ran out into the street and shouted, it was a shout of joy."

"I doubt it," Takahiko said. "But after a family commits suicide, sometimes the house just remains vacant, with no one ever living in it."

"The neighbors must hate that."

Shizuko pictured the empty entrance she'd just seen.

"For a while you would still feel like someone's living there," Takahiko said.

"The way Mr. Tanabe did things is best, I think," Shizuko said.

"How so?"

"He decided to completely rebuild his house and rent out a couple of rooms on the second floor to young people."

"So, there'll be one of those strange metal staircases next to the main entrance?"

"So, even if the old couple passes away, at least someone will still be living there."

"When I was a child, I saw something kind of weird," Takahiko said. "I was walking down a broad street that ran parallel to the railroad tracks, and all of a sudden it ran to a dead end."

"Road construction?" Shizuko asked.

"No, it wasn't that. The road ended, and there was a house standing there. Nowadays, you see the opposite a lot."

"So, there was private land that cut the road in two?"

"It was a really nice road leading to the next train station. As I got closer, I realized they were in the midst of moving the house itself."

"Moving the house?"

"The whole house, foundation and all, was up on something, and they were moving it across the road. I was pretty small, so I don't remember all the details, but they had it up on some kind of roller and were pulling it. I was very surprised to find out you could move houses. Wooden houses basically just sit on the ground."

"I wonder if our house could be moved."

"Of course. Shall we have them pull it all the way to Akita for us?" Takahiko looked seriously at Shizuko.

She felt the unspoken question—*Would that make you happy?*—hanging in the air.

"I wouldn't like that," she said. "The house has to be on this land, surrounded by this neighborhood."

"But if the surroundings change, it's the same as if the house moved somewhere else. When we built this one, the spot where the Kiuchis live was just a vacant lot covered with weeds. And the Yasunagas' next door to them was just a dug-up piece of land."

He was right, of course. When the children were still small, they enjoyed having a safe place for them to play in just across the street. But these reminiscences were always tinged with the fact that these vacant lots had disappeared, as houses had gone up, one after another. She hadn't planned to soften her stance toward her husband, but a stronger emotion now took hold of her.

"Things have changed, all right," she said. "Of course, the land for all our houses originally belonged to Mr. Oda's father, or maybe his grandfather. I'll bet the land itself's pretty astonished at how fast things change."

Shizuko touched the flower petals on the three-tiered lamp with the pads of her fingers. How hot would the glass shade get after being on so long? But it was, surprisingly, only gently warm. The shadow of her hand fell on the *kotatsu*, shaded, like an evening shadow, with a faint reddish glow.

With Takahiko's little grunt as he stood up, Shizuko roused herself, realizing she'd forgotten all about getting the bath ready.

"I'm sorry, but the bath's not ready yet."

Takahiko, his back to her, was just opening the door to the toilet and didn't seem to hear.

Left alone in the living room, Shizuko headed to fill up the bath when her eyes were suddenly drawn to the curtain at the window. Guiltily, quickly, she approached the window, edged the curtain aside slightly and peeked. She almost gasped.

The Kiuchis' front door, which she'd pulled tightly shut, was open again. Dark-reddish light streamed out onto the concrete carport. The front gate was still closed; no one seemed to be about. She was about to call out to Takahiko but swallowed back the words. She couldn't help but think that, even if she went over again to shut the door, it would remain as it was now—open.

* * * * *

In her mind, Shizuko could clearly picture, hours later in the dim light of morning, the Kiuchis' empty house, its door silently open.

night guest

The sound of footsteps flitted by, just beyond the television.

It was Friday evening, and the TV screen showed the white interior of a beauty parlor. The footsteps passed behind the screen so distinctly that they seemed almost to shake it. Hurried steps, strained, as if they were forcing themselves not to break into a run.

Her husband was home early for a change. After dinner, he said he felt as if he were catching a cold; his head felt heavy and he went to bed. It didn't sound as if the children were coming back to pay a visit. The road in front of their house was a cul-de-sac, and very few people passed by, especially at night.

Maybe it's someone visiting the Odas across the street, Masayo thought, sitting on the sofa, listening carefully.

The gate, not latched, rattled open abruptly; unconsciously, Masayo glanced over at Yoshiko beside her on the sofa. Yoshiko's legs were tucked up under her; head slumped forward, she dozed.

Dully, something bumped against the front door.

"Good evening! Good evening!"

Whoever it was didn't ring the door chime but knocked. A woman's voice called out impatiently. "I'm sorry to bother you, but would you please open up?"

Masayo stood, wondering for an instant whether she should wake up Yūzo, who was sleeping in the next room. Deciding not to, she walked to the front door. . . . Bathed in the glow of the streetlight, a woman stood outside, clutching a knife. This imagined scene touched Masayo's mind for an instant. Fear, and strangely, anticipation, sent chills up her spine.

"Who is it?" Masayo's voice stiffened as she laid her hand on the doorchain.

"Please let me in for a minute. *Please!*"

The voice, not that of a young woman, sounded tense and cornered. Urged on, Masayo opened the door. A small woman, clad in a black overcoat, fairly tumbled inside.

"Lock it—quickly!"

Her face was pale and drawn. Masayo swiftly locked the door and latched the chain.

"What's going on?"

The middle-aged woman, shoulders heaving, leaned heavily against the wall. Her hands clasped not a gleaming knife but an oversized, almost shapeless handbag.

"A strange person was following me."

"A man?"

"I was walking in this direction from behind the station, and I didn't realize it for a while."

"A young man?" Masayo asked.

"When I turned the corner of the road over there, he suddenly got closer."

"Did he do anything to you?"

"He was trying to pass me."

"Would you like some water?"

"No, thank you. It's enough that you let me in." The woman finally stood up away from the wall. Fingering the buttons on her duster coat, she looked toward the closed door.

"So did he go away?"

"I don't know. He walked by me, then stood at the corner waiting for me."

"I wonder if he's still there."

Masayo slipped into her sandals and was quietly about to open the door.

"Masa-san—don't open it. It's dangerous," Yoshiko said in a subdued, hoarse voice from behind. Her faced peeked out from the shadows of the pillar.

"If he's still there, I'll call the police," Masayo said, carefully opening the door a crack.

On the road outside, where the light from the street lamp melted into the dark, a man's figure stood facing the low cinder-block wall of the Takigawas' house.

"Is that him?"

Masayo, her hand on the doorknob, turned, facing the woman. Rooted to the spot, the woman, eyes closed, just shook her head; it was less a response to the question than an attempt to deny all that had just happened. Masayo peered back through the crack in the door. The man, of medium height, wearing jeans, slowly walked away from the wall. Without avoiding the full light of the street lamp, he turned the corner around the Takigawas' house and disappeared in the opposite direction from the station.

That's not him. . . . The man's brazen actions made Masayo shudder, yet she felt somehow deflated as well.

"Maybe I should call 911," she said. If the police came right away, they might be able to catch the man as he walked down the main road toward the large public-housing complex.

"Is he still there?" the woman asked.

"He was standing in front of that wall like he was peeing or something, but he left and I can't see him anymore."

"It's OK, I was just so—startled."

Masayo took a good look at the sheepish woman standing under the foyer light, her hands at her chest. The woman's eyes blinked repeatedly; as if revived, a little color had returned to her cheeks. What she'd been holding inside ever since she'd stumbled through their door seemed to be surfacing.

"It's not even 10:00," Yoshiko said spiritedly. "When the weather gets warmer, it seems that's when the weird people come out of the woodwork. It's just like our cat—hardly ever at home these days, out chasing after other cats. . . ." She invited the woman to rest on the step leading up to the main level of the house. But though she relaxed her posture, the woman remained standing.

"Did he try to grab you?" Masayo asked, trying to draw her attention away from Yoshiko.

"No, he didn't do that. It's just that he . . ."

Masayo, trying to suppress the feeling welling up in her, waited spitefully for the reply.

"When I got to the streetlight at the corner, he passed me, and then came to a sudden stop."

"Did he say anything?" Masayo asked.

"Not a word. . . . And my legs just turned to rubber."

"And that's when you ran over here."

"No, then under the streetlight . . . he suddenly turned toward me."

"Good heavens," Yoshiko said loudly. Masayo ignored her and urged the woman to continue.

"And his front was open. . . ." The woman raised a hand to her throat, swallowing deeply, and closed her eyes.

"I was frantic. I turned the corner and saw the light on at your front door. And I pretended I was just visiting you. . . ."

"How terrible, opening himself up like that . . ." Yoshiko looked the woman over as if what she had seen was somehow plastered on her body.

"We have streetlights, but very few people pass this way at night, you know," Masayo said in way of warning. At the same time, she experienced an odd sensation crawling up the back of her neck.

"You know," Yoshiko said, "Masayo had a similar thing happen to her once, too."

"Goodness! You did?" the woman said moistly.

"And if memory serves, it was on a night just this same time of year."

It wasn't pleasant to hear Yoshiko telling a stranger what had happened to her. And what's more, Masayo felt that hidden behind the words of sympathy directed to the woman, was a message aimed at *her*.

"It was a little later than it is now," Masayo said, cutting off Yoshiko.

"Do you think it was the same man?" the woman asked.

"I'm not sure, but I don't think so." It was definitely someone else. They both had acted suspicious, but it wasn't the same man.

On that day, Masayo had gone shopping near downtown Tokyo and suddenly felt like she didn't want to go home. She knew the time was drawing near to start getting dinner ready, yet she couldn't bring herself to head for the train station. With nothing in particular that she wanted to buy, she went in one store after another, first a clothing store, then a shoe store, and so on. Each time she came outside, the darkness had deepened a little more. She sensed the shop windows and shop lights growing gradually sharper.

I should be in the train now, she thought, out at the station exit, waiting for the traffic signal to change at the street where all the buses are parked, now turning the last corner, and arriving at my front door. She could imagine herself at each moment, yet her body showed not the slightest movement to go home. A desire welled up, hard to suppress, to scoop up in her hand a small amount of the freedom that flowed down and filled the city streets; she would let herself loose, as if she were a small fish named Masayo, free to swim in the flow.

When it was finally too late for her to prepare their usual dinner, she was able to bring herself to call home. The kids were already going to college, she thought irritatedly, so why do I have to feel so constrained?

Yoshiko had answered the phone. After Masayo's made-up excuse for not being home in time for dinner, a moment of silence fell. Yoshiko's voice quickly turned ingratiating—No need to rush back always, she said. Yūzo has a meeting, Masayo said, so could you and the children just order some sushi? No one's home yet, Yoshiko said gently, so don't worry, I'll just share some fish with the cat. Don't say that, Masayo replied, and after a little more arguing back and forth, she hung up.

Ten yen's worth of conversation, and that's all it took to muddy the water she held in her palm. It'll take more than this to get me down, she told herself, and set off willfully from one store to the next.

As night came on, the number of women walking along with department-store shopping bags—numerous until then—suddenly decreased. Masayo watched them detachedly, as if they were comical animals roaming the streets. The fever that had taken hold of her so suddenly cooled, and around 10:00 P.M. she began the trek back home. The streets had taken on yet another face, the passersby now nearly all men. Hardly any women were walking alone. Realizing how late it was, she hurried to the station.

After she got off the train and walked across the overpass, still quite a lot of people were around her. And still quite a few as she exited the station and crossed the street. But as she turned from the road where the buses ran, with each corner she rounded, the number of people dwindled, until she reached the intersection near her home. In front of her was just the row of streetlights, glowing palely.

My big mistake was assuming I was alone, she remembered. In front of her was just the quiet street, but behind her a pedestrian had turned the same corner. The lengthy strides were a man's, but not the sound of shoes—sandals maybe, or zoris, lightly grazing the surface of the road. The strides were hurried, occasionally faltering.

Masayo was too nervous to look behind; instead, she strode on purposefully, eyes fixed ahead. She thought about making a break for it but decided that would only attract attention. Also, since she was so late in getting home, at the very least, she wanted to present herself respectably, a figure who could calmly open her front door. A part of her refused to believe anything was wrong.

"Ma'am? . . ."

Right behind her, the man's voice called out. The darkness burst open. She tried to run, but her legs had lost their power.

Suddenly, she was pushed into the hedge beside her. A mix of smells assaulted her—the pungent odor of the cedar, the stink of alcohol. She reached out desperately, trying to push the man away. Out of the corner of her eye, she caught a glimpse of a streetlight way up high.

"Just once, lady, just once is all I ask."

She could hear his voice, but her own shout refused to rise up from her throat.

"Just once and I'll stop. Just one kiss."

He was drunk, that was clear, but there was something else, an earnestness that was not just the alcohol speaking. And this made Masayo even more afraid.

"My old lady, she doesn't even let me kiss her."

Quite suddenly the voice of this man, forcibly attacking her, collapsed into tears. She tried desperately to push his face away and found that her thumb had slipped inside his mouth. He might bite my finger, she thought. The man flinched, and instantly Masayo slipped it past his teeth and violently pinched his cheek from the inside. The man tried to pull his face away, still repeating in pained words his desire for just one kiss. With enough force to rip open the skin, Masayo twisted his cheek, which she held firmly clasped, inside and out.

"OK, OK . . . boy, you're strong, lady. . . ."

His body suddenly moved away, her finger popped out of his mouth, and the man stumbled, his head collapsing in the hedge. He was not a young man, by any means.

Masayo ran off toward the corner of her street, and at about the same time the man roused himself and started to run. Not after her but in the opposite direction—Masayo didn't realize it until she arrived at the front door of her house. Strangely, only the image of the man's clothes remained with her—coatless, he had had on a black vest over a white shirt.

Though she wanted to, she found she couldn't just walk in as if nothing had happened. She hurriedly rang the doorbell, and her son Tōru answered. At this she relaxed and couldn't hold back:

"Some drunk just tried to grab me." Tōru slipped on his sneakers, grabbed a baseball bat from the umbrella stand, and flew outside to look. He soon came back, reporting that no one was there.

"He's pretty fast for a drunk," Tōru mumbled, returning the bat to the stand.

Masayo sat down on the step going up into the house, her shoulders heaving.

"Did you hurt your finger?"

Until he asked, Masayo hadn't realized she'd been flexing her thumb.

"Don't be silly. I was just frightened, that's all."

"It's dangerous, you know. I don't want you walking alone at this hour."

She nodded lightly to her worried son and then took off her shoes. A weird sensation seized her, that her right thumb was no longer part of her body. Tōru locked the door, telling her that his father wasn't home yet. Yoshiko wasn't in the living room and seemed to have gone to bed.

For some time, Masayo couldn't rid herself of the feelings—the lukewarm sensation of her thumb stuck deep in someone else's mouth, the slow movements of the man as he pushed her down against the hedge. The next day on her way to the supermarket, she could barely pass in front of the spot where it had all happened. She feared that the branches of the unkempt, overgrown hedge would be parted, flattened down like crumpled bed covers. Trying to avoid looking there, she walked along, head down, passing schoolchildren on their way home and the mailman on his bicycle. She felt as if she could still hear the man's strangely plaintive voice from out of the thick shrubbery—*My old lady, she doesn't even let me kiss her*. That drunk might be around her husband's age, she suddenly realized. An inexpressible gloom and a faint nervousness clung to the road.

"Do you live very far away?" Masayo asked the woman in front of her, shaking away the memories.

"Just behind the public-housing complex. When it's late, there aren't many buses, and taxi drivers at the station make a face because it's so close, so I just got impatient and started walking."

The emotions that the incident had brought to the surface had quieted down, and an expression more in keeping with her age appeared. The woman was on the small side, so at first Masayo had guessed her to be in her thirties. But now she looked past forty. "I'm sorry to have bothered you," the woman said, bowing her head, the toes of her low-heeled shoes primly arranged.

"I really think you'd better wait a while. He might be hiding somewhere," Masayo said, remembering the leisurely way the man had set off under the streetlight.

"With such a peculiar man loitering about," Yoshiko added, "it might be a good idea, for the future, if we did call the police."

"I'm fine, really. So, please, don't go to any trouble."

"My grandchildren are both in college," Yoshiko said, "and normally we could ask one of them to escort you home, but unfortunately they're both out right now."

"No, I couldn't have you do that."

"But there're too many dark places from here to the apartment complex."

Thinking she should wake up Yūzo, Masayo cut in on Yoshiko and the woman's conversation. Yūzo claimed he was catching a cold, but he's such a gregarious sort he might very well walk with her all the way home.

"No. I'll have my husband come and get me," the woman said, as if anticipating Masayo's thoughts. "Sorry to trouble you, but if I could use your phone . . ."

"Oh, that's a good idea," Yoshiko chimed in, turning to look toward the living room where the phone was. "I'll call for you," said Masayo, stepping up quickly into the house. The woman told her the phone number, bowing again. "My last name is Itō," she added hurriedly to the retreating Masayo, who walked past Yoshiko into the living room.

On the TV screen, a customer, hair dryer in place, was leafing through a woman's magazine, while off to one corner of the beauty shop two beauticians engaged in a rapid-fire exchange about a young male colleague who'd disappeared. The show looked to Masayo as if it were a scene in a miniature box.

"Hello, the Itō residence."

A low, refined voice came on the other end of the line. Masayo related how his wife had been accosted by a strange man on her way home, run into their house, and now wanted him to come take her home.

"A strange man?"

"A pervert, I guess you'd say. That kind of person."

"And did something happen to her?"

"No, she was just frightened and ran into our house since we're nearby. No cause for alarm."

"Sorry you had to go to all the trouble. I'll be over right away," he said. She gave him the directions and hung up. His voice had been smooth and pleasant.

On the TV, a male beautician, the collar of his coat turned up, was hurrying to the hospital where his wife, unbeknown to anyone else, was an inpatient.

"Who is it? A visitor?" The door to the next room opened and Yūzo stuck his head in to where they were. A nightgown was draped over one shoulder, and he squinted in the light.

"A lady was accosted by some weird guy and ran into our house."

"Hmm . . . and what about the man?"

Yūzo fumbled to put his arms through the nightgown sleeves, when Masayo stopped him. "The man's disappeared," she said, "and the woman has just called her house and is waiting for her husband to come get her." Hearing this, Yūzo sat down, as if disappointed, on the sofa.

"Is she young?"

"Younger than I am."

Yūzo pretended to watch the TV but seemed preoccupied

with what was happening at the front door. Assuring him there was nothing to worry about and that he should go back to bed, Masayo returned to the foyer. The woman was talking with Yoshiko and her expression softened when Masayo told her that her husband was on his way. Masayo wondered what this woman's house smelled like. The subdivision homes behind the public-housing complex each had a forced uniqueness to them, but in essence they were identical, all neatly lined up in a row, their walls nearly touching. She could picture the front door—inside, there'd be a vase on a narrow shelf with some wilted flowers. With a faint smell of fried food stagnant in the air, dirty dishes tossed in the sink, a teenager's underwear balled up on top of the washing machine. Somehow, the man's low voice didn't fit that scene. . . .

Though it would take about ten minutes to walk to their house, the woman restlessly wanted to go out on the street to check. "Your husband will come all the way to our house," Masayo said, trying to stop her, but she wouldn't listen. Giving in, Masayo unlocked the door.

From the narrow street in front of their house to the main street where the streetlights were, outside was quiet, a placid evening.

"Leave the door unlocked, please," Masayo said to Yoshiko; she left it open and went out to the front gate. She and the woman walked side by side under the faint light of the street lamps, whose glow reached into their cul-de-sac. Masayo looked over at the Takigawas' wall, where until a short while ago the man had been standing, his back to her. The asphalt below it and its cement blocks were white and dry, no wet stains were apparent. That made the man even creepier.

Walking slowly, they reached the corner of the main street. A faint light shone through the curtain at the Takigawas' window. At the Kiuchis' across the street, a cream-colored car crouched in front of the entrance, its rear bumper nearly grazing the wall.

"Seems like everything's all right," Masayo said, looking

around the deserted street lit by the neatly spaced streetlights. The woman nodded faintly but didn't look around. Her gaze was fixed to the right, toward the apartment complex. Masayo had no coat on but hardly felt cold. A faintly sweet scent hung in the night air, as if flowers on a nearby tree were in bloom.

"Do you have any children?" Masayo asked, to put the quiet woman at ease.

"No, we never had any," she replied, her eyes fixed on the end of the road.

"But there's still a chance . . ."

"Two years ago, I reached the point where I can't have any."

"Is that right? . . . But sometimes, you know, I think it's better if I didn't have any children."

"Only people who have children say that."

"Still, sometimes I think about how differently my life would have turned out, without children."

Masayo said this not just regretfully for having asked the wrong thing; it was something she'd clearly wanted to get out.

"I wonder."

Masayo's words seemed to fly right past the motionless woman.

A figure appeared from the direction of the station, turning at the intersection. A tall man approached, appearing in the rings of light, then sinking back into the dimness. Glancing dubiously at Masayo and the woman standing at the entrance to the cul-de-sac, he hurried by. He disappeared to the right, into the break in the Takigawas' wall. The dull clang of feet bounding up a metal staircase was mixed in with whistling, followed by the sound of a door slamming shut. He must be one of the young men renting a room on the second floor of the Tanabes' newly rebuilt house.

His nonchalant homecoming left behind a certain softness that hung over the streets.

"Do you always pass by here?" Masayo spoke, as if to draw closer to the gentle ambience left behind by the young man. "There are a lot of hedges so it's actually quite nice here in the daytime."

"In the daytime, yes . . ."

Masayo was about to talk about the hedge but dropped it. The cedar she'd been pushed into was just two light poles or so down toward the station. The leaves had grown out since then and protruded darkly out toward the street. It was just around there, maybe; Masayo turned, and at that moment heard the woman's subdued voice in her ear.

"That must be him, I'm sure."

At the end of the road to the apartment complex, something very small was moving.

"You'd better make sure first."

Masayo held the woman back, who was about to walk off.

"He's overweight but he walks fast—very fast."

She was right. As the small shadow reached each streetlight, it grew visibly distinct.

"It's my husband," the woman said decisively. Masayo felt a strange emotion about to arise. The man was now clearly visible. He had on a white shirt and a black vest.

"Are you sure?" Masayo asked tensely, wanting the man to come even closer to make absolutely certain.

"Yes, it is," the woman replied, her voice as strong as Masayo's. "I'm really sorry to have worried you. Thank you for all you've done. And please thank everyone back at your house. Well, I'd better say good-bye, then."

The woman's tone was hard. She trotted off toward him without waiting to hear Masayo's reply. He had stopped at a streetlight a little ways off and waited for the woman. She came up so close, almost bumping into him; they exchanged a few words, then the woman turned toward Masayo and bowed. Carried along, the man in the black vest bowed to her, vaguely.

"Take care," Masayo murmured, returning the bow. As the man and woman walked off side by side, Masayo noticed he had on neither shoes nor geta but grey-colored sandals.

A lukewarm sensation of her right thumb being inside the

man's mouth seeped up, the dull strength she felt inside the shrubs pressed down on her—the sound of sandals scraping along the road . . .

"Good evening."

Masayo flinched at the sudden voice behind her, taking a moment to realize that the slim woman standing there, wearing a light-weight, white coat, was her neighbor Mrs. Oda. She had walked down from the station and appeared before her.

"Is something wrong?" Mrs. Oda seemed surprised at Masayo's reaction.

"Oh, thank goodness, Mrs. Oda. There was a strange man lurking about here, and a woman passing by ran into our house."

"Goodness, is that so?"

Mrs. Oda's expression abruptly changed, and she looked around her.

"Nothing happened to her; the man just stood at this corner and was going to show her something."

"Sounds like some sort of pervert . . ."

"You should be careful when you come back late."

"I heard that you had a similar experience," Mrs. Oda said.

"But that was a drunk, not a pervert."

"There're certainly all kinds in the world, aren't there? It's terrible."

"You're much younger than I am," Masayo said, "so you need to be extra careful."

"But going out, sometimes it seems like too much trouble to come back home," Mrs. Oda said, and headed toward the end of the cul-de-sac. Perhaps irritated at Masayo, who didn't reply, in a low voice Mrs. Oda fairly spit the words out: "Not that there's really any place to go out to . . ." Reaching the end of the cul-de-sac, they said good-bye, one going to the right, the other to the left. Behind her, Masayo heard the gate being gently latched and a key fitting softly into a lock and turning.

As if to rid herself of the image of the husband and wife disappearing down the street-lit road, Masayo slipped past the front door that was slightly ajar, stepped inside her house, and turned the lock tightly.

"Is that you, Masa-san?" Yoshiko's high-pitched voice came from the living room.

No. It's not—Masayo was seized by a sudden desire to yell it out. But she didn't, and just stood there on the concrete floor.

the two-story house

The phone in front of her began to ring.

It rang like a living creature, unable to endure sitting there being stared at. *Just as I thought*, Kiyoko mused, a dark sense of victory passing through her as she watched the telephone ring two, three times.

"Mom, the phone!" Kōichi called out, annoyed, from the sofa facing the TV. Mayu turned, puzzled, to her mother who sat in the chair beside the phone yet didn't lift a finger.

"Mommy, it's ringing."

"I hear it."

"Well, then, why don't you answer it?" Kōichi asked irritatedly.

"I just want to hear what it sounds like."

"Quit joking around." Irritations quickly got on Kōichi's nerves and he had a quick temper, the same as his father. Unlike his father, though, he didn't try to hide his feelings or put up for long with annoyances.

Brrring! Brrring! Mayu imitated the sound in a small voice, her little *brrings* following each ring, her way, perhaps, of telling her mother to pick up the phone.

"Hello, the Oda residence." Kiyoko slowly reached out, picking up the receiver, her voice deliberately cold.

"It's me. I'm running a little late at work here."

Exactly as she'd imagined, her husband's voice filtered out through the phone and lodged itself deep within her.

"I see. What about dinner?" Kiyoko asked. In the background, a faint stir grazed her ears.

"I've got to go meet Masuda in a while, so I won't need any dinner."

"So, not in the office, then?"

"What?"

"So, you're working outside the office?"

"I might meet him somewhere or go over to his office. We'll decide that later. Why do you ask?"

"Well, if you're at the office, I can always get in touch with you in case anything happens."

"Is something up?"

"Not at all."

"Everybody OK?"

"Yes, we're all well."

"Well, I'll see you later then."

Back in its cradle, the phone was just an object once more. They'd had similar conversations, any number of times, but at some point they'd started to worry her. It wasn't as if she had doubts when he called like this to say he was working late. But Kiyoko's mental image of her husband had, for some reason she couldn't quite lay her finger on, become opaque, as if covered by a membrane. She was upset with herself for being so fixated about this. The time they spent together before they got married was much shorter than the time since, but it seemed to her she knew less about her husband now than before.

Maybe it happened because she quit her job and stayed home. When she was working at a company, she and her colleagues would go out after a late evening at the office, and she could still feel the bracing night air of the city, as if it were a swell on the ocean, on her skin. Now, no matter how often she went out on her own to seek the same experience, it was no longer the ocean she found but insipid water. A free, strong swell that would grab her body and pull her along had now passed her by, leaving her adrift. The more it happened, the more often Kiyoko sought excuses to go out to the city.

"Was that Daddy?"

Mayu hadn't seemed to be following their conversation, but during a break in her TV show she turned from the screen to her mother.

"That's right. He said he's going to work late, so you should go to bed."

Not visibly upset, Mayu hopped on one leg into the room next door, where her brand-new study desk was lined up next to her brother's. She acted thoroughly at ease in the home she was used to. The same could be said of Kōichi, sprawled out on the sofa in front of the television. But for Kiyoko, the identical house was the narrowest of enclosures, restricting all movement.

You're too happy, one of her friends had told her. But don't you feel like you can't breathe? Kiyoko asked good naturedly. Well, I would like to live in a bigger place, her friend, who lived in a public-housing complex, replied calmly, entirely misreading Kiyoko's words.

After cleaning up the children's dinner dishes, Kiyoko sat alone at the kitchen table, chopsticks in hand, but with no appetite. Suddenly, she stopped and listened. A sensation had brushed her, just behind her. The second time, she heard the sound and recognized it as a siren. The third time, the noise swelled up abruptly.

"Turn off the TV!"

Kōichi, startled by her voice's intensity, leaped to turn the volume knob down. The harsh scream of the siren rushed into the silent home and just as quickly, stopped.

"It sounds really close, doesn't it?"

Kiyoko pushed her chair aside and stood up, and Mayu rushed over, clinging. Through the kitchen window, a small, red light shone through the trees in the house behind theirs, blinking on and off.

"It's the Tanabes!"

"A fire engine!"

Mayu hugged her mother tightly around the waist, and Kiyoko could feel her little heart pounding. Kōichi ran over, leaned over the sink, and opened the window. A dark, strawberry-colored light seeped through the frosted glass and pulsated sharply on and off through the shadow of the camellia leaves. Just beyond the hedge in back, a rumbling grew as silver-helmeted figures moved about the Tanabes' garden. From the roadside out front they heard a hoarse, shrill voice crackling over a two-way radio. A loud thud came from the second floor of the Tanabes' house and a shout.

Everything was happening all at once, but no flames could be seen anywhere.

"It's not burning and the fire engine's here, so everything's going to be all right."

Kiyoko plucked Mayu's tight little hands from around her waist, grabbed one, and ran to the front door. Kōichi had already pushed it open and was peering outside. He yelled out. Several silver-coated figures rushed up the cul-de-sac and were opening their front gate.

"Just a second, I'll open it," Kiyoko was about to say, when the firemen got the latch undone and surged into the garden. Kōichi stood stock-still, breathlessly at the gate; a flat hose snaked by his feet.

Instantly, the scene outside their home was transformed. Apparently more than one fire engine had arrived; through the kitchen window—another red light could be seen blinking at the entrance to the road. In the street just beyond, a scattered crowd had already gathered under the streetlights. In back, branches of the hedge had snapped off, one after another. Someone banged on a door. White smoke curled out from below the eaves of the second floor of the Tanabes' and slowly spread upward.

"Because there's no wind. I hope there's no wind." Not sure what she was saying, Kiyoko repeated herself, her arms around Mayu, her other hand tightly clasping Kōichi's arm. Her voice was shaking, she realized, and she coughed hurriedly to cover her confusion.

The firemen concentrated their efforts on the north side of

the Tanabes' house. Shouts, people running on the metal staircase, the shatter of glass could be heard. All that was visible
through the trees from Kiyoko's house, though, was the smoke
drifting from the eaves and the shadowy movement of silver-
colored figures in the darkened second-story windows. Worried
that she may have left the kitchen window open, Kiyoko hurried
back inside. Mayu, hand still tightly grasping her mother's, went
with her.

Kiyoko closed the window on the commotion outside,
breathing a sigh of relief, not that she'd stopped fearing that the
flames might shoot up. The air in the house, shut off from the
noise outside, suddenly wrapped about her thickly.

"Don't worry. It won't burn up."

Mayu's eyes, looking up at her mother, were fearful, and
Kiyoko drew her close.

"There's a bucket in the bathroom," Mayu said in a small
voice, her forehead pressed against her mother's apron.

"The firemen will put it out, so there's nothing to worry
about."

Another thud sounded. Suddenly the kitchen window was
aglow in red, the flames licking at their windowsill—the vision
ran through Kiyoko's mind—the tall flames pushing their way
inside, the thick *fusuma* sliding doors bursting into flame, the
flames leaping to the ceiling. The fire no longer was outside their
home; it ran through their house as if it owned the place. *No way!*
Pushing aside Mayu, Kiyoko put a large pot in the sink, and
turned the faucet on hard, and water gushed out.

Hearing a sudden bang on the door, Kiyoko yelled out to her
son.

"There're a whole lot of people in the garden!" he cried out.

"Firemen?"

"Spectators."

Kōichi looked excited and Kiyoko went out with him again.
She couldn't believe her eyes. From the gate, running along the
inside of the cement-block wall, there must have been thirty

people squeezed into the tiny space. In a flash, the garden had become a public thoroughfare. As if it were the most natural act in the world, the crowd had amassed uninvited into a stranger's walled-off property. They whispered to one other, pointing to the second story of the Tanabes', standing with their arms folded, looking back at the fire engines. Kiyoko was dumbfounded. Momentarily, she was struck by an illusion, that these were all guests she'd invited to a public fire. The small garden, usually quiet along with its four-person family, set back under the far-off light of the street lamps, was now thrown open to all these people. For some some reason, she found it invigorating.

"I wonder if they've put it out," someone said, sidling closer. It was Mrs. Yasunaga from across the street, who'd come over to be next to the gate with all the other gawkers. Her manner seemed different than usual, oddly more familiar.

"I just hope it doesn't burn up any further," Kiyoko said in response.

"It's right behind your house, isn't it?"

"I think they're renting out the second floor to some young people."

"Well, I've seen young men and women going in and out a lot."

"I guess they've got to consider how they'll make ends meet in their old age, and—"

"Hmm?" Mrs. Yasunaga interrupted, turning to look at the gate.

"What is it?"

Kiyoko, overly sensitive now, shuddered as she followed Mrs. Yasunaga's gaze. Deciding nothing else was to be seen, the bystanders were leaving one by one through the gate.

"That man, in the black vest! . . ."

"What about him?"

The figure of a man in a black vest was walking quickly outside the wall away toward the main road.

"Was he wearing sandals?" Mrs. Yasunaga asked.

"Hmm . . . I didn't notice. An acquaintance of yours?"

". . . Perhaps . . ."

Mrs. Yasunaga thrust her head out over the low wall to follow the man's retreating outline. She didn't go back to the front door where she'd left Kiyoko; suddenly coquettish, she bowed politely and hurried back to her house, disappearing inside. She looks frightened to death, Kiyoko thought, and gazed down at her feet. The white hose lying there, running across the garden, was squashed flat.

"Darn. We should have charged admission."

"Kōichi!"

"Five hundred yen a person, and we'd have made more than ¥10,000."

"You realize there are people suffering because of this fire, I hope."

"I wouldn't get it from them. From the bystanders."

Kōichi's pout revealed a lingering tension.

"Look, up there," Mayu pointed upward. A fireman slowly made his way along the roof of the Tanabes' two-story house. The smoke had thinned out almost completely.

"It's out. Let's go inside."

"I'm going to go out front to see."

Kōichi rushed out the gate, and Mayu, wanting to follow, tugged at her mother's hand. Someone should stay in the house, Kiyoko protested, but she allowed herself to be led out to the main road. The street was flooded in water, and three fire engines were now parked in front of their neighbors' houses, red lights spinning and flashing.

Mr. Tanabe! Mr. Tanabe! Are you there? Shouts came from behind the trees in his garden. *Mr. Tanabe!* The voices moved about from right to left behind the hedge. Among the onlookers who were still surrounding the fire engines, a rumor began to circulate—*Someone's missing!* The circus atmosphere enveloping the bystanders had turned ghoulish. There weren't even any flames, so how could someone possibly burn to death? Kiyoko thought, desperately trying to erase the grisly images that came to her.

Mr. Tanabe had known her husband since he was little and still treated him like a child. Everytime they ran across him in the street, the diminutive old man would be sure to bother them with some fidgety chatter. Kiyoko didn't claim to like him, but the thought of him collapsed on the muddy ground was more than she could bear. She imagined, too, that this old man with his snorting, impatient way of talking, now just a soaked body, was lying twisted in the corner of some dark hallway.

"What's the matter with Mr. Tanabe?" Mayu asked, her eyes alarmed.

"He probably just went out somewhere," Kiyoko answered. "Let's go home," she called out to Kōichi, then turned and walked briskly home.

In the now nearly deserted garden, a fireman was coiling up the white hose which, in the end, didn't get used. Kiyoko stood at the entrance and looked around, feeling she might give him a word of thanks, when she noticed with a start the figure crouched at the edge of the hedge, separating her house from the Tanabes'. Not a bystander, she sensed. Was it the old man?

"Mr. Tanabe? . . . ," Kiyoko said timidly, but the figure standing up in front of her, slightly bent over, was unexpectedly a young man's. Below his jeans, he was barefoot.

"Are you all right?"

"I just twisted my foot a little."

"You live on the second floor of the Tanabes'?"

"No, I was visiting a friend and then all of a sudden I heard there was a fire. . . ."

The young man hurriedly tucked his black shirt into his pants.

"You jumped from the second floor?"

"I grabbed onto a tree and then jumped, so it wasn't as high as you'd imagine, but it really startled me." He started to walk off, dragging one foot, then stopped.

"Is your friend all right?"

"Yeah—just ran out the door." The man lifted his foot off the ground, gazing up at the dark second floor. Ah, Kiyoko somehow knew—so his friend is a girl.

"Is the fire all out now?" he asked, somewhat embarrassedly. So if it was a girl, it meant that she and the man ran out separately—one out the door, the other out the window.

"It stopped before it really began burning, thank goodness. By the way, did you happen to run across old Mr. Tanabe?"

"Mr. Tanabe? You mean the landlord?"

"Yes."

"No, I was so startled I just . . ."

He inclined his head, took a couple of steps in the direction of the gate, his bad foot gingerly touching the ground, then halted.

"Why? Did something happen to him?"

"They don't know where he is, and the firemen are searching for him."

As if suddenly worried, the young man cut across the garden, dragging his leg. The fireman and the hose were gone; the garden was once more empty and dark.

"Let me lend you some shoes or something. You might hurt yourself, going barefoot."

The man looked down vaguely at his feet; they're dirty already, he murmured shyly.

"But there's broken glass around."

"Thanks."

The man held onto the half-opened gate to put on the sandals Kiyoko brought out from the entrance. He gave a clumsy bow and hopped off on one foot into the road.

Hiroshi! A woman's voice, surprisingly loud, bounced off the wall. *Where were you?* the voice continued, suddenly trembling and breaking into a sob. Muted, his reply was hard to catch. Looking out the gate, Kiyoko saw him, his hand resting on the young woman's shoulder, turning the corner where the Takigawas' house was.

"Daddy doesn't know about the fire, does he?" Mayu said from behind her, breathing in deeply.

"No, he doesn't. He wasn't here, after all."

"I'll bet he'll wish he'd been here."

"I wonder . . ."

Kiyoko had never left the children alone at night, but if a fire broke out nearby when she wasn't there—the thought sent a shiver down her spine. She felt a heavy weight plastered on her back.

From the corner where the young man and woman had disappeared, Kōichi came running back.

"They found him—old Mr. Tanabe."

"That's wonderful. Where was he?"

"He was at the Ōmoris' house, the one behind his."

Well, then, where was *Mrs.* Tanabe all this time? Since no one was searching for her, she must have taken refuge too. Again, Kiyoko found it strange that a couple would run to different places.

Kiyoko latched the gate, leading the children back into the house. Outside wasn't cold, but stepping inside, they could feel that the air was warm and stuffy. Kiyoko stood blankly at the dining table and listened to Kōichi boasting to his sister—how the plants in the Tanabes' garden were all trampled, how water had cascaded down the metal staircase like a waterfall. The chopsticks on her half-eaten bowl of rice, the empty soup plate in which she hadn't yet poured in the corn soup, the slightly burned cream croquettes, and salad bowl—all seemed so distant now. She couldn't believe she had been in the middle of eating. She tossed the leftover rice into the garbage receptacle in the sink; covered the salad with plastic wrap, putting it back in the fridge; then made some instant coffee, gulping it down like medicine. Through the kitchen window, the red lights of the fire engine continued blinking, and a stir of people could still be heard from the Tanabes' in back. But the interior of her home, framed by its walls and window, felt protected, as if it were a small, safe burrow.

"It's all over," Kiyoko whispered. A hot breeze flushed through her, and she saw the young man who had hurt his foot, jumping from the second floor; the young woman sobbing out

Hiroshi; and the small old man seeking shelter with the Ōmoris. The dull moan of the refrigerator behind wrapped itself around her.

It wasn't much of a fire, but in daylight, you could easily tell that the second floor of the Tanabes' was no longer inhabitable. The fire had apparently broken out in the corner room furthest away from Kiyoko's house. With the roof stripped off, the blackened timbers were visible; the outside wall was sooty, discolored in patches. The fire hadn't reached to the first floor but inundated as it was by water the first floor was no doubt unlivable, too.

That evening, Kiyoko told Fusao, who had returned home late, about the fire. Asking repeatedly if their own house was all right, he went out without coming in, straight over to the Tanabes'. But Fusao reported back to her that the gate was roped off and a policeman stood guard. Fusao seemed relieved. From the outside, at least, the two-story house was still standing, basically intact.

His sobered-up face pale, Fusao sat at the dining table and Kiyoko recounted the events surrounding the fire and the confusion when old Mr. Tanabe had been missing for a time. As she spoke, the scene came back to her of the men's voices in the garden, their calling out the old man's name; again, she recalled the awful vision she'd conjured up.

"It might have been better for the two of them to live quietly in their old house," Fusao murmured. "Having apartments is dangerous," he added, "with young people coming in and out; you have no idea what might happen."

Kiyoko, on the verge of telling him about the young man crouching in a corner of the garden, for some reason swallowed back the words. He'd hear everything from Mayu tomorrow; in the meantime she wanted to hold onto the image of the young couple for a bit longer.

The next morning, before leaving for work, Fusao went over to the Ōmoris' house, where the old couple had been reunited and taken refuge. "Mr. Tanabe seemed all right," Fusao told Kiyoko, "but for Mrs. Tanabe, it was apparently a terrible shock."

Fusao left home again, and Kiyoko saw him off. The old couple had spent the night at the Ōmoris'. But where had that young couple slept? Kiyoko couldn't let go of the thought.

* * * * *

Three or four days after the fire, when things were just starting to settle down, Mr. Tanabe showed up at Kiyoko's house. Mayu had gone to play with a friend after school, and Kiyoko had sat down on the living-room sofa, just opening the newspaper, when the front doorbell rang.

"Coming," she replied, and went out, finding the front door unlocked after Mayu had gone. "Just a second and I'll open it," she called out. But whoever was outside, ignored her, ringing the chime over and over. Standing there was a small old man wearing an oversized, white dress shirt with the creases still crisp. The sleeves were too long, half hiding his hands. Before uttering any words, he snorted deeply and shook his head.

"Is the lady of the house at home? The grandmother, that is."

"What? You mean my husband's mother, Mrs. Oda?"

"The grandmother. Yoshie-san." He insisted again impatiently.

The name vaguely reminded Kiyoko of a photograph. A sepia-colored photo, stiffly mounted, of a woman, a severe look to her. Her hair was done up in an old-fashioned style. Kiyoko had no idea if the photo had been taken when she was young or middle aged.

"Fusao's grandmother, you mean." When Kiyoko finally figured out who he was asking for, she became flustered.

"The grandmother." The old man tapped impatiently on the pillar at the entrance, peering past Kiyoko into the house. She had the weird sensation that someone was standing right behind her.

"If you're looking for Oda Yoshie, she died a long time ago."

The old man stared back at Kiyoko, disbelief on his face.

"This happened a long time ago, before I moved into the Odas' house. I never even met her."

Kiyoko, nervous, tried to figure out how to convince him that the person he had come to see was long gone.

"Is that right. I see."

The old man nodded, shaking his head slightly and closing the door—leaving Kiyoko standing there blankly. She felt uneasy; clearly, he hadn't believed her but had just given up, deciding that talking to her was getting him nowhere. The only sound lingering from behind the door was the man's unhurried snorting, which made Kiyoko feel even more creepy. When she told Fusao later that evening about the old man's visit, her husband looked puzzled. "When I went to see him right after the fire, he seemed all right," Fusao said doubtfully.

The next day, the front doorbell rang again, around twilight, just about the time for Kōichi to come home. Kiyoko was about to open the door, a cheerful greeting on her lips. As she slipped off the chain, about to unlock the door, the thought struck her—it's someone else. Sure enough, there stood old Mr. Tanabe again.

"Is the lady of the house in? The older lady?"

He had on the same white shirt as the day before and as always his words were restless, accompanied by that sound that welled up from somewhere between his throat and nose.

"Do you mean Oda Yoshie?"

"Yes, Yoshie-san."

"Grandmother died a long time ago." Kiyoko spoke more authoritatively than the day before.

"And you would be Tomiko-san?"

She couldn't tell if he understood her reply or not as he gazed with great interest into Kiyoko's face.

"I'm Fusao's wife," she said.

"Oh, Fusao. He really has turned out well, hasn't he?"

She could only nod vaguely at this.

"And you had something you wanted to say to Fusao's grandmother?"

If she could find out what he wanted, she might be able to try a different tack, Kiyoko thought, but soon regretted her words.

Now, he'd be sure that the person he sought was still alive. The old man suddenly straightened and politely bowed his head.

"I've really caused you a lot of trouble, and I wanted to apologize."

"I understand your wanting to see her, but grandmother has passed away and is no longer here."

"Oh . . ." He straightened up and looked doubtfully at Kiyoko.

"She died of a cerebral hemorrhage."

"I see."

Kiyoko felt impatient, seeing her words go right over his head.

"Do you understand?"

Making that wet sound deep in his throat, which made even Kiyoko feel it was hard to breathe, the old man turned around and left without another word.

"What did Mr. Tanabe want?" Mayu asked from behind Kiyoko as she locked the door.

"He thinks Daddy's grandmother still lives here and came to see her. She used to live in the old house, but passed away."

"I know all about it—the old house."

"Don't tell fibs. Not even Mommy knows about it."

"One night, Daddy told me. There was a toy room right here. And a deep well under the kitchen."

"Don't be silly. Old Mr. Tanabe is just confused after the fire."

She scooted Mayu back to the living room. Having the old man visit so often is making us *all* a little strange, she thought irritatedly. Uneasily, she felt that if she stepped out for a while and left the children alone, Mr. Tanabe might force his way in and make them listen to a weird story. Perhaps, if Fusao talked with him, he'd be convinced, she thought. She decided to ask Fusao to do so after he returned from work that evening. This decided, she stood at the sink to begin getting dinner ready.

Fusao got home late and for two days didn't have time to visit the old man. Fortunately, Mr. Tanabe didn't show up during this period. The after-fire cleanup seemed to be progressing bit by bit.

And occasionally what sounded like the old man's voice could be heard from the garden in back. When restoration on the house begins, Kiyoko thought with relief, his spirits will pick up, and he'll be back to normal.

The next afternoon, on the way back from shopping at the supermarket with Mayu, Kiyoko discovered a pair of old sandals neatly lined up at the entrance. On top of them, a small piece of paper had been placed, with the words *Thank you very much* written in a round, slightly wide hand. The letters were drawn in such a playful script that Kiyoko couldn't tell which of the two—the young man or woman—had written the note. If they returned the sandals, she thought with a smile, they must still be getting along all right. She regretted not having kidded the young man about abandoning his precious girlfriend and escaping through the window.

Fusao got home after 9:00. Kiyoko reheated his dinner, and was just telling Mayu to take a bath, when the doorbell rang.

"Who could it be?"

Looking at her husband's face, she saw the image of the old man standing at the door flash through her mind. This is perfect, she thought—now Fusao can speak to him directly. As she started for the door, Fusao stopped her.

"I'll get it."

Kiyoko followed him. The chain rattled, as he had some trouble getting it open. She sensed that it wasn't the old man standing there but someone else.

A white-haired old lady stood quietly. Mrs. Tanabe.

"I'm sorry to bother you so late."

Lifting her head after bowing, she quickly gazed around the foyer.

"What's the matter?" Fusao said, inviting her inside.

"No, thank you. I just thought that perhaps my husband was visiting you."

She didn't take a single step forward and blinked repeatedly.

"No, we haven't seen him. Mr. Tanabe isn't at home?"

Fusao looked back at Kiyoko, at a loss what to do. He seemed confused about connecting what she had told him about the old man's visits and the old lady's appearance now. "He's come during the day," Kiyoko started to explain, but the old lady spoke first.

"Almost every day he goes out, saying he's going to visit the Odas, so I just thought . . . I'm sorry to bother you."

She bowed again, about to leave, when Fusao stopped her.

"Just a moment. When did you see him last?"

"In the evening, after he came back from your place and had some dinner. . . ."

"But he hasn't been here, either yesterday or today." In spite of herself, Kiyoko's voice was harsh. It made her a bit angry, even uneasy, to think that Fusao might think she wasn't telling the truth.

"This evening, did he say he was going to visit us?" Fusao's voice got a bit louder.

"I just noticed at night that he wasn't there. . . ."

"That's no good. I wonder what happened. Actually, after the fire, he came here twice to see my grandmother."

"Your grandmother?"

"Yes, Yoshie-san. He wanted to apologize for the fire."

"Goodness . . . ," the old lady said in a small voice, moving her hand to her mouth.

"At any rate," Fusao said, "I'm a little worried, so I'm going to go look for him. The Ōmoris wouldn't know anything, would they?"

Fusao changed from sandals to shoes, as the old lady watched him blankly. "I'll stop by them and then look around the neighborhood," Fusao said, guiding Mrs. Tanabe out, and he left. As she listened to their footsteps, intermingling, then receding, Kiyoko had a strong feeling that old Mr. Tanabe might show up out of the blue at their door.

*   *   *   *   *

The clock on the wall gulped back a muffled sound, signaling that the minute hand had reached the twelve. If its vocal cords had been healthy, then eleven gentle, metallic chimes would have rung out. Two hours had already passed since Fusao left. It'd be a lot faster, Kiyoko thought, if he called the police after one quick look around the neighborhood. Her irritation was about to boil over when the front gate clattered open. No matter what's happened, she told herself, it's better than waiting like this, not knowing what's going on. She ran out to the front door.

"We found him. But it wasn't easy." Fusao said playfully, shaking his head.

"Where was he?"

"I called all the places Mrs. Tanabe could think of, but he wasn't anywhere."

"So where was he?"

"We thought that maybe he was just wandering nearby, so someone from the Ōmoris and I split up and walked around looking for him."

"Where did you find him?"

Finally taking off his shoes, Fusao hurried into the living room.

"At the railroad crossing."

"*What?*"

"Can I have a glass of water? I'm parched."

He gulped down the entire cup of water Kiyoko gave to him and sat down exhausted on the sofa.

"You know that small railroad crossing on the west side of the station? Where all those real-estate office buildings are bunched together? There used to be a farmhouse there and a bamboo grove growing along the railroad tracks."

"And then?"

"He was standing next to the bamboo grove facing the railroad tracks."

"But there isn't any bamboo grove there."

"So, he was standing in this tiny lot between the real-estate buildings, facing the other direction."

"Why?"

"I made sure no train was coming, and I said, 'Is that you, Mr. Tanabe?' He turned around really slowly."

"I wonder what he was doing." Kiyoko didn't want to put into words what she had been imagining.

"He moved sluggishly, not like he usually does, as if something had come loose inside him."

"Did he know who you were right away?"

"When I told him it was late and we should go home, he followed me without a word."

"That was a close call, wasn't it."

"When the bamboo grove was there, you couldn't see things well, and many people died there. There was a warning bell, but no crossing barrier."

"Did he say anything about your grandmother?"

"On the way back he did. I had no idea . . ."

Fusao faltered, finding it hard to go on. Kiyoko felt, along with the night, the heavy dampness of a bamboo grove settling on her husband's shoulders.

"After my grandfather died, my father was transferred and the whole family moved out. For a time, my grandmother lived alone in that big house. It seems that the Tanabes looked after her."

"It's the first time I've ever heard this." For Kiyoko the revelation was as if it were something that was taking place in another world, before she was born.

"And when she lived alone, it seems my grandmother sometimes went over to the railroad crossing by the bamboo grove and just stood there."

"Is that really true?"

"It's what old Mr. Tanabe says, so it's hard to say for sure, but I believe it."

A gentle calm descended on his words. Kiyoko could picture it—the tall, sepia-colored woman, her hair done up high, standing all alone at the railroad crossing, the thick bamboo grove behind her.

"Maybe since I turned him away, Mr. Tanabe went over there to see her."

"Or else he was going somewhere even further away . . ."

They were silent, and from the next room they could hear, faintly, Mayu grinding her teeth in her sleep.

behind the window

He was just going out the gate when someone called to him.

In the road, a young man in shorts and a black T-shirt stood in the fierce noon glare.

"Mr. Kiuchi. This was in our mailbox."

A weak sort of look gathered round the young man's eyes as he hesitantly proffered a postcard to Masaki. The long fingers that held the edge of it were bent back unnaturally, pale white, as if they were like some internal organ that never sees the light of day. At his fingertips glittered a rectangle of an intense indigo sea.

"Thanks," Masaki nodded, accepting the postcard from the young man, whom he remembered as his neighbors', the Yasunagas', younger son. Masaki quickly flipped the card over to check the name of the woman who sent it. "Thanks. I appreciate it."

He read the short message, written in a bold hand in ballpoint, and sighed with relief.

"Was it an important postcard?" the young man asked, ingratiatingly.

"No, but I'm glad you didn't just put it in our mailbox. She might have read it."

"You mean your wife?"

"Right."

"But there's nothing really written on it."

"You read it?"

The young man had fallen in step with Masaki naturally as if he too were headed toward the station. Masaki turned to look at him.

"I'm sorry. I just thought it was a beautiful card, and I wanted to see what ocean that was a picture of, and I ended up reading it."

"Well, if you insisted you hadn't, that would be hard to believe, wouldn't it? But this isn't something I mind other people reading."

"Because it's like a kind of code just the two of you understand." Realizing he wasn't going to be scolded for having read the postcard, the young man revealed his curiosity in a friendly tone of voice.

"You're the younger brother, right? You're attending college?"

"Yes. I'm Tōru. I'm a sophomore."

The boy's childish way of answering was amusing. Gently, he wiped away the sweat from his forehead with the base of his thumb as if he were brushing water droplets off a leaf.

"What did you feel when you read the postcard?"

"At first, I thought it was sent from abroad. The picture is the Mediterranean, but it was sent from Tokyo."

"It's a message that she's back."

Masaki patted his face with a colored handkerchief and put on his sunglasses, which were about to fall out of the shallow pocket of his polo shirt. The world around him was suddenly bathed in softness, far away. Hidden behind the grey lenses, he was struck by a desire to tease the college student beside him.

"Does she often travel abroad?" Tōru asked.

"It's part of her job."

"Why is it awkward for that postcard to arrive?"

"Well, if she's back that means we can see each other."

"Oh, I see. Actually she didn't need to write anything on it."

"That would be a little too obvious," Masaki said.

"But a totally blank postcard would be pretty erotic, I think."

"Erotic? . . ."

"It's like when some college students wear their school uniforms and girls think it's totally sexy."

"So a blank postcard and a school uniform are the same?"

"Well, they're somehow similar. Don't you think so?"

His confidence deflated, Tōru's long fingers tugged at the thin chain around his neck.

The two walked for a while in silence down the hot, sunny road.

"I didn't see your sports car. Did your wife go out?"

Being asked about his wife made Masaki uncomfortable. This boy from next door must have been curious about them for some time. Masaki felt a twinge of regret that he'd talked to him as an equal. "Yes, she's gone out for a while," he replied. "You're a college student, so you must have a lot of girlfriends," he continued, changing the topic.

"Yeah, a few, I guess."

"No, I mean someone you're pretty involved with."

"Not really. If you'd like, I could introduce you to one or two girls."

"No, I'm fine. Just make sure 'you're' doing OK"

"But now I know your secret, Mr. Kiuchi."

The boy's teasing tone made it hard to tell if he was joking or serious.

"Well," Masaki continued, "I'm going to take the train, so I'll be seeing you." Tōru held his hands to the sides of his shorts and stiffly from the waist up bowed his head slightly. His narrow eyes slanted upward and reminded Masaki of a fox. The boy turned the corner of the department store in front of the station and strode off. Masaki folded the rectangle of sea in half, stuck it in the hip of his cotton trousers, and buttoned his pocket. Inside it felt warm and damp from the sweat seeping through his underwear.

* * * * *

Masaki ate cold summer noodles at a *soba* noodle shop, a makeshift breakfast and lunch, and then stopped by a coffee establishment where he meticulously read three porn novels serialized in three different sports newspapers. In one, a young man was sleeping with the female super of his apartment, whom he'd apparently just met, when a widow started banging on the door. In the second novel, a nurse was being assaulted by a doctor in a consultation room. In the third sports paper, a man had taken two women on a yacht, was making love to one, who'd taken off her swimsuit, from behind, while the second woman eagerly watched the proceedings. Masaki felt momentarily excited, but a familiar bleakness took hold of him. The more the novels proved to be unfulfilling, the more he felt as if the lower half of his body were wrapped in a filthy rag, discarded on the floor.

He checked the front of his trousers to make sure nothing was obvious, put on his sunglasses, and left the shop. It wasn't far to home but by the time he got back, drips of sweat had clammily crawled their way down his chest under his polo shirt. With each step, his underwear clung to his behind.

In the shower, Masaki rubbed the hair below his stomach with a large bar of imported soap. Among the bubbles his scrubbing had produced, his penis stood at haft mast, neither totally up nor down. The quiet of the home, where he was alone, urged him on. Remnants of the novels he'd read at the coffee shop clung to a dark corner of his body. He rubbed his half-erect penis, which now stuck out from between his tightly clenched legs, with the slick soap film. Gradually, it began to harden and point toward the ceiling. He felt no pleasure at all, his body endured a dark red loneliness. What the heck do I think I'm doing? he thought. I'm not some twenty-year-old student. Michiko's dry body didn't come to mind. And neither did the body of the girl whose name was written on the back of the postcard. He put his mouth to the shower head, rinsing it out with lukewarm water. He let the water overflow and, mixing it with saliva, dribbled both down his chin to his stomach. He found it comforting.

Outside the glass door, the phone rang. Feeling as if he had been spied on, Masaki, flustered, wrapped a towel around his waist and picked up the receiver with a wet hand. The empty house was suddenly filled with promise. He imagined a single black line at the bottom of a dark blue sea, heading straight off into the distance.

Before he had even put the phone to his ear, though, the hurried voice on the other end crushed his hopes.

"It's me. What were you doing, Masaki?"

Masaki felt confused, as if his wife's gaze had shone fully on him when he was in the bath.

"It was hot, so I was taking a shower. What's up? Did you meet Mr. Koike?"

"I met him, but it didn't work out. He already hired some young girl last week. That's why you can't just sit on that kind of information—you've got to act on it. You know this, but still you didn't do anything. . . ."

Michiko's voice took on even more the acerbic tone she always had when nagging Masaki.

"The job wasn't that great, anyway," he said. "You're better off waiting for something else."

"That's not true. You're not doing anything and just want to get me out of the house. I know what's going on. Whenever you're up to something I get in the way."

Masaki pressed down firmly on the front of his bath towel to keep it down, but all he encountered was a vague flaccidness.

"That wasn't what I intended at all. But that's too bad about the job—are you still at Mr. Koike's?"

"I left a long time ago. Can't expect me to hang around in a place where I'm not wanted."

"So you're coming home now?"

"Why do I have to come back?"

"Huh?" Masaki asked in spite of himself. Drops of water still clung to his body, and he shivered in the air conditioner's breeze. "What do you mean, 'Why?' . . . This is your home."

"Sometimes I wonder about that."

With these clipped, rising inflections, the phone clicked off. Using the bath towel around his waist, he carefully wiped off the receiver, wet with a mixture of sweat and shower droplets. At least for the moment, he was free from having to think about anything. Replacing the receiver, he heard her voice suddenly echoing in his mind.

Why do I have to come back?

Why do I have to come back? . . .

Well, why indeed? Masaki cocked his head to one side, the gesture childish. "Why, indeed?" he said aloud now, getting into it, crossing his arms at his chest, hugging his chilly shoulders. *Under the big chestnut tree . . .* He remembered a dance that accompanied this children's song but couldn't recall if he'd learned it himself in kindergarten or had seen some other children performing the dance.

So-so-ra, so-ra, sora. The rabbit's dance . . .

He stuck his index fingers up to both sides of his head and skipped around the room. His bath towel fell off and slipped to the floor, but he kept on dancing.

El-e-phant, el-e-phant, my, your trunk is very long. . . .

Naked on all fours, he crawled along the floor. Unfortunately, nothing he had dangled down far enough to make a good elephant trunk.

He's lost, he's lost, poor little kitten . . .

He sang the half-remembered lyrics but couldn't remember what sort of actions accompanied the song. Where is Michiko right now? he thought, as an uneasy chill ran deep within his chest. He stopped singing.

Michiko's second phone call came soon after Masaki had reluctantly settled down at his desk, vaguely flipping through an English magazine he couldn't have cared less about. Two places in the hefty business journal, published in New York, were marked with red Post-its; Masaki took care to avoid just those pages. If he did open them, he'd come face-to-face with the work he could not avoid any longer. Or rather, he'd come face-to-face with himself, who hadn't even begun the work he had to do.

The deadline was the next day. Masaki had quit his job

without much thought. After his unemployment insurance ran out, his college friend Masuzawa talked his company into sending some translation work his way. Masaki knew full well he couldn't let the deadline pass without finishing. His English needed work and his translations tended to be full of guesses or omissions where his linguistic skills failed him. The least he could do for his friend was to get the work done by the deadline. More than from a sense of duty, though, his motivation was fear—fear that he'd lose his only source of income. The phone rang again.

Feeling saved by the bell, he left his desk. Beyond the closed window, the sun was sinking, but hot yellow light still clung to the leaves of the feeble magnolia growing on the edge of his small garden.

"—on a drive."

The voice spilled out of the receiver before he'd even gotten it to his ear.

"Where did you say?"

"I got angry, so I bought a swimsuit, and that's why I'm driving toward the sea now."

"Where along the sea?"

"What does it matter? I have a right to go to the sea, don't I?"

"Going to the sea is fine, but at this hour?"

"The sea knows no time."

"You won't be back for dinner?"

"_____"

Michiko didn't reply.

Was this because the sea knows no dinnertime, either? Or because she really was worried about dinner? He couldn't tell.

"Hello? Are you still there?" He was afraid that if he didn't say something she'd hang up. "Are you with someone?"

"Well, you have Aoki, don't you?" Michiko shot back, as if she'd been waiting for the chance.

Masaki realized how out of place his words had been.

"That's all over, and first of all, she's not even in Japan."

"But she came back, didn't she?"

"That's impossible."

As he spoke, Masaki unconsciously searched the hip pocket of his trousers. His fingers touched the pliant postcard.

"No—she was due to come back a little while ago."

Her strangely confident reply made him flinch. A sudden thought struck him: maybe Tōru from next door had run across Michiko. *I know your secret, Mr. Kiuchi*, he had joked, words that had more immediacy now. Maybe he wasn't joking after all. *I didn't see your car. Is your wife out?* Tōru had asked. When Masaki heard him, he didn't give it much thought—the young man was interested in us from before, he thought, but maybe there was a deeper meaning hidden in his words. What if, for instance, Tōru had made a promise to meet Michiko somewhere this afternoon?

Masaki didn't really believe any of this, but the delusions rushed at him like a landslide. And strangely, they were mixed with a touch of pleasure.

"So, what time do you think you'll be able to come back?" He changed the subject, trying to keep his voice calm.

"I have no idea. . . ." Her voice was no longer scathing but subdued, closing in on itself.

"But you will be back?"

"I don't know. . . . I'll think about that after I get to the sea."

"Don't do this. Come on home."

"But I have no idea why I should come back."

Because I'm here, he wanted to say, but the words stuck in his throat. He felt himself, waiting at home like this, strangely insignificant and shallow. And the house that surrounded him was like a house made out of cards, plunked down on the ground.

"I don't care if you're late—just come back. I'll be up no matter when you come back."

"I have to go. Make sure to eat something for dinner."

He could picture Michiko turning away and hanging up the phone. *Make sure you eat something*—her final words were all that he had to cling to.

She'll be back. Things happen, like a kind of joke, and if you treat it like a joke everything will be OK, Masaki murmured. With nothing else to do, he walked to the window on the east side of the house. From there, past the cement-block wall, he could see part of the verandah of the Yasunagas' house. Sticking out from the shadows of the wall was one end of a clothes pole, with white laundry, underwear perhaps, hanging down. The suspicion he'd had that his wife was going to the sea with someone else vanished. He was sure now that she was alone. And that was even more frightening. If Michiko ran further and further inward, inside herself, she might indeed never return. If that was the case, he thought, breathing out heavily, he'd much prefer her to have met Tōru. On the verandah, something moved and the washing was snatched away.

When the phone rang the third time, Masaki was standing in the kitchen under the fluorescent light, eating a bowl of cold rice and bottled *namedake*, mushroom paste in soy sauce. He didn't feel particularly hungry but anxiously felt that he should put some food in his stomach. An uneasy feeling that something might be about to happen made him bolt it down. The slimy *namedake* felt like his own anxiety, poured out over the rice.

At the sound of the phone, he hurriedly set his bowl aside, gulped down a mouthful, and picked up the receiver.

"Hello—is that you, Masaki?"

Instead of the rushed words he'd been expecting, he heard an extremely laid-back voice of a man.

"Hey, you still at the office? Working overtime?" Masaki replied, a bit of mushroom paste still stuck beside his tongue.

"They shut off the air conditioner so it's hot, about time to head on home. I really need to get that work I asked you to do finished by tomorrow, so I just thought I'd double-check."

"Sorry you had to go to the trouble, but I think I'll finish on time. I'm right in the middle of it."

"Just don't have a beer and forget about it."

"Like I could."

"What do you mean?"

"I don't know, I'm just feeling jittery."

No, no. The one on the right's supposed to be set up the same as the one on the left. Masaki could hear Masuzawa giving instructions to someone nearby. The image of a busy, after-hours office on the other end of the line crossed Masaki's mind, and he felt pathetic, even dirty, standing in the kitchen eating cold rice.

"I'm sorry. What did you say?"

"You sound really busy," Masaki said.

"I'm almost through. Oh, when you come by tomorrow, if I'm not here, just leave your translation with one of the girls in my office."

"OK. You won't be there?"

"Yeah, well . . . it's my wife, she's in the hospital."

"She hasn't delivered yet?"

"There's a good chance it'll be tomorrow. What about you guys? No plans of your own?"

"Well, you gotta do something before that's possible."

"Dummy. They say doing it too vigorously isn't good, either. Maybe that's your problem."

"Certain conditions have to be met first, and we haven't met them."

"What are you talking about? I live in a company apartment, but you've got your own home, with a lawn, even."

"Can't make children with lawns."

Masaki felt his feelings soften; the phone call, which had started with urging him to finish his work, had ended up being about his house.

His friend said he'd stop by the hospital to see his wife after work, and hung up. Masaki realized all the more how deserted his house was. The rice in the bowl with the leftover mushroom paste looked like animal feed, and his appetite vanished. He rinsed the leftovers into the garbage receptacle in the sink and drank luke-warm water from the bowl to which some mushroom paste still clung. His stomach contained the same contents he'd just thrown into the garbage, he realized, suddenly nauseous.

He returned to his desk with the magazine spread out over it but didn't get to work. He couldn't shake the memory of what Masuzawa had described to him the last time they met, namely, his wife's swollen belly. As her pregnancy progressed and stomach swelled, her navel got shallower; the bottom of it gradually poked out to the point where it protruded.

Masaki recalled Michiko's white stomach and her deep navel. Desire seemed always silently lurking within that vertical, long, and shapely hole. If she were pregnant, would her navel, too, swell up like that? Certainly, it wasn't concern over losing her navel that made Michiko refuse to have children, was it? . . .

Even so, where was that lovely navel running to? If she were heading to the Shonan coast, she would have reached the sea a long time ago. Masaki turned to look out the window into the darkness. Michiko's absence seemed to hover in the gloom, just where the concrete wall beyond the tiny lawn floated palely. Masaki averted his eyes. Raucous music intruded over from the house next door, with the sound of a woman singing—nearly screaming. Tōru must have come back.

Masaki counted on his fingers the hours remaining and finally got down to work. But after a short while, he got up from his desk again. This time he was certain the phone call was from Michiko even before he picked up the receiver. His work had not gone well; all he'd done was look up words in a dictionary. He threw it all aside and leaped to the phone.

"What's the matter? Where are you?" he asked in a rush of words, before he could make out what she was saying. With their words clashing together, perhaps she didn't hear him.

"*What?*" she asked.

"Where are you, I'm asking."

". . . I don't know where I am."

"But you went to the sea, right?"

"I'm not going to the sea."

"But didn't you say you were, Michiko?"

"That was a lie."

"You said you bought some underwear, so you were going to the sea."

"A *swimsuit*. That was just nonsense."

She didn't scold him for his mistake; her reply in a faraway voice left him confused and abandoned.

"OK, so where are you now?"

"I don't know myself. . . . The only thing I know is I've gotten farther and farther away from home. . . ."

Her voice did sound fainter than the earlier calls.

"Do you have any money? The car was pretty low on gas."

If he didn't talk about something concrete, she really would vanish into the vast expanse of night. Are you on the Daisan Keihin? Or the Tōmei Highway? Or are you headed north on the Tōhoku Jūkan? He ran off a list of possible routes, but she just replied *uh huh* to each one.

"I'm not going to call anymore," she muttered. She hadn't heard any of his questions.

"Wait a second. I don't know what's happened, but I need to talk with you, face-to-face, not on the phone."

"Nothing happened. Did something happen to you?"

"No, nothing. But if nothing happened, then you don't need to go off so far away."

"I'm going to hang up now."

"Wait. What about me?"

"There's some bread in a paper bag on top of the fridge. You can—"

Her words were cut off abruptly as if she were calling from a pay phone. Masaki couldn't lay the phone down quite yet.

"I don't care about breakfast. Are you really some place so far away you can't come back tonight?"

He continued to call out to the black receiver, his substitute Michiko.

"_____"

"Well, I guess there's nothing I can do, then. Be careful, there're a lot of speeding cars at night."

"_____"

"No, I don't think I'll be able to sleep. I have some work for Masuzawa I've got to finish and deliver by tomorrow."

"_____"

"Maybe so. But sometimes, there are things a person just can't do anything about."

In the fathomless silence, as if he were pressing his ear against a wooden board, he felt his words becoming antagonistic.

"Yes, but at our age, to have our own house with a garden, we're really blessed. I'm grateful to your father. We're not living up to his expectations, though."

"_____"

"But that's a completely different problem. Don't you think you're being a bit selfish?"

"_____"

"Don't be stupid. OK, now it's my turn—what was all that with Mr. Tomita the other day?"

"_____"

"You say things to me, but you don't realize what you're doing yourself."

Masaki felt someone was right next to him, listening to his intense words. He laid a hand on his waist and stood up straight.

"_____"

"You idiot. You think you can make a fool of me? I haven't said anything, but what do you think's been on my mind every day?"

"_____"

"Fine, don't come back. You're the one who left, so that's fine with me. Even if you do come back, don't expect me to let you in."

"_____"

"Shut up. Go to hell. You're not worth me begging you to come back."

He shouted this final sentence and slammed the phone down. He couldn't stop shaking. Sweat bubbled up on his neck. "Well, I guess I told her," he muttered and breathed a long sigh, drained. Thirsty, he reached for a nearby measuring cup, filled it, and drank it down in one gulp. As the chlorine taste hit his throat, he was struck by an anxious thought. Did she really hang up? When their conversation was over, there had been an audible click, but maybe Michiko just stayed on the line, silently listening to him. His composure suddenly collapsed, and he looked around the room.

* * * * *

Masaki worked until dawn, finishing about half the translation. Usually as the night deepened, he would turn off the air conditioner and open the shutters wide to let in the cool air. But now hot night air lay heavy over the whole house and he left the air conditioner on. Masaki writhed between two opposing emotions—the hope that Michiko would be coming home and the fear that she would never return. He concentrated on his dictionary work to drive the unease from his mind.

Every time a car drove by the road in front of his house, though, his hand halted. Whenever the white light of a headlight shone over the concrete wall, he half rose. But none of the cars slowed down or began to stop. It was doubtful whether he'd finish the work by the set time. After 3:00 A.M., he grew exhausted, going back and forth between the hopes raised by the passing cars and the analysis of consumption patterns of American housewives. He threw aside his pen.

He was taking a shower when the frosted glass lit up slightly. The light grew steadily brighter, and a shadow of the iron bars outside the bathroom window slowly slipped above the glass. The shape imprinted itself on his eyes for a moment, then disappeared. He hurriedly turned off the water. The car engine rumbled lowly. A car door shut.

See, she's back, after all. Masaki ran naked from the bathroom, his feet dripping. He waited for the sound of the gate being opened, so the car could drive in. Instead, an engine revved noisily and the car drove away.

Heavy footsteps staggered outside the wall.

"Hey there, Tako. So you waited up for me."

A thick, loud, drunken voice filled the narrow road. A cat's reedy "meow" answered.

"Thank you very much for waiting up," the man continued. "You're the only one who really understands."

After that the voice quickly hushed; the gate of the Yasunagas' shut, and the neighborhood grew silent again.

A flutter rose in Masaki's throat and his body felt agitated. He rinsed himself again with hot water, turned off the air conditioner, closed the shutters, and collapsed into bed. If Michiko were there, she'd insist on closing the windows and curtains, too, but with her gone there was no need. Without Michiko, there was nothing worth stealing in the house.

"At least *some* people come home. . . ," Masaki muttered, staring at the ceiling.

Once again a light from a car driving by swam across the shutter above his head.

This house is too big for one person to live in.

He himself didn't know if he was serious or joking.

The depths of the sky were beginning to glow palely.

* * * * *

See you later! A child's shrill voice pierced Masaki's ears, and he woke up.

You have your handkerchief and Kleenex? An even more shrill woman's voice followed.

It took him a moment to recognize this as the usual morning goings-on at the Odas' house diagonally across the street.

In the stretch of light shining in from the garden, Masaki turned to the bed beside him. The lavender bed cover lay flat, untouched.

So, Michiko never came back—the thought soaked into his head, heavy from lack of sleep. His mind was groggy from only sleeping three hours, but strangely that one thought rose up with great clarity. As if the part of his brain that thinks about Michiko never slept.

They'd quarrel or rather Michiko would get angry and end up driving off in a huff—she'd done that any number of times. It was always at night, and she always came back by morning. But this time was different. Michiko had left in the morning, when Masaki was still sleeping, without a word. So maybe, she had no idea when she should come back, and went further and further away.

He rolled over, the light covering catching between his legs. The front of his body was uncomfortably stiff.

Morning phallus / rising gallantly / And you have left me.

A haiku verse he'd written as a student rose to his lips like a burp. When he showed it to a friend, he had asked what word indicated the season, a must for haiku. Morning phallus, the young Masaki replied. So what season is it, then? his friend insisted. Summer, of course, Masaki answered. His friend was silent, but later when Masaki happened to check in a haiku seasonal manual at a bookstore, of course he couldn't find any such rule.

This haiku, perhaps better termed a *senryu*—comic haiku—had its origin in something that happened in the summer. At first he'd used the words "rising in vain," but that seemed a bit too obvious, so he changed it to "gallantly." That's better, he thought—more tragic. This was more than ten years ago. Now the verse struck Masaki as awkward and strained. He hated the feeling that the twenty-year-old youth who'd composed it was making fun of the thirty-something man he'd become. A man who, presently, lay sprawled in bed, clutching a bed cover, all alone.

He wanted to sleep a bit more, but the relentless sunshine and his anxiety about his wife forced him out of bed. The pale sun shining down on the patchy lawn was already steamy.

Masaki took out the bread from the bag on top of the fridge that Michiko had mentioned. He was struck by its sour, yeasty smell. It wasn't the yeast so much as it was the bread growing moldy. He spat out the mouthful he'd taken in and reached for the milk in the fridge door. The carton was nearly empty.

The kitchen would get hot if he boiled water, so he made some instant coffee with tap water and drank it. Undissolved granules of coffee stuck to his tongue, surprisingly bitter.

Still in his sweaty pajamas, Masaki went outside to gather the paper from the mailbox. As he turned back to go inside, he saw the face of a white-haired woman staring out the window of the Takigawas' house across the road. He nodded vaguely to her and hurried inside. Without the car outside, the front of the house seemed exposed and helpless.

There were no reports of traffic accidents in the paper. If he didn't go back to sleep, there would be nothing else to do but wait for her return. Reluctantly, he sat down at his desk where the English magazine lay open, just as he had left it. When he worked for a company, he'd never started work this early. Maybe, he thought in all seriousness, this is the kick in the pants I need to get me back on track. But soon after getting up, he felt no strength in his hand; trying to grasp the ballpoint pen tightly only made him irritable.

It was nearly noon when, hungry, Masaki got up from his desk. No telephone calls had come, not even a wrong number. Not a single person cared about him. He was all alone in the house, a thought that saddened him. He stood up and stretched as hard as he could; he felt dizzy, his legs unsteady. He realized he hadn't had more than a bite to eat since the cold noodles at the noodle shop the day before. She's been gone one whole day, he sighed.

He hadn't noticed it in the morning, but now Masaki's eye was caught by a bit of white cloth that had fallen on the lawn next to the wall separating his house from the Yasunagas'. It wasn't particularly windy, so the laundry hadn't blown over. He opened the creaky shutter and, as if deliberately abusing his enervated body, stepped out into the blinding sunlight of the garden.

What he found was a long cloth made up of three Japanese hand towels sewn together in a long strip. These days it was unusual enough to see a faded Japanese hand towel, but why three of them were sewn together he had no idea. From the position where the cloth fell, it could only be from the Yasunagas'. An old woman lived in their house. For all he knew, there was a special use the old people put these cloths to.

It was all a bit strange, and he was thinking about laying the cloth on top of the wall when Masaki looked at the house next door. Today, no laundry had been hung out to dry on the south-facing verandah. The window of the corner room was wide open, and he could see an old woman's back. He couldn't tell what she was doing. She wore a simple sleeveless shirt and from time to time leaned forward slightly. Michiko nervously disliked mosquitoes and flies and wouldn't allow the shutters to remain open; Masaki felt a twinge of envy at how cool it must be to open the window like that and let the breeze blow through. If he balled up the hand towel it would fall off, so Masaki roughly folded the piece and laid it on top of the concrete wall. He turned to go back inside to get out of the fierce sunshine.

In contrast to the one where the old woman sat, the room directly facing him now was quiet. Both the large window facing the garden and the bay window fronting Masaki's house were shut tightly, which caught his attention. It seemed to be a kind of room for receiving guests; he'd seen it occasionally over the wall and knew the room was Western-style, with paintings on the walls.

Shadows moved inside, tightly protected by the shining glass windows. A small bit of the lace curtain at the edge of the window facing the garden was drawn back. From where he stood, Masaki could clearly see into the room. Tōru might be in there. Remembering yesterday's events, Masaki was about to raise his hand in greeting as he looked in. But suddenly he pulled back and hid himself in the shade of the magnolia leaves. A second shadow moved in there, and the way it did told him something out of the ordinary was taking place.

A short girl with long hair stood with her back to him. With slender fingers she held her long hair back; rubbing its way up her hair from the side was the face of the young man that Masaki met the day before. Pushing away his head, which was about to conceal itself in the hair, the girl bent forward to do something to the front of her body. Tōru's face disappeared beyond the girl, while she stood there, in her earth-tone slacks, legs slightly apart. Masaki, staring intently, thought he saw the girl's body shake slightly. Before he could make sure, though, the girl turned, and Masaki glimpsed her suntanned, unexpectedly childish profile. Tōru appeared from the shadows and the two made their way to the sofa next to the wall, disappearing from view.

Masaki pretended to be checking for bugs on the magnolia tree so that no matter what angle people saw him from, no one would suspect a thing. He steadily edged closer to the wall. The magnolia wasn't tall enough to block the sun, although its broad leaves did a good job of concealing his face as he peeped over the wall.

He changed position and could now see about half of the sofa. The girl's head, it appeared, rested on the dark-brown armrest. Tōru wasn't visible. Irritated, Masaki rested his hands on the branches of the magnolia and stretched up; just then, naked white buttocks protruded out over the armrest. Whose, he couldn't tell, but clearly, they had stripped off their underwear. Masaki swallowed hard and wiped the sweat from his eyes with his arm. His forehead throbbed and he found it difficult to breathe.

A soft white object fluttered at the edge of the curtain. Aren't they afraid of being found out? he wondered. For a moment, Masaki turned his eyes to the corner room with its shutter and window flung wide open. The old woman sat as before, continuing to move forward occasionally as if swimming.

The girl's head, which was all he could see now, suddenly

sank down beyond the armrest to be replaced by a limb—an arm or leg—jutting upward, which soon disappeared as well. Just then, the lace curtain blew over to the left side of the window, where the sofa was, blocking Masaki's view.

He stiffened, wondering if he'd been seen, and still clutched the magnolia branches. He could sense, beyond the lace curtains, signs of some new, gentle motion. But if he really wanted to see, he'd have to climb the wall and go into his neighbor's garden. He considered waving the hand towel and calling out to the old woman. If he did, the young girl, naked, might leap up in confusion from the sofa and run to the side of the window where the curtain was slightly open. He could picture her body, cornered, without a stitch on, plastered against the large window glass facing the garden. With her breasts, mashed against it, even the hair below her belly might be clearly visible. Masaki waited breathlessly, hoping against hope that something would disturb the room. An earthquake, a fire, even a phone call would do.

Masaki was still staring fixedly at the scene beyond the curtains when the sound of a car engine passed by like the wind, an automobile with a cream-colored roof. The car braked violently to halt right against the gate of his house. Over the concrete wall of the small garden, he could see a familiar head of wavy hair alighting. Something very nettlesome had returned, Masaki felt, finally letting go of the magnolia branches. The metal gate swung quickly open with a heavy rasp.

Wondering what sort of expression he should put on, he ran barefoot across the lawn into the house. He leaped to the front door to unlock it.

women shopping

The floor of the supermarket drew closer.

As the first floor of the department store disappeared above, the basement supermarket spread out before her, still uncrowded; it was early for people to be shopping for supper. Only half of the line of registers were open, with hardly anyone waiting.

Stepping sprightly from the escalator, Masayo grabbed one of the shopping baskets piled up to eye level.

She suddenly remembered what Tōru had asked her to buy. Instead of turning right as she usually did, to the long stretch of food shelves beginning with the dairy section, she turned left at the aisle and headed for miscellanies.

Since it's not summer anymore, Tōru had commented, he needed a milder shampoo. But there's still a large bottle of shampoo in the bathroom, she'd replied.

"Hmm . . . so you change shampoos with the seasons?"

"You don't know anything, do you," he said. "In the summer, a shampoo that evaporates quickly feels good 'cause you sweat, but in the fall you want something gentler."

"That's news to me. Your father and brother manage with the shampoo we have, and I haven't heard any complaints."

"And that's the problem."

What's the problem, Masayo was about to ask, but held back. She knew the answer. Her husband Yūzo and eldest son Tsutomu were content to get their hair cut at the barber shop near the station, while Tōru insisted on going to a stylist downtown. And only Tōru used the men's eau de cologne someone had given them, on the shelf above the washroom sink.

"All-natural products are popular, why not try something different, like washing your hair with vinegar?"

"Give me a break. You think my head's a pot-au-feu stew pot you're going to eat with vinegar sauce?"

Masayo walked past the shelves crowded with all kinds of colorful detergents, toothpaste and toothbrushes, milky lotions, toilet lotions, soaps; all the while she smiled wryly as she recalled their conversation. She'd wanted a daughter and when Tōru was little there was a period when she treated him like a little girl. And maybe that accounted for his personality, which was the exact opposite of his brother's.

From among the host of shampoo bottles, Masayo picked a pink one with sloping shoulders and tossed it in her shopping basket. She walked past the tissue paper, disinfectants, toiletries and sponges, and slippers, coming out at the food section, where she was greeted by high stacks of saran wrap on sale.

It had grown colder these past few days, so maybe a nice pot-au-feu stew for dinner wasn't such a bad idea, she thought, passing the meat section and stopping in front of the seafood. Until the year before, the seafood section of the department store's supermarket had been the liveliest spot in it. There were always three or four shopkeepers in rubber boots and aprons, their hands swollen red from the water, counting fish, stuffing minced fish into plastic bags and wrapping them up in a flash, writing the price with red pencil on pieces of Scotch tape and handing these over to customers—all the while keeping up a hoarse banter designed to lure in more shoppers. One young employee had close-cropped hair; another, an older man, was fat with salt and pepper hair and always ready with a dirty joke; while a third wore gold wire-rimmed glasses and a serious look.

One day they had all vanished, replaced by a row of shelves stuffed with various fish in white polystyrene trays and plastic wrap. Where had all those happy, boisterous men gone? Masayo wondered, discouraged as she stood vacantly in front of the fish market. No, fish market wasn't the right word anymore, for along with the seafood—the shrimp, shellfish, squid, and sliced cod—there were vegetables—*shungiku* (garlands of chrysanthemums), shiitake and *enokidake* mushrooms, carrots, leeks—all wrapped as *yosenabe* sets you'd just toss into a stew pot. The meager plates of vegetables made Masayo lose her appetite, and she left the seafood section.

Retracing her steps, she put two packages of thin-sliced, top-grade beef into her basket and as she made her way to the register, added some *nattō* (fermented) beans, tofu, lettuce, and spinach—and finally a bunch of bananas wrapped tightly in blue-vinyl tape.

Time must have passed while she pondered the evening menu; the number of customers had grown since she had looked down at the place from the escalator. Short lines were beginning to form at the checkout counters. She looked for one in which the customers had few items in their baskets and stood right behind a short woman wearing a coat. She seemed to have stopped by the supermarket after a trip downtown. The woman raised her hand to her forehead and murmured, confusedly, as if she couldn't decide whether to go back to get something she'd forgotten to buy or to give it up as her turn to pay grew closer. Masayo herself was starting to get irritated by the woman's hesitation and hoped she would make up her mind. Finally, the woman put her shopping basket on the ground and, apologizing, turned toward Masayo.

"My!" the woman exclaimed, putting a hand to her chest. She wore glasses with a light-brown tint. Masayo was sure she'd seen her before.

"Mrs. Yasunaga?"

"Yes . . ." A disagreeable feeling moved through Masayo.

"I'm Mrs. Itō. You remember—the night there was a strange man in the street and I ran into your house—"

"Of course, Mrs. Itō. I didn't recognize you with the glasses."

The two images overlapped—the woman in the black coat who banged on their door and ran in and the person standing before her now. Because it had been night, Masayo didn't have a strong memory of the woman's face, but she was sure it was the same person. The only difference was the glasses. The coat she wore now wasn't black, but a light cream color, nearly white, and her makeup was heavier.

"I really must apologize for not thanking you properly."

"Oh, please, don't worry about it," Masayo said. "It was the least we could do."

The customer in front of them finished paying and the line moved forward; the woman hurriedly lifted her basket from the floor and placed it near the cash register.

"Was there something else you wanted to buy?"

"Ohh, no—I'm fine."

Masayo was hoping they could just say good-bye then and there, and the woman's words seemed to mirror similar thoughts. As she slid the basket in front of the checkout girl, she appeared to be trying to hide something in it.

When she opened her bag to take out her money, Masayo noticed it wasn't the big black handbag, nearly shapeless, that she'd had that night but an expensive, light olive-colored leather purse with a shiny gold clasp. The poor-looking, little pouch she pulled out of the handbag made an amusing contrast—a shabby little affair she'd probably sewn together herself out of pieces of felt.

Masayo didn't like to peek into other people's kitchens, so she tried to look away from the shopping basket. But as the checkout girl called off the prices of each item and placed them in a second, empty basket, she found her attention naturally drawn in that direction. Chopped pork, *chikuwa* (rolled fish paste) pickled Chinese cabbage, cleanser—the clerk lightly read out the prices, finally intoning "760 yen" as she placed a lightweight box, wrapped in light-blue wrapping, inside the basket. All the other items, covered in clear plastic, were visible for all to see; only this one was wrapped, which made the box stand out all the more. Masayo knew right away what was inside. Once—when they'd seemed to have forgotten all about such things—Yūzo, not forgetting at all, had bought a similar box. Where did you buy that? she asked him. Not in a supermarket, I hope. In a drugstore, he replied simply. Didn't you feel strange buying it? she asked. I'm not a high school student, you know, he said curtly. But when you're getting on in years a little it's embarrassing, too, isn't it? she asked mildly, and glanced at Yūzo's head. For his age, his hair was getting pretty thin. Same as buying cold medicine, her husband murmured casually. He'd paid ¥1,000 for the box then, she recalled. Buying it like this, in a supermarket, made you feel you weren't just peeking into someone's kitchen but into their bedroom. Masayo was taken aback by the woman's boldness.

The woman went over to a nearby counter to pack all her purchases into a plastic bag printed with the supermarket's name. After finishing, she stood, apparently waiting for Masayo. Masayo tried hard to keep her disgusted feelings from showing as she finished paying and walked over to the woman, basket in hand.

"How nice to see you again," the woman greeted her again.

"We live so close by, it's a wonder we don't run into each other," Masayo replied, quickly packing her purchases into the plastic. But that wasn't strictly true. Since that evening a half year ago when the woman took refuge in Masayo's house from a flasher, she'd seen her a number of times walking down the street, head always down. Masayo had avoided being seen. It wasn't that she minded saying hello but rather that she didn't want to remember the events of that night. When Masayo had seen the woman's husband, whom she'd called to come get her, under the streetlight wearing a black vest and sandals, she was frankly shocked. The husband's clothes resembled those of the man who'd attacked her, though she thought it must be someone else. As long as there was no way to make sure, though, Masayo preferred to have nothing to do with the couple and tried to put the incident out of her mind.

"Are you in a hurry, Mrs. Yasunaga?" the woman said as they went up the escalator side by side.

"No . . . not particularly . . ." The answer seemed to be dragged out of her against her will.

"Good. Please let me treat you to tea, then. Just a simple cup of tea—don't worry about it being a way of thanking you or an apology or anything. . . ."

"You don't need to go to any trouble. . . ."

"No trouble at all. I'd just like to invite you."

The woman's words suddenly took on an intimacy, and she rubbed her shoulder against Masayo's.

"Well, if we go Dutch treat, then I don't mind."

Masayo had wanted to draw the line somewhere but instead found herself pulled along by the woman, even to the point where she assumed her tone of voice.

The woman led her, with practiced steps, out of the department store and down a steep staircase to the basement level of a cozy little building that had recently been remodeled. Surprised to find a coffee shop in such a place, Masayo followed closely behind. A thought began to take shape in her mind: having followed the woman this far, maybe she could use the opportunity to draw out more information about her husband.

Sitting along the wall in the coffee shop, which was unexpectedly spacious, they ordered coffee and turned to face each other. The woman took a pack of slim, imported cigarettes from her bag, lit one up with a red lighter, and drew a deep drag on it before offering the pack to Masayo.

"Have you always worn glasses?"

Masayo didn't smoke and turned down the offer of a cigarette; instead she took a sip of water. She couldn't get used to the woman's face with its gold-framed glasses, the top part of the lenses tinted brown. Seeing her with glasses just didn't fit the image she had of the woman who had run into her house to escape.

"They're nonprescription. Somehow, I feel safe wearing them, like I've got a little bit of extra protection."

The woman took them and laid them on the table. Her

somewhat worn-looking features she'd shown as she had stood frozen under the entrance-hall light reappeared.

"You've been wearing them ever since that happened?"

"Yes, ever since then."

"But that's the only time that kind of thing happened, right?"

"After dark now, I always take a bus or a cab. Your house is a bit too close to take a cab, isn't it. But how about you, Mrs. Yasunaga—no problems after that?"

She elongated the ends of each word, and they seemed to cling to Masayo's skin as if they were stroking it. Masayo merely nodded, wanting to change the subject back to the woman and her husband.

"I envy you having such a kind husband. He must have been worried about you, the way he ran right over."

"When I got home, he asked a lot of questions about what the man did. Not that I saw much in detail or remember much."

"So you told him about it?"

"As much as I could."

"And then?"

"He said it was too bad I didn't have a Polaroid camera so I could take some pictures."

"That's terrible! Of course, maybe you could have used the bright flash to scare away the man."

The two of them burst out laughing so loudly a young man sitting in back, a salesman by the look of him, turned around to stare.

"Men seem to get excited, even if it's their own wife it happens to."

The woman lowered her voice, moving her head so close their hair almost touched. The acrid odor of a saliva-wetted cigarette struck Masayo.

"Well, so something good happened that night after all." Masayo was surprised at her vulgar words.

"Anyway, that's why I don't want that kind of experience ever again."

"It happened because you two get along well," Masayo said, encouragingly.

The woman, looking less than pleased, asked Masayo about her husband.

"Well, he's getting along in years. He just says I'm silly, and that's the end of it."

"Come on, you're not that old yet," the woman said with an arched smile.

"I think I saw your husband once or twice after that," Masayo said.

"Did he say hello?"

"Does he often wear that black vest?"

"It's his favorite. He always wears it. Except for the summer."

"And he had on sandals."

"Well, he works at home and when he goes out, he usually dresses that way, kind of sloppily."

"Does he like to drink?" Masayo asked casually, taking a sip of her coffee.

"He hardly drinks at all at home but likes to go out drinking. When I'm going to be out late, he'll have a drink at one of those *yakitori* shops in an alley on the other side of the tracks. You know where I mean?"

The feeling of a man's mouth crawling up her right hand, the one holding the cup, to her thumb came over her, and Masayo unconsciously put the cup back on its saucer. Did he ever come back with a cut somewhere around his mouth? She couldn't quite get the question out. Graphically, the feeling came back to her of the man's weight pushing her down into the cedar hedges. *My old lady—she doesn't even let me kiss her.* The man's sobbing voice as he tried to force a kiss rang in her ears. Masayo could barely keep from shouting at the woman in front of her: *He pushed me down— a total stranger—into the bushes—and told me he wanted just one kiss!* She had no definite proof, though, and, if the woman denied it, Masayo would be left with nothing to say. The most she could expect would be an entirely fruitless argument. *You're so carefree about buying condoms, well, why don't you try satisfying your hus-*

band? Masayo took a drink of water to swallow back the words rising up in her.

As the cold water forced its way down her throat, a thought hit her: *Wait, just a minute.* She remembered the woman's words that night as they waited under the streetlight for her husband. Hadn't she said she couldn't have children, implying, in a sad tone, that she'd had an operation? If that's the case, then why buy that light-blue box, that ¥760 purchase? Maybe she used the contents of the box with someone other than her husband. . . . Masayo soon realized the illogic of this. If the problem is with her body, it wouldn't matter if it was her husband or another man. Was the woman lying? Or was there some other use for the contents of that box that was beyond Masayo's comprehension?

So absorbed in her own thoughts, Masayo found herself pulled abruptly back to reality by the woman, who was again leaning in closer and whispering.

"Huh?"

"I really would like to have you over sometime." As she spoke, the woman turned a bit to one side and, holding her now empty coffee cup close to her chest, carefully wiped off the lipstick stain on it with her thumb.

"But your husband works at home, doesn't he?"

"Yes, but he's often out in the morning, and sometimes is gone for the whole day."

"And do you work as well?—"

Masayo's words were cut short as she felt someone tapping her on the back.

"Well, well. Imagine finding you here!"

The loud voice belonged to Tōru, who was sitting right behind Masayo and had turned to face her. Masayo, who felt as if she'd been caught doing something bad, felt even more flustered as she noticed a girl with long hair sitting opposite Tōru. The girl was looking directly at her and gave a vague nod of greeting. The girl's face was small and cute but her eyes glittered with an excess of curiosity.

"Well, what about *you?* What are *you* doing here? If you're meeting your friend, you should come to the house." Masayo hid her agitation behind these peremptory words. The seats directly behind her hadn't been occupied when she came into the coffee shop, which meant that Tōru and his friend had come in while Masayo was absorbed in talking with the woman. Tōru acted as if he had only now noticed her, but he was the kind of boy who didn't mind a little playacting. Masayo searched her memory to figure out which part of their conversation she wouldn't want him to overhear but couldn't come up with a good answer.

"This is Miss Katase," Tōru said, introducing the girl, "we're in the same club." Once more the girl nodded her head slightly in a vague greeting. Masayo recalled hearing the name in a telephone call for Tōru.

"This is Mrs. Itō," Masayo said, briefly introducing the woman to her son. Then she stood up and took the check from the table.

"Please drop by our house," she said to the girl as she walked by Tōru's table. The girl just nodded silently. "We don't have time," Tōru said irritably.

"What a nice son you have," the woman said fawningly as she spoke to Masayo, who mounted the stairs ahead of her. The woman had let Masayo pay for the two coffees, completely forgetting, it seemed, her original intention of treating Masayo.

"Sometimes, I don't know why he's going to college. . . . All he does is play around."

"How nice to be young. But you know, those two make a nice couple."

They came out onto the darkened street, and Masayo turned to face the woman. Her face was framed by the tinted, gold-frame glasses.

"You were facing the opposite direction so you wouldn't have noticed, but I was watching them since the two came in. They're pretty close—you can tell."

"I really don't think—"

An unpleasant feeling hit Masayo, as if the tip of the woman's tongue was worming its way inside her. On the one hand, she wanted to tell her to mind her own business; on the other, anxiety welled up. Her insides burned with a reckless desire to drag Tōru forcibly out from the underground coffee shop where he still sat, facing the girl.

"With a boy, you can expect things to happen, but if it were my daughter, I'd be a bit worried."

Along with a desire to resist the woman, who'd already made up her mind that something was going on, a vision abruptly seized Masayo of the young girl, wearing an apron, her long hair hanging down slovenly, standing around aimlessly in their kitchen. It was an awful feeling, like suddenly seeing some strange creature around the sink. The woman said something else, but Masayo replied curtly that she had more shopping to do and said good-bye. Leaving the woman at the top of the stairs to the coffee shop, Masayo strode off toward the station without glancing back. I wish I'd never talked to her, she thought regretfully. The woman's syrupy voice seeped into her skin, and even after saying good-bye she felt a twinge as if that voice were oozing out of her pores, from her underarms, and the backs of her knees.

* * * * *

Tōru was only down the street, but even after dinner was ready, he still hadn't returned. The rice cooker, rice done, had switched off, and chunks of tofu floated on the surface of the finished miso soup. She placed the seasoned spinach in a deep plate, put the grated radish in a small bowl, and set a heavy frying pan on the gas range.

"Looks like no one's coming back, so why don't we go ahead and eat," Masayo said to Yoshiko, who was sitting on the sofa in the living room, legs tucked up under her, watching television.

"Everyone's going to be late today?" Yoshiko spoke over the TV. She didn't sound hungry.

"Tsutomu has experiments today, but I wonder what's taking Tōru so long."

"I thought he said he'd be back early today."

Masayo, slicing onions to go with the *nattō*, turned around to find Yoshiko already at the dinner table.

"No, but when I went out shopping I saw him near the station with a friend of his. He should be home." She couldn't bring herself to tell Yoshiko it had been at a coffee shop.

"With his girlfriend?"

"Huh? What do you mean?"

"That little girl with the long hair? . . . He'd said she was just a friend," Yoshiko added, looking knowingly at Masayo.

"Mother, you knew about this?"

"He's brought her here a couple of times."

"My goodness—I never knew anything about it." Masayo looked at Yoshiko in surprise.

"Now that I think of it, it was always when you were out." Yoshiko seemed to be relishing Masayo's reaction; she rearranged her chopsticks on the table as she spoke.

"Well—you should have said something."

"I don't think he deliberately chose those times." Yoshiko was trying to protect Tōru, but there was also a hint of sarcasm in her words, directed at Masayo's going out too often.

"He never tells me anything."

Acting out her sense of betrayal, Masayo moved toward the gas range, roughly turning the knob. A blue flame whooshed up under the frying pan, and her nose was stung by the dry odor of burning iron.

"I was going to bring tea in for them, but the room seemed too quiet."

"They were in Tōru's room?"

"In the sitting room. Something felt out of the ordinary, so I didn't open the door and went back."

"*Mother . . . ,*" Masayo called out, the words boiling out of her. The woman's knowing words about Tōru and the girl as they left the coffee shop came back to her. Irritation and anxiety both struck—was she the only one who didn't know what was going on? She couldn't stand the thought. Tōru, the girl, Yoshiko, that woman—Masayo was tormented by the thought that they were all conspiring behind her back.

"If something happened to the girl, what would we do?"

"Tōru knows that," Yoshiko replied.

"He says he does, but still—"

"Nowadays, there are all kinds of convenient places outside the house they can go to. . . ."

A mental picture of Yoshiko, tea tray in hand listening outside the parlor door, came vividly to Masayo. What is happening to this house? Yūzo comes home late, drunk, every night, and never says a word to anyone—that's what's wrong.

"The frying pan is burning," Yoshiko said lightly, turning around to look at the gas range. Masayo turned the can of salad oil upside down and tapped out the last drops into the frying pan. The pan sizzled and smoke poured up; not worried about the splattering oil, she ripped open the plastic wrap and dumped in the chunk of beef. She sprinkled some salt and pepper on it, unconcerned whether she did a good job or not, stirred the piece a few times and tossed the meat on a plate, placing it in front of Yoshiko.

"I'm going out to find Tōru."

Not waiting for a reply, Masayo pulled off her apron and hurried out of the house.

Dressed only in a light cardigan, she felt the cold. She regretted not having worn something else but didn't feel like turning back. She rounded the corner, where the Kiuchis' house stood, the car gone and the place looking deserted, and she came out onto the main road leading to the station. The early evening air hung over the road and on the one or two people approaching, on their way home, in the streetlight. Masayo looked carefully at each one to see if she could make out Tōru's large figure.

"Good evening."

Suddenly greeted by one of the shadows passing by, Masayo halted.

"Out shopping?" It was their neighbor, Mr. Oda, dressed in a duster coat, a pleasant expression on his face as he bowed slightly to her.

"Just going down the road a bit," she said evasively and slipped past him, still bowing. *You should have seen Mrs. Yasunaga walking off to the station—I've never seen her like that.* Masayo flinched as she imagined herself the topic of dinner-table conversation at the Odas'. As she did, though, she had enough presence of mind to check out a second shadowy figure coming up after Mr. Oda.

Masayo arrived at the intersection where the *soba* noodle shop and the bakery faced one another and stopped. As long as you didn't take the long way round, you would have to pass here because there was only the one road; but beyond it, a second one branched off to the right. Masayo usually took the first, but once she'd seen Tōru walking down the one on the right. The shopping district was well lit and it was easy to see someone, but they very well might have taken different roads and missed each other. But she'd come this far and the coffee shop was nearby, so she decided she'd best give up worrying, just go in and grab Tōru by the scruff of the neck, and take him home. The cold seeped into her and she clasped her arms and ran across the intersection. As she walked down the steep stairs into the coffee shop, Masayo realized she wasn't sure what she should say to her son. She was driven by one thought—that she had to drag Tōru away from that girl and bring him home.

Pushing open the door, Masayo was greeted by one of the waitresses. The atmosphere in the shop had changed dramatically from when she had been there. Quiet then, with few customers, now it was packed and filled with smoke and the clamor of voices. Two young men in identical business suits sat where Tōru and the girl should be. A waitress came up and told her, in a bored voice, that she'd have to share a table or else sit at the counter.

"It's OK," Masayo said, craning to look around the shop, "I'm looking for someone." From far back at the counter, a long hand fluttered up, motioning to her. So that's where you are, she thought, and took a couple of steps down the aisle, only to be stopped in her tracks by the laughter of some men she'd never seen before, who were occupying the seats at the counter.

"Stop it. That's mean."

When she heard that voice above the raucous clamor, it finally dawned on her that the men were laughing at her expense. Pretending not to have seen the hand, it was all she could do to mutter—*hmm, that's strange*—and retreat to the entrance. She pushed open the door and ran up the stairs as if fleeing. Blood rushed to her head, and her face twisted in humiliation. Why do I have to be insulted like that by those men? she wondered. She pressed her hands against her face and set out furiously down the brightly lit street toward the station. It's all that woman's fault, she thought. If I hadn't run across her at the supermarket, none of this would have happened. That woman, that Mrs. Itō—*she's* the one who should be pushed down on some pitch-black street by that sandal-wearing husband of hers—

The train from downtown had pulled in and a stream of people hurried down the shopping district streets. Where could he have disappeared to? she wondered. The roads were overflowing with people but Tōru was nowhere to be seen.

After she brought her chilled body back home, she found Tsutomu waiting for her, leaning over the kitchen table engrossed in eating. "You're back early," she forced herself to sound cheerful, and Tsutomu, his mouth full, nodded silently.

"Tōru's not back yet?" she asked casually, turning on the gas range to heat up the miso soup Tsutomu was eating cold. "He called, I think," Tsutomu said, indistinctly between mouthfuls and pointed with his chopsticks to the living room where Yoshiko was.

"Tōru called?"

"Just after you left," Yoshiko replied. "He said he was going to take Miss Katase home so he'd be a little late." Her feet were up on the sofa, eyes glued to a historical drama on TV.

"Really? And you didn't tell him to come home soon?"

"It's not often he even calls to say he's going to be late," Yoshiko murmured in satisfaction, evading Masayo's question.

"I wonder where that Katase girl lives. . . ."

"Over in Urayasu, I think," Tsutomu said, more to himself than her; now, though, relaxed after having eaten, he looked up from his plate of food.

"That's all the way across Tokyo. Do you know this girl?"

"No. Tōru's talked about her, that's all."

"What did he say?"

"How she said how hard it is for her to dry her long hair after she washes it."

Tsutomu thought it was pretty stupid.

Masayo had no idea under what circumstances the girl had said this, but the vision suddenly crossed her mind of Tōru and the girl bathing together. Maybe it was the girl who had put that idea into his head about changing shampoos with the seasons, Masayo thought, suddenly even more upset.

* * * * *

That evening, near midnight, Tōru came back just a few minutes after Yūzo. "You're pretty late," Masayo managed to say, but afterward, listening to Yūzo and Tōru's friendly conversation comparing which trains they'd taken, she lost the chance to confront her son. "I put the shampoo you wanted in the bathroom," she mentioned meaningfully, but Tōru just parried this with a light "Thanks!" Masayo hesitated to ask her husband before she'd had a chance to question Tōru himself. Even if she did consult with Yūzo, he probably wouldn't have a definite opinion one way or another; it was even less likely he would have anything to say now that Yoshiko had gotten involved. Yūzo, wanting to stay clear of the accumulated frustrations of Masayo's life, would try to run away or shut himself up with a huffy silence. Yūzo and Tōru were talking now about having a beer. If they had trouble getting up the next day, it wouldn't be her responsibility, she told them sharply as she opened the door to her bedroom.

This isn't some kind of you-know-what motel, you know, so don't bring a girl here and do anything funny—the words she'd wanted to direct at Tōru spun around and around in her head after she lay down under the covers and closed her eyes. But she wasn't sure herself if that was what she wanted most to say to her son. *The truth is, you're lonely.* She felt these words whispered low in the darkened room. Behind her closed eyes, images of Tōru when he was little marched past, one after another.

The next morning, events of the previous day faded. At exactly 6:00, the shutters of Yoshiko's window clattered open. While Masayo was dressing in the dim room, she heard the front door being unlocked noisily and the sound of the morning paper being retrieved. Masayo went out to the kitchen, quickly lit the kerosene space heater, and put the kettle on the stove. No different from any other busy morning, the time passed quickly, with Tsutomu and Yūzo finishing breakfast and leaving the house one after the other. As usual, hardly a word was spoken.

After the two had left, Tōru, his face puffy from lack of sleep, lumbered into the kitchen. Seeing that face in the morning sunlight, her desire to have a good talk with him now that they were alone evaporated. I have to attend an early morning class, Tōru mumbled unhappily, as he chewed apathetically on a piece of toast. All vestiges of the day before were wiped clean from his face.

No, it wasn't that Tōru was acting differently yesterday, Masayo concluded; rather, incited by Yoshiko's and the woman's words, hadn't she conjured up her own image of her son? The woman had spoken with such brazen confidence, but her words were merely conjecture, and as for Yoshiko, assuming she wasn't telling a fib, it was quite possibly all just an old person's addled misunderstanding. Masayo realized she'd been fooled into running around, and suddenly yesterday's events appeared idiotic.

Dutifully running off to the coffee shop only to be made fun of by strangers was not just stupid but comical.

The days passed by without incident, and Masayo's conviction grew stronger that this was indeed much ado about nothing. Once, when Tōru was out, the girl called. "My name's Katase, is Tōru at home?" she asked, a sort of childish innocence still detectable in her rapid-fire speech. Masayo felt a warmth welling up toward the girl that she hadn't felt when they met. "Oh, you're the Miss Katase I met in the coffee shop once," Masayo replied cheerily. "Well, Tōru's not back from school yet." "I'll call back later, then," the girl said, as if running away and about to hang up. "Next time, why don't you drop by when I'm here?" Masayo said expansively, and the girl said "OK" in a small voice. "Thank you very much," is what you're supposed to say, Masayo muttered as she replaced the receiver. She wondered how she appeared in the girl's eyes.

In early December, Yoshiko came down with a cold and fever. Fearing that it might develop into pneumonia, Masayo made sure her room was heated enough and brought meals to her. She urged Yūzo to come home early, but he replied with a smile that his mother was all right. He continued to come home late.

The son turned out to be right about his mother. In three days Yoshiko's fever had subsided, and a week later she was able to do things around the house pretty much as before. While she was taking care of Yoshiko, Masayo had been tied down at home, able only to dash off for shopping nearby.

A few days before, they'd received an ad for a sale at a department store in downtown Tokyo. Masayo decided that Yoshiko had recovered enough and told her she had to go out to buy some end-of-year presents for Yūzo's colleagues.

"So it's already the end of the year, isn't it," Yoshiko sighed, lightly nodding her assent. "I'll be fine," she said.

The day was clear and warm. Masayo felt happy to be liberated for the first time in a long while and went out dressed in a beige, light wool coat and high heels. She enjoyed the sound of the heels, clicking down the almost glaringly bright asphalt streets. As she walked toward the station, the noon sun right in front of her shone directly into her eyes, making it hard to see. But turning around, she could make out the sharply etched scene of the road, stretching out toward the residential area to the north. Our house is near the station, yet it's a quiet neighborhood, she mused with a swell of pride. I guess I shouldn't nag Yūzo so much.

Two figures approached from in front. As if they'd just been to the supermarket, the man held a paper sack and the woman a white shopping bag. The woman slowed and the man's pace slackened, too. Their faces were in shadow and she couldn't make them out clearly, so Masayo walked on as before.

"Mrs. Yasunaga!"

When the woman called out to her, she was too close for Masayo to pretend she didn't hear.

"Thanks for the other day. . . ."

Bowing her head, Masayo instinctively stiffened and looked at the man's sandals.

"This is my husband." The woman, without her glasses today, turned slightly to the man beside her.

"My name's Itō. Thank you so much for having helped my wife that time." The man, slightly overweight, clad in a brown leather jacket, greeted her in a low voice. The jacket, open in front, revealed a V-neck, knitted, black-wool sweater.

"It was nothing, really. We have to look out for each other, after all," Masayo said casually, but faltering over what she meant by looking out for each other.

"No, you've been very kind and we're grateful."

The man wasn't so tall, but his features were finely chiseled. His face was somewhat expressionless, though, as if within its strong symmetry lay buried the collapse of its very balance. Masayo remembered, spitefully, what the woman told her the other day about how her husband had questioned her at length and how he'd gotten aroused.

"Once, a while back, something like that happened to me—not far from here a strange man pushed me down into the bushes."

"Oh?" the man said in a deep, throaty voice and blinked.

"In my case, the man was drunk and was going on and on about how his wife didn't pay any attention to him."

"Even if he's drunk, still . . ."

The man nodded vaguely, looking at his wife; there was some white mixed in the hair above his ears.

"If only they got along as well as the two of you, going out shopping together."

Masayo aimed her final words at the woman, who stood demurely beside her husband, looking like a totally different person from the other day.

"Well, this is a real exception. Today we just happened to be . . ." The woman replied in a studied, calm manner. The man took a cigarette from the pocket of his leather jacket, and even though there was no wind, exaggeratedly cupped his hand around his lighter as he lit it. A sudden impulse seized Masayo to stick her thumb inside that mouth. At once she felt all over again that sticky feeling and, flustered, rubbed her thumb on her coat.

"I can see you're on your way out, Mrs. Yasunaga, so we won't hold you up any longer."

The woman lightly tugged her husband's sleeve. The man hurriedly took the cigarette out of his mouth and mumbled, bowing.

Masayo walked on a ways, then turned around to watch the two figures, the man abruptly putting his arm on the woman's shoulder, as they grew distant. The road was bathed in winter sunlight. Masayo tried hard to conjure up the face of the woman the other day, the one with the gold-framed glasses, as she walked quickly toward the station.

water thief

Below the tap, a column of water trembled in the air.

Back home from shopping, Shizuko groped in her bag for her key when she noticed the water coming out of the faucet pipe, its length running along the garden wall. More than just a drip, a fair amount twisted down, splashing onto the cement sink below.

She couldn't remember using the faucet that day and wondered perhaps if the rubber ring inside needed to be replaced. Stepping over the thick, lustrous bush beside the sink, she shut the faucet off; the water stopped completely. Maybe when she'd watered the potted plants yesterday, she hadn't shut it off properly. This much water coming out all night—what a waste, she thought, but soon forgot about it as she went inside, bustling about in the kitchen.

A few days later, locking the door on her way out to go shopping, Shizuko noticed the water turned on again. The tap had been left on. The day before it had rained all day, so she knew she hadn't used the faucet in the garden. If the rubber ring in the faucet was worn, maybe it would twist back even if shut off. Shizuko had no memory of using it. A bit concerned, she recalled a friend's story about how an underground leak in one of their pipes had sent their water bill skyrocketing.

Two or three days later, in the afternoon, Shizuko was writing letters at the *kotatsu*, now turned off and used as a desk. Suddenly, she heard a loud splash outside. Imagining the pipe was bursting and water was shooting up in the air, Shizuko stood up quickly. Her back went out and a sharp pain stabbed through her. She'd experienced it before and ended up immobile, so she lay on the tatami, breathing quietly, waiting for the pain to pass. Now that she lived alone, if she were unable to stand or walk she'd be in dire straits. *See? What did I tell you?* she could imagine her husband Takahiko saying. She rested awhile and tried slowly to bend her leg; her forehead was covered in sweat. She put her hand on the tatami and sat up; fortunately, there was no pain. Once, when her back had gone out, the orthopedic doctor examining her said, half-jokingly, that for humans walking on two legs puts the most stress on the back. "It'd be a lot better if people walked on all fours," he said, "I've never heard of a dog or cat having its back go out."

She got to her knees, gingerly crawling to the window on the south side of the house. Before she realized it, the violent rush of water had stopped, replaced by a mild, streamlike gurgle. An uncomfortable feeling remained in her back, but the pain was gone. She was able to stand and walk.

Even so, that evening after 10:00 when the phone rang while she was locking up for the night, Shizuko took longer than usual to return to the living room.

"Were you taking a bath?" It was Takahiko's voice, a bit impatient.

"No, I was at the front door, locking up for the night."

"What a big mansion you have there."

"Had a bit to drink, have we?"

"No way. I've even brought work home with me. Everything all right there?"

"Yes, everything's fine. The water outside, though, sometimes comes on."

"Call a plumber."

"I don't think it's broken. When I shut it off, the water stops."

"That's strange. Is somebody using it?"

"I think so. I've noticed something unusual the past few days, and then this afternoon—" She hadn't planned to tell him, but perhaps her fears over her back made her fainthearted, and she related all the events of the afternoon.

"So, how is your back doing?"

"It hurt just that one time, and now it's fine."

"You silly, if you don't watch out, it'll be your doctor's bills not the water bills that you'll need to worry about."

She was happy that her husband seemed more concerned about her back than the water, but at the same time she was also a bit vexed.

"Still a while before we're on Medicare, right?"

"If you were here with me, I could take care of you."

"But you're at work all day."

"If you stay there, you're alone at night, too, right?"

"That's true. . . ."

Once again their conversation fell into the usual pattern of mutual reproach; Shizuko changed her tone to break the spell.

"I'll have to catch him in the act," she said.

"Who?"

"The person who's sneaking in and using our water."

"It's got to be a child from the neighborhood."

"Even if it's a child, I have to catch him red-handed."

"What would you do if it turned out to be a weird man?" Takahiko's voice still sounded a bit peevish.

"Would anybody really do that—go into someone else's property, just to use the water?"

"A water thief."

"No way," Shizuko said.

"Well, you're by yourself, so just be careful." From his tone, clearly, the phone call was drawing to a close.

"I'll be fine. How is it there, still cold?" Finally, she was able to express some sympathy for her husband, living so far away.

"It doesn't look like we'll be taking our coats off for a while."

"Will you be able to come back for a visit next month?"

"I'm planning on it. Good night," he said, and hung up.

The house was suddenly quiet. Away from the phone, she wasn't sure whether she was looking forward to her husband's short visit home. Whenever a bit of trouble occurred, she did think it'd be nice if he were with her. But she also was depressed at the thought that he would someday move back for good and disrupt the carefree single life she'd grown used to. If Takahiko passed away, would she be able to live such a worry-free life? It would surely make her feel lonely, and helpless, so perhaps their present situation, living apart, was the happiest she could hope for. Outside, a hard tap of shoes clicked on the road coming from the station, fading away, past their west-facing wall. Tonight, I'll take a good hot bath to relax my back, she thought, and slowly made her way to the bathroom.

* * * * *

Water splashed outside the window.

It was two days after she'd talked with Takahiko. *He's here!* a voice cried out within her. She was about to stand up suddenly when the memory of her back from the other day brought her to a halt. She crawled over to the TV she'd been watching vacantly and switched it off, listening carefully.

The rush of water on the cement sink soon stopped, but then dripped.

Straining to listen, Shizuko finally couldn't bear it and stood up, taking care not to aggravate her back. Approaching the glass door on the south side, she looked diagonally out. Takahiko's words—*water thief*—came back to her. The Odas' wall next door stood right nearby through the scrawny trees that substituted for a hedge, and the water pipe was visible at the entrance to the narrow path in front of them. From the faucet, a thin line of water wavered, shining dully in the afternoon sun.

I don't know who you are, and I don't mind you using it. But when you're done, turn the water off, will you?

Shizuko, angry with her invisible foe, regretted she hadn't looked outside as soon as she noticed the water, regardless. She slipped on some sandals to go out into the small garden. The Odas' house stood silently, with no sign of anyone about. She leaned over the dark-green leaves of the silverleaf bush and shut the faucet off as hard as she could. The cement sink below was darkly wet, evidence of how much the water had been gushing out a few minutes earlier. She turned around to check the gate, but the bolt was firmly in place. That meant that if the thief weren't hidden somewhere in the garden, he must have gone through the sparse trees onto the Odas' property.

You *water thief,* you! . . .

Relieved not to be dealing with the strange kind of man Takahiko had mentioned, Shizuko nevertheless felt perturbed. It wasn't the water bill or the way the person had slipped away so quickly that bothered her. What she couldn't stand was having the water in her own house left running like that. Blood rushed to her head, and her heart beat quickly. For a moment she was struck by the desire to grab that little thief and ring his scrawny neck. Though it was just water from a faucet, for some reason she couldn't suppress the rage rising up inside her.

Shizuko breathed deeply, looking around the small garden. The sweet daphne just inside the gate was well past its peak and ugly; its small, crinkled-up petals, like birds' claws, clumped on the branches. Next to the wilted blossoms, thin, fresh green leaves pushed out brazenly. Even with her nose next to them, she could smell no fragrance. Next to the sweet daphne were lackluster yellow flowers scattered on the thin branches of the fragrant olives. This year she'd failed to notice when they were in full bloom. Maybe because of the weather, they hadn't fully come out.

Slowly calming down, Shizuko decided now that she was in the garden to take a look at the plants Takahiko had left behind. They were less true bonsai than his own creations, plants of all different sizes he'd stuck like straws upright in pots, shabby-looking little things—a ginkgo in one, a small flowering dogwood sticking out of the soil in another. Among them were also the nicer plum and pine that he'd purchased at the local nursery on his day off once, when he went for a walk near the public-housing complex. But somehow it was the clumsy cuttings he'd stuck in the pots that reminded Shizuko most of her husband.

The bonsai were on a shelf, a concrete slab on top of two cement blocks set on the ground in the garden; though *garden* might be an exaggeration—it was just a narrow strip of dirt between the house and the surrounding wall. Sometimes, Shizuko had the feeling that the bonsai plants watched her. Takahiko, nearing retirement, had been sent off to Kushiro in Hokkaido to serve on the board of a subsidiary company, but Shizuko refused to accompany him. Perhaps the last thing he had said to her before he left had to do with his bonsai.

"Don't let my bonsai wither up, OK?"

With these words, she began her new life.

After a few moments of silence, Takahiko had muttered: "I never thought at this age I'd be a bachelor again."

With their children all grown up and on their own and no bedridden relatives to care for—from any perspective, it would be natural for Shizuko to go with her husband. The home office would rent out their house; when they returned to Tokyo, the office would have it ready for them to move back in. Despite all this, she just couldn't bring herself to move to Hokkaido with her husband.

Though concerned about the bother of moving and whether she could stand the cold, she knew deep down these were not the real reasons. She sensed, as if right beside her, the Shizuko who, if she gave in once would, grumbling all the while, go along with Takahiko. And that's why she felt even more strongly that she had had to insist on not going.

"Things from the past interfering here?" her husband had asked, weakly.

"If that were the case, then I wouldn't have been able to live like this all these years, now, would I?" she said, curtly dismissing his doubts. But really she wasn't clear about her own feelings. Maybe this is good practice for when I'm a widow, she thought, but couldn't say it aloud. If you get used to a little inconvenience now, she might have replied, you won't have so many problems after I'm gone. Which explanation would be crueler to her husband, she didn't have the leisure to contemplate.

"Just once in my life let me get my own way."

With these words, tears had flooded out. Not knowing why, she felt sorry for herself. And for her husband for having such a pitiful wife. And these unexpected tears had, perhaps, led to those words from her husband about the bonsai.

"Don't wither on me, guys. I'll get in trouble." She addressed the scrawny bonsai, just as the phone rang inside the house. Forgetting all about the water pipe, she scurried to the entrance. A slight twinge of pain in her back made her slow down. Just as she reached the living room, the phone stopped in mid-ring.

* * * * *

Every time she went out or came home, she checked the water, but for some time later, she didn't notice any water running. Maybe shutting it off as hard as she could had done the trick. Hard as it was for her to turn it on, no halfhearted efforts would be able to do it. Was that all there was to it? she wondered, thinking how foolish she'd been to get so worked up.

All this made her feel even worse the day the life-insurance saleswoman came and told her about the water dripping.

"We have plenty of life insurance, so no thank you," Shizuko said, bowing. The woman, standing at the entrance, a bit overweight in her tight yellow suit, replied that she wasn't looking for new clients but rather canvassers.

"You mean you want me to introduce you to people who might want insurance?"

"No, we're looking for people like myself to work for the insurance company."

"You're asking me, at my age, to work as a door-to-door, life-insurance saleswoman?"

"Goodness, Ma'am, you're still young. We have a lot of people working for us who are much older. You won't have set hours, so actually it is more suited for people who aren't so young."

A little overly friendly, the woman started to come in the house. Gold teeth glinted in her wide-open mouth. She'd said Shizuko was young only to turn around and say the job was suited to older people. Her skewed logic bothered Shizuko.

"I'm a little too busy, I'm afraid."

"But your children must already be working, and your husband, too. . . ." The woman, pushing forward, was half inside the door. She studied Shizuko through her glasses.

"I don't really think so. I had no plans to do that kind of thing, and besides I'm not that well, my back is bothering me."

"Really? One of my clients has a bad back too and had that laser-type kind of treatment and she said it was amazing. . . ."

Waving her hand in refusal in front of this woman, who prattled on, Shizuko finally was able to shut the door. Alone again, she caught her breath, when the woman's words came back to her. Maybe she thought I'm a widow—the doubt raised its head. She felt as if the woman had insulted her.

"Ma'am!"

She thought she'd gotten rid of her, but the woman's voice came from the garden.

"I'm not going to open the door again," she stiffened.

"The water's on outside."

It sounded as if she were walking in the alley, calling out over the wall.

"Thank you. Something's wrong with the faucet."

Mind your own business, Shizuko thought, managing to force herself to sound apologetic.

"Got to be careful about the water bill, right?"

Shizuko waited for the woman's cheery voice to fade into the distance, then quietly opened the door. She could hear water running in the garden. She stepped over the silverleaf bush, turned the faucet handle, and the water easily stopped. You turned it on as you left, didn't you! she wanted to shout at the woman. But she knew she was just venting her anger on a convenient target. She'd relaxed her guard a bit, and now the whole thing was starting up all over again. She couldn't stand the thought. And today she'd happened to be at home and still hadn't noticed. She twisted the faucet a couple of times to make sure it was shut tight and stood up. The postman on his bicycle rounded the corner into their road. After putting a letter into the mailbox of the Yasunagas' diagonally across the street, his red bicycle hurried past the wall. They got less mail now that Takahiko wasn't living here; his mail was forwarded to Hokkaido, a thought that made her feel vaguely lacking.

As if the life-insurance woman's visit had been a starting point, the water came on again. It didn't matter how hard she shut off the faucet. What was worse, before she'd always noticed as soon as the water splashed; but now, she didn't even notice.

"It's hard to believe that a child would take such precautions."

During one of their evening phone calls, now a twice-weekly habit, Shizuko again raised the topic of the water.

"That's why I told you before," Takahiko said, "that it might be some strange man."

"I just don't think so."

"Then you think it's a child playing a trick?"

"I wonder."

"A child just trying to harass us . . ."

"But why would someone try to harass us?"

"I have no idea. I said that because of what you said—that it wasn't just some childish trick. But kids from the neighborhood don't get into our garden that much, do they?"

"That's right. And that's why it's bothering me."

"Has the water bill gone up a lot?"

"Yesterday, the man came to read the meter and it didn't look like it."

"Then what's the problem? Just let it be. If you don't worry about it, before long they'll give up."

"But that's why I'm bringing it up—because I'm worried about it." Shizuko's voice was loud now, and Takahiko didn't respond.

". . . I know, maybe we should make a real wall between us and the Odas."

"Because of the water?" Takahiko asked.

"If it's children, that's the only place they could come in."

"Unless they climbed the wall."

She hadn't considered that. Even if they built a wall and the same thing continued to happen—that would frankly be awful. Unendurable. The matter would escalate from being a minor annoyance to something almost ghastly.

"It's too expensive to talk about on the phone. Let's talk about it the next time I'm home." Takahiko's tone had changed with the topic of building a wall, Shizuko noticed, and she felt a bit comforted by that fact.

* * * * *

One day, Shizuko aired out her wool coat, which had been hanging on the hat rack in the entrance, in preparation for storing it away. The white radish flowers she'd put in a glass vase lay scattered on top of the shoe shelf. When she'd cut them from where they grew in a corner of the garden, they'd been a pretty light purple, but now, off their stalks, they'd shrunken to a deeper hue. The petals had spilled off the mat on which the vase stood and littered the floor.

Putting the coat out in a sunny spot, Shizuko began cleaning the entrance for the first time in a week. She put the shoes and sandals, now reduced in number, upside down on the step leading into the house, took the umbrella stand out into the garden, drew some water from the faucet there, and set about scrubbing the foyer's decorative stone flooring. When Takahiko was living at home, he'd make her scrub with water and polish it a couple of times of week. Now she only picked up her broom when she felt like it. She did have to admit though that she enjoyed seeing the well-scrubbed stone floor, dark and shiny. She took the bucket out, set it up under the faucet, shut the faucet off tightly, and went back inside.

A few hours later Shizuko stepped down onto the verandah to retrieve her wool coat. A bit of laundry she'd set out there had dried. She checked the mailbox, empty, and looked up at the young shoots on the white plum tree, which hadn't produced many flowers this year. She happened to glance over at the faucet.

The water was on. It might have been the way the faucet had been turned on, but the water wasn't twisting about this time. Rather it flowed silently in a single, rounded line, smugly, seemingly as if it were taunting her. She could still feel how hard she'd twisted the handle at noon and found it difficult to keep her composure. She felt as if her own nerves were flowing down. If she were going to have to experience this regularly, she might as well destroy the whole water pipe. She could even imagine reaching the point where her mind would start to go and she'd take to her bed. Why not just let the water run? If from the beginning she was the one who left the water on, it wouldn't be half as irritating. But she knew she wasn't the type to do that.

Shizuko decided to make tea to calm down but found that even picking up the light pot set her nerves on edge. She roughly poured water into the teakettle, set it on the range, and turned on the burner. In Kushiro in the winter, she wondered vaguely, do the pipes freeze?

From the kitchen, she could hear a faint clang of metal being banged. Shizuko, her ears now sensitive, instinctively leaned out over the sink, her face pressed against the shutter. All she could see were the trees forming the boundary between her house and the Odas' and their wall. Tiptoeing out of the kitchen, she approached the glass door on the south side of her house. Quietly, she opened the shutter and looked in the direction of the sound.

A little girl stood there, dressed in a red shirt and jeans. Her fist held a rock, too big for her hand, and she was banging the rock against the side of the pipe leading to the faucet. Shizuko had expected something like this, but still the scene went beyond what she'd imagined. While she was wondering what she should say to the child, water gushed out of the pipe as if the girl had smashed it open with her rock. Surprised, she stepped back, then leaned forward to shut off the faucet. The stream of water trickled; she loosened the faucet a bit and the water came out again, more forcefully, then carefully she adjusted the flow. Finally getting it the way she wanted, the girl rested one hand on the faucet, twisting her face and opening her mouth wide under the stream of water. Face upward, she gulped down the water, then twisted back to open her mouth again. Her shoulders moved as she breathed, and the way she drank made the water look delicious.

Satisfying her thirst, the little girl turned her back on the still-running water, about to slip through the trees, when she came face-to-face with Shizuko watching her through the glass door. Surprised, the girl halted and looked up at Shizuko, undaunted.

"You're little Mayu, from the Odas', right?"

The girl wiped the back of her wet hand on her pants and nodded silently.

"You're in elementary school?"

"Second grade . . ."

The girl's voice was rheumy and husky. "Just wait a minute," Shizuko said, hurriedly, looking for a pair of shoes. Confused, she felt a strange mixture of letdown and excitement.

The girl stood stock-still. She was thin, and her bowl-cut hair was gathered in one place with a yellow polka-dotted, rubber hair tie. Beside her, the running water sounded gentle.

"Why don't you turn the water off after you drink it?"

Mayu smiled bashfully, went over to the faucet and shut it off, her hand turning white with the effort. A few drops fell out, then stopped.

"See, you can do it."

"I forgot my key."

"I don't mind you drinking the water. But I want you to shut it off after you're done."

"All right."

Shizuko was surprised by the straightforward reply.

"In your own house, do you leave the water running after you drink it?"

"No, I turn it off. . . ."

"Well, then, you'd better do the same with this water."

"We don't have a faucet in our garden."

"Like I said, it's OK for you to drink the water here when you're playing outside."

The girl had been expecting to be scolded for using the faucet, and Shizuko found herself a bit impatient.

"It's a problem for me if you leave the water running. So promise me you won't, all right?"

Looking down, Mayu nodded.

"Is your mother out?"

"Yes. I often forget my key, so I can't get in. . . ."

Mayu shrugged her skinny shoulders in a suddenly grown-up fashion.

"And so you always come over here to get a drink?"

"When I get thirsty."

Instinctively, Shizuko looked up at the wall of the Odas' house. It stood there silently, abandoned.

"Will your mother be back soon?"

"Sometimes she's late."

"It's going to be evening soon, so you're in a fix, aren't you?"

"When my brother comes home, he has a key."

"But what about dinner?"

"It's already made."

She pictured the empty kitchen table with plates and cups lined up. On days that their father was late, the children must eat alone. When you forget your key and can't get in, come over to my house—Shizuko was about to say but held back. She couldn't completely believe everything the child said, but if the number of times the water was left on equaled the number of times her mother was out and she'd forgotten her key, that would mean Mayu would be coming over several times a week.

"Is your mother working?"

"She's not working; she goes out to study and stuff . . ."

"Really, that must be hard for all of you."

"We're used to it." Mayu said precociously; then as she was about to lean against the trunk of the thin persimmon tree, she stumbled and laughed comically.

Usually Shizuko waited for Takahiko to call to take care of what they needed to discuss, but that evening she called him, waiting until after the special evening rates began. Probably too early, for he wasn't home. Listening to the phone ring in the deserted house, she imagined a cold plate, a meal for one, all alone on a kitchen table. A woman came several times a week to clean and do the laundry and would make dinner and leave. But Shizuko couldn't remember which days of the week they were. He must be out eating and drinking somewhere, she thought. Deciding to put it out of her mind, she turned on the television.

After 9:00, Shizuko couldn't wait any longer and dialed her husband's number.

"Well, what do you know!" Takahiko answered halfway through the third ring.

"I found out who the water thief is."

"One of the kids next door, right?" Shizuko was excited but Takahiko's reply was nonchalant.

"Right. The Odas' little girl."

"A girl, huh? . . ."

"Her mother goes out, and Mayu forgets her key and can't get in the house. She gets thirsty and comes over to drink water from our faucet."

"Mrs. Oda goes out that often?"

"The little girl said she goes out to study. I imagine she's at one of those Culture-Center type of places."

"If she forgets her key that much, she won't make a very good latchkey child, now, will she?"

"Maybe that's not the only time she comes over to drink water—"

"Why doesn't she turn off the tap afterward?"

"She's careless, I suppose. Not well brought up."

"If she doesn't care because it's someone else's tap, that's hard to take."

"But I'm glad we didn't get in a panic and put up a wall. It'd be like destroying a fountain for little birds."

"If it were birds, they'd find another spot to drink."

"So everything's OK now. I told her to make sure she shuts the water off tightly when she's finished."

"We'll see."

Takahiko's doubtful tone bothered her. She remembered how Mayu had responded to her questions; whether she was childish or precocious for her age was hard to tell.

"The last thing we did was link little fingers and make the 'thousand needles' promise. You know, if she didn't turn off the water in the future she'd have to swallow a thousand needles. She said so herself."

"Well, then, you'd better lay in a stock."

Her husband wasn't taking this seriously, and Shizuko felt displeased. She had no idea how big a bundle a thousand needles would make, but an image came to her of herself, with needles like the toothpicks that they sell in stores, forcing the whole bundle down the girl's wide-open mouth.

"At any rate, I'm sorry to have worried you about it," she said. "I just called to let you know that this water business is taken care of for now . . ."

"Well, that's certainly better than having it remain a mystery."

He wasn't particularly happy about it. This was because they lived so far apart, she thought irritably. But who knows, he might be the same even if they were together. She began to get concerned about the phone call, which cost nearly 100 yen per minute.

At least she'd gotten everything off her chest and felt better. Before turning in for the night, she checked the front door as usual. She locked it, then unlocked it again, and looked outside at the faucet, less to make sure it was all right than out of what was now long-standing habit. The faucet stood silently in the entrance light.

Good night. Nodding in satisfaction, she addressed this to no one in particular.

Shizuko woke up, feeling bothered. She twisted her neck from her pillow to look at the digital clock: the green numbers read 3:17. A long dream she'd been having was still half with her, but after she opened her eyes, her mind was unexpectedly clear. There was a dull tension in her abdomen. She thought about getting up to go to the bathroom, but her body wouldn't move. It had started to rain. She'd taken in her laundry and coat, so there was nothing to worry about. The light futon covering over her had grown warm and cozy.

Shizuko rolled over, giving up the idea of going to the bathroom, and closed her eyes, thinking she'd sleep a little more. But then, with a start, she realized if it were raining, she should hear the patter of raindrops on the eaves—but didn't. Just water, as if it were flowing past her feet where she lay in bed . . .

The faucet in the garden, she thought in alarm and sat up in bed. Clearly, she could make out the monotonous sound of water, a stream, seeping into the dark room. She reached out for the long cord hanging from the fluorescent light on the ceiling but pulled back halfway. She straightened up the front of her nightgown and sat up properly, knees together, in the darkness.

She knew what would happen next. She'd stand up and open the sliding screen to the next room. Walk out, bare feet on the cold wooden floor, to the entrance. With her toes, feel around for sandals, put them on, unlatch the chain on the front door, turn the lock, and grab the knob. Push the door open gently and stick her head out from the crack; she could see the faucet, lit by the pale streetlight. From the faucet, a straight line of water, twisting around itself, would be silvery and glistening.

Standing next to the dark bushes, crouching there darkly was the girl she'd talked to during the day. In one hand she held tightly onto a rock and in her mouth, opened as wide as it would go, was a bundle of needles thicker than the child's leg. The heads of the thousand needles spilling out of the girl's mouth shone darkly and stung Shizuko's eyes. The girl, unblinking, stared at Shizuko, moving her cheeks just a little. Thinking she might be trying to say something, Shizuko stepped forward as the heads of the needles, all in a round bundle, ever so slowly, yet surely, moved further into the girl's mouth. . . .

Should I watch this or not? Confusion filled Shizuko as she sat motionless in the dark room. The sound of the water grew louder.

the letter

The window at the entrance gleamed dimly.

Behind the frosted glass, the glow meant that the fluorescent light in the living room was still on. It's like a pale moon, Fusao mused, sunk deep in a pool of water. And why in the world do I have to go inside that little watery box when the breeze outside is so wonderful? The hesitation he often experienced wrapped itself around his weary feet. Having come this far, the heavier his body felt, the more it was pulled, even sucked, in the direction of the front door, like the tide, beyond his control. Is this how birds feel, he wondered, when they return to the sky?

Standing before the front door, Fusao rubbed his face hard with his palms. Then gave his cheeks a couple of slaps to rearrange the features he acquired outside into something more fitting for home.

Ringing the doorbell, waiting for it to be opened, he glanced past the wall at the entrance to the Yasunagas' house opposite. Their house was still, except for the small moth fluttering around the light outside. Mr. Yasunaga, who often came home late at night, drunk, had yet to go through his own little homecoming ritual.

He'd been expecting Kiyoko to open the door but it was Kōichi.

"You're still up?"

Breathing a sigh of relief, Fusao started to relatch the door chain.

"Mom said she's on her way back."

"She's still not home?"

Fusao let go of the chain and looked at his watch. The thin hands of his watch always seemed to point to his own guilty feelings at being late; now, suddenly, they reproached his wife.

"She called just a little while ago from Shibuya. Said she was on her way home."

"And so you stayed up?"

"No, I have an English test tomorrow."

"What a surprise, you studying for a test."

"You want some tea?"

Kōichi, unusually briskly, went into the kitchen and put the kettle on. Looking at him from behind, Fusao could feel the gentle sense of relief flow out from his son now that his duty of standing guard over the house was over. Fusao took off his overcoat and loosened his tie and peeked into the next room. At the foot of the two study desks lined up beside the window, Mayu was asleep, her head pushed up against one of the chairs.

Usually, Fusao found it too much trouble to undress until he took his bath. But this evening, as if to underscore the fact that he'd come home before his wife, he quickly changed into a fresh T-shirt and cotton briefs.

"Mom said she left that letter over there for you to read." Kōichi pushed a cup of terribly strong tea toward his father and motioned with his chin at a white envelope on top of the television.

"Mother left after you came back?"

"No. Mayu told me."

"So, she went out after Mayu came home."

"I guess so."

Kōichi nonchalantly answered his inquisitive father, then gingerly lifted the hot teacup and took a noisy sip. Maybe because of the lateness, and the fact that Kiyoko was not home, he was unusually affable. If my wife left home, Fusao wondered vaguely, is this how we would spend our evenings? Uncomfortably warm evenings, father and children alone, and the uneasy feeling that something was missing.

After listening to Kōichi's enthusiastic report on the day's major-league baseball games, Fusao waited until his son disappeared to take a bath before he reached for the white envelope. Addressed to Mr. Oda Fusao and Mrs. Oda Kiyoko, the letter was, as Fusao had surmised, from his mother in Nagano. The top of the envelope had been cut open sharply with scissors, a thin white strip still attached; Fusao could picture Kiyoko stiffly pulling the letter out of the envelope.

* * * * *

It has been so hot and steamy, but now it's turned chilly again. This year the weather is so unsettled, and I hope you are all well and have managed to avoid catching a cold.

It's June, but it doesn't look like we'll be putting the kotatsu *away any time soon. Fortunately, Father has gotten much better and is even able to go outside with me occasionally. So please don't worry.*

I've called a few times hoping to talk with you about the matter we discussed a while ago, but you both seemed so busy. When I've called in the evening it's just the kids who are there, so I decided after all it would be best to write.

* * * * *

From the spaces between the smudged handwriting, Fusao could hear his mother's restless breathing. Filtering in from the bathroom came the sound of loud splashing, and Kōichi's voice, which had started to change, was singing out of tune a song in English. Outside the window, everything was still, with no sign of Kiyoko's return.

* * * * *

We weren't really sure what we should do, but when I consider the future, I think, maybe, after all, it would be best if we all live together.

Even if we stay here, Father can do hardly any work at all now after his operation, and even though he's better now, no one knows what the future holds. In Tokyo there are lots of big hospitals, which is a comfort, and being near you would be a relief. And Father seems to want to spend his final years in the place where he was raised.

Since you were kind enough to make the offer, I think we will take you up on it.

Your house isn't that big, and I'm not thinking of actually living under one roof. It'll make the garden smaller, but I think it would be a good idea to build a small guest cottage on the east side of the entrance. Since it'll be just two old people, even an eight-mat little cottage would be fine. Don't worry about the money for it, since we'll take care of that. I wonder if you would see Mr. Suzuki, the carpenter, since he's nearby, and get an estimate.

If we do move there, we'll get rid of most of our things, but it might be a good idea to build a small shed in a corner of the garden to put things in. . . .

* * * * *

So—it's finally come, Fusao thought, biting his lip and tossing the letter back on top of the television. Kiyoko's emotions, her message to him to read the letter, lay heavy on him. Surely, the letter was to blame for her going out like this, leaving the children alone 'til past midnight. It's true that every time his mother called with forlorn reports about his father's condition, Fusao had suggested they move back to Tokyo. But that was just so much talk that happened to come up in the course of the conversation. Kiyoko hadn't gotten angry or objected each time he made his glib invitation, but it was easy enough to tell that deep down she didn't welcome the prospect. Maybe she didn't take it seriously, figuring there was no way they could carry out that plan on their small piece of land.

Fusao had to admit, however, that the thought of living together with his elderly parents ignited a small flame within him. It brought back so many memories of the old house and life as a child with his parents and grandparents. The square stepping-stones running along the hedge between their house and the Tanabes'. The long-handled well pump. The toy room. The lush persimmon tree growing outside.

His grandfather had been a difficult person, always redolent of cigarette smoke, but his grandmother was like a door opening onto a strange and wonderful hallway, something Fusao never felt about his mother. When he helped his grandmother or ran an errand for her, she'd take out her large purse and give him some spending money; his mother never gave him more than his allowance. And Fusao would scurry off to the toy store or the stationery shop, feeling as if he'd struck it rich. In front of his grandmother, he could act in ways he would never dare in front of his mother. It might be too late for Kōichi, who was already in junior high, but at least Mayu could experience this enviable feeling of having a secret path open to her, one that her parents knew nothing about—

Of course, all of this was a dream premised on its never really coming true. Fusao couldn't help but be taken aback at all this talk about an eight-mat room and a new shed.

"Mom's still not back?" Kōichi, towel draped over his shoulders and still undressed after his bath, came into the living room, glancing up at the clock on the wall. He tried to act casual, but he was uneasy.

"She'll be back soon." Now, it was Fusao's turn to act casual.

"How long does it take from Shibuya to our house?"

"About an hour. But you should get to bed or you'll oversleep."

He didn't want to talk about Kiyoko with Kōichi. Any complaints the son might have about his mother would, finally, end up as criticism of him, the father. And this could only lead to husband-wife matters, something the children were better off not knowing.

"All set for the test?"

"No problem!"

Kōichi put his hands on his shoulders and nodded a couple of times. "Good night," he said in a forced, low voice, and shut the door to the room next door. *Hey, you, get off my futon,* Kōichi's mutters drifted in; Mayu groaned as she was pushed back on her own futon, and then the room next door was silent. In the living room, only Fusao and the white envelope remained.

The wall clock made its usual choked sound as it noiselessly struck 12:30. If I'd known this was going to happen, Fusao thought, I wouldn't have had to rush back home. But what if he'd gotten home even later? Did Kiyoko plan to leave the kids alone until the middle of the night? She'd been taking a one-night-a-week class for the past year at the Culture Center, but she'd promised to be home by 9:00. And today wasn't even the day she had her class, so what could possibly be keeping her? As if to push aside the anger and unease he felt toward his wife, the letter from his mother on top of the TV caught hold of him. If the letter is what caused Kiyoko to stay out this late, then what's going to happen to this family?

A little after 1:00 A.M. a key turned hesitantly in the front-door lock; light from outside shone in the open doorway and lit up the glass door to the living room. She must have taken the very last train of the evening. Fusao was about to get up from the sofa but, thinking it over, settled back down again. He had to let her know in no uncertain terms how angry he was. He and Kiyoko were going to have uncomfortable words about the letter, and no matter how that turned out, it was best to start off from a position of strength.

After the door opened, the entrance was still. No matter how long he waited, there was no sound of movement. A terrible vision struck him—of Kiyoko, attacked on the street, crouching, covered with blood. Throwing all his strategies to the wind, he rushed out to the entrance.

Kiyoko stood, eyes closed, facing the half-open door, leaning lightly against the pillar.

"What's the matter?"

Fusao quickly felt for the light switch and turned on the overhead lamp. Kiyoko slowly opened her eyes and seeing him standing above her threw both arms up and shouted, "*Yesss!* I'm an *A.M.er!*"

The abrupt, childish shout startled Fusao.

"Kiyoko! You'll wake up Mayu. It's past 1:00, you know."

"That's why I'm an *A.M.er*. I've always wanted to be one."

Without shutting the door, she staggered and sat down heavily on the step leading inside.

"Are you drunk?"

Spirits dampened, Fusao reached past her to push the door shut. He was struck by the strong odor of liquor.

"How could I be drunk?" she said accusingly. "You're the one who's drunk."

"No way. I didn't drink anything tonight. I've been home for over two hours."

"Pardon me. You're home early, aren't you."

Before he had a chance to wonder whether she meant it sarcastically, Kiyoko linked her hands behind her head, leaned back onto the wooden floor—eyes closed, legs still stuck out on the floor of the foyer.

"Pull yourself together! Where did you go drinking?"

He put his hand on her shoulder, trying to guide her to the living-room sofa; just then she opened her eyes, stared at the ceiling, and muttered in a surprisingly sober voice: "What's wrong with that? It happens sometimes." An ad hoc plan sprang to his mind, to use her drunkenness as an excuse to avoid talking about the letter and pass the rest of the night in peace. But now, hearing this calm voice, he knew this wasn't going to happen.

Kiyoko sat up and calmly began to undo the laces of her sandals; she stood up in front of her husband and walked briskly into the living room. She sat down in the hard wooden chair opposite the sofa and for a time was silent, head bowed.

"Would you like some water?"

Fusao spoke cheerfully, unable to completely abandon his plan of a few moments before. Instead of answering, Kiyoko opened her shoulder bag and took out a red pack of Lark cigarettes. She clumsily pulled out a cigarette from the open pack and lit it with a disposable lighter.

"You're smoking?" Kiyoko hadn't had a cigarette since she was pregnant with Kōichi.

"I don't need any water but you can get me an ashtray."

"Where is it?" he asked.

After reading a newspaper article about second-hand smoke and its effects on the family, Kiyoko had made him give up smoking. Since then the only time they had used an ashtray was when guests came. Fusao had no idea where it had been put away.

Following his wife's instructions, he stooped down beside the door in the bath and looked at the shelf under the sink. Three mismatched ashtrays lay in a stack, covered with a dry white powder. A small black shadow suddenly ran by his outstretched left hand. He cried out and pulled his hand back only to bang his elbow on the pillar next to the sink; numbness shot through his arm. What the hell am I doing? he asked himself, rubbing his elbow with his hand.

He put the heavy-glass ashtray that they'd received as a wedding gift from a friend on the table. "Thanks," Kiyoko said in a low voice, and nervously tapped the side of her cigarette. The stained-glass ashtray looked cloudy under the living-room light. Fusao hesitated, then reached for the pack of Larks. Without a word, Kiyoko pushed the lighter over to him.

"You know, I've decided to live in the shed," she said after exhaling a thin trail of smoke.

"What are you talking about?" Fusao feigned ignorance. Unused to the cigarette, he felt dizzy.

"You read it, didn't you? Your mother's letter."

"Yeah, I read it."

"Then you know what I'm talking about."

"No, I don't."

A sharp crease ran through her face. You think I could ever admit that I know what you mean? he thought, trying to bolster his courage.

"You really don't understand?"

Her voice suddenly became high pitched and desperate, a voice he had heard any number of times in memories he'd rather not linger over.

"I don't."

"OK, then, I'll tell you."

She crushed out her long cigarette in the bottom of the ashtray and began speaking, strangely serene.

"You invited your parents many times to come live with us. And never once did you consult me about it."

"Well, you know, I just said that to cheer them up, that's all—"

"Look—you said you didn't understand, so be quiet and listen. This land is your father's. When we built the house, we got a loan from your company, but your father also helped us out. It's just you and your elder brother, and he doesn't live in Japan anymore. If the one son left invites his parents to live with him, and they think that's a good idea and say they will, can you then refuse?"

"If my family's against it, of course I can."

"No, you can't. You never had any intention of refusing. You knew that even if I complained you'd get your way. And that's OK. That's the way it should be. Wait. Just listen to me. Mr. Suzuki will come over, show us some plans, give an estimate, and then the carpenters will go to work. The eight-mat cottage will be finished, then the prefab shed, and their things will arrive from Nagano. Your father and mother will move here, and three generations of Odas will sit around the dinner table having a lively time. What a wonderful thing. Mayu will probably enjoy living with her grandparents. . . . But I won't. It has nothing to do with me. No one consulted me, so don't expect me to take any responsibility. When their things arrive, you can put them in this house. There's a lot more room here than in a shed. In return, give me the shed. There's enough space in it for a person to live. Kōichi and Mayu are related to me, so I think I have the right to live in a corner of this land. That's why I came back tonight."

"Hold on. If you just give your side of the story, you're putting me in a tight spot. The reason I asked my father and mother if they would come here was—"

"You won't be in any tight spot—watch out, you're getting ashes everywhere—because you're a good, considerate son."

Her words weren't the vehement outburst you might expect from someone in a rage but rather were spoken ominously, as if she were coolly observing herself from a distance. The voice of a woman who had already left the house and was living alone in a shed in a corner of the garden.

"But I want you to know right now," she continued, "that if the two of them come to live here I'm going to find a job and start working."

Fusao could picture Kiyoko silently walking from her shed across the garden and out the gate on her way to work. The scene was strangely vivid and real. He was overcome less with a sense of how ridiculous that would be than with the dread that chilly scene engendered.

"This isn't easy for you, honey, but it isn't for me, either. We're in the same boat."

Fusao realized he hadn't called her honey for years, since before Kōichi was born.

"No, you're wrong. You're their child and they're your parents."

"But we're husband and wife," he said.

"So what?"

"If you feel that way, then what am I to you?"

"Hmm, that's a good question. . . ."

Her answer was not what he expected. Seeing her lost in thought, Fusao didn't know what to think.

"No matter what happens," he began, "you would always be my—"

Just then, they heard a soft thud in the next room. Tiny fingers appeared at the edge of the door and slowly pushed it open.

"Smokey."

Her face grimacing against the light, Mayu pointed to the smoke hanging in the air.

"Oh, I'm sorry. Daddy, put the cigarette out right now. You have to tinkle?"

Kiyoko's voice calling out to the little figure shuffling off to the bathroom was no different than usual. She took the ashtray with its thin line of smoke trailing upward out to the kitchen, where she yanked on the ventilation fan. Mayu came out of the bathroom and she and Kiyoko exchanged a few words in front of the sink. Kiyoko suddenly bent backward and laughed. *What just happened here?* Fusao wondered vaguely. He felt exhausted and let his head sink back against the sofa.

* * * * *

As if they had dug a hole and buried it, the letter disappeared as a topic of conversation. Not that it had been forgotten, even after being shoved to the back of the letter rack that hung next to the television. But Fusao did his best to avoid looking in that direction. He spent his days clinging to the hope that, without a reply, his parents would somehow understand the mood in his home.

The weather was rainy for a while, and then stopped. Today was a Sunday, not a sunny day exactly, though the sun did peek through the high clouds that covered the sky. The blare of an ambulance siren grew nearer. Fusao heard it turn the corner at the intersection on the road leading to the station; the wail drew closer. He lifted his eyes from the sports article he'd been reading in the morning paper and looked outside. He waited tensely for the siren, filling the road, to rush like the wind past the entrance to their little cul-de-sac. But the siren, too loud for a residential area, passed by the Takigawas' next door and abruptly stopped.

"I wonder what's up."

He put down his newspaper and stood up.

"Yes, what could it be?" Kiyoko said, without much interest as she took laundry out from the washer.

"Daddy, there's an ambulance at the Tanabes'." From outside Mayu's excited voice rushed in.

When he went out to the main road, the vehicle, surrounded by a smattering of children, was parked out front; its rear door was open. Here and there, worried faces peeked out over hedges. Perhaps an accident had happened to one of the people renting rooms on the second floor. Or to the old man himself. Fusao had no way of knowing, and he hesitated to step into their house.

He was about to ask the white-helmeted driver who was standing next to the ambulance, when white uniforms flitted past the trees from the garden. A stretcher, bearing what looked like a not-very-heavy load, was carried out the front gate. Despite the mugginess of the day, the figure on the stretcher was swathed in a blanket. It was old Mr. Tanabe. The old man's eyes were wide open, staring up at the sky. His expression, fixed seriously, kept one at a distance. A small old lady hurriedly ran after the stretcher.

"What happened to him?" Fusao called out before he realized it.

"He was eating lunch and suddenly felt sick. He lay down and I didn't know what to do. . . ."

"Will you be all right? Would you like me to go with you?"

The old lady busily waved her hand in front of her in refusal, as if she didn't recognize him; one of the stretcher bearers, having placed the stretcher in the ambulance, helped her get in from the back. The siren started again and the ambulance was once more an anonymous, indifferent vehicle, leaving the spectators behind and driving away.

"Did Mr. Tanabe die?" Mayu asked, looking up. He hadn't noticed she'd been holding onto his hand.

"If he were dead, they wouldn't put him in an ambulance. They'll take him to a hospital and the doctor will treat him and he'll be fine."

As he answered his daughter, Fusao wondered how old the elderly Mr. Tanabe was, his thoughts betraying his words. A grey van, which had been waiting for the ambulance to move on, slowly drove closer and came to a stop next to Fusao.

"Did something happen at the Tanabes'?"

The head sticking out of the driver's side belonged to Mr. Suzuki, the foreman of the construction crew that had built their house.

"His wife said he felt sick all of a sudden, so it must be his heart or blood pressure."

"Mr. Tanabe's getting on in years, that's for sure. . . . But his timing in rebuilding was good. 'Course they had the fire, but as long as they rent out the rooms, they'll have money coming in."

Mr. Suzuki squinted up at the two-story house.

"So you built the Tanabes' house?"

"That's right. Mr. Tanabe sure had a lot of special requests, I can tell you."

Mr. Suzuki slapped both hands on top of the steering wheel and smiled. Looking at that face, with its deeply etched wrinkles around the eyes, Fusao remembered the white envelope in the back of the letter rack.

"Now that you mention it, a couple of days ago I got a letter from your mother in Nagano," Mr. Suzuki said.

"From my mother? To you?"

"She asked for an estimate about how much it would cost to put up an eight-mat guest cottage in your garden. I've been meaning to stop by, but I've been so busy. . . ."

"My mother sent a letter directly to you?"

A weight he'd been trying to forget began oozing its way forward. He could picture his mother, pen in hand, irritated by the lack of a response.

"You knew about the guest cottage, I assume?" A trace of anxiety grazed the builder's features.

"My mother wanted me to ask you, but I've been coming home late every day."

"I hope so, otherwise, I'm afraid I've gone and shot my mouth off."

Mr. Suzuki gave a knowing smile, the kind he might show when tramping into their place in wet feet; a glint of a gold tooth showed at the corner of his mouth.

"So, are your parents then planning to move here?" he asked.

"Nothing's been decided yet. . . . Do you think it would be possible to build a second story on our house?"

It wasn't the first time Fusao had thought of this. But he also wanted to shift the conversation away from the guest cottage.

"Well, when we built it we weren't thinking about that, so I'm not sure about the beams. It wouldn't be impossible, but we'd need to put in some thicker support, next to the others."

"So it might be impossible?"

"No, if we tried, it might work out. . . ."

The builder's words were evasive, but clearly he didn't relish the idea.

"I really hope Mr. Tanabe is all right." Mr. Suzuki forced these words out. "I have to go to a building site now," he added, promising to stop by soon. He put his van in gear and drove off.

Fusao watched the van, with Suzuki Construction Company stenciled on its side, drive off, then he turned with heavy steps toward home, Mayu's hand still in his.

"Did the ambulance get to the hospital already?" she asked.

"No, I bet it's still going *pee-po, pee-po* down the street."

A mental picture came to Fusao of old Mr. Tanabe staring fixedly at the ceiling as the ambulance jolted down the road. He remembered the night the fire broke out on the second floor of the house and how he and the Ōmoris had searched all over for him. The old man looked so very small then, standing alone by the railroad tracks.

He also recalled the dumbfounded look on Mr. Tanabe's face when, two years before, he'd stopped by to tell them about the construction at his house and found out they'd built their kitchen on top of the old well. The old man had asked about his parents then and, as he recalled, said something about how it was better, when the parents were still healthy, to live apart.

Fusao began walking faster as if to avoid the image of Mr. Tanabe's face, with its wide-open eyes, transforming into something else. He turned the corner around the Takigawas' house, and there was Mrs. Takigawa, white haired, broom in hand, standing at the front door. She called out to them as if she'd been waiting. Fusao explained what had happened at the Tanabes' and she nodded, her face knitting in concern. As he did, he remembered that she was living alone, her husband stationed someplace far away. She stood there, hand on her slightly bent waist, her thin features lined with wrinkles. Fusao was seized by a desire to ask her why she was living apart from her husband. He finished talking, and her face broke into a sudden smile. She called out to Mayu in a high, unnaturally friendly voice.

"So, you're with your Daddy today. That's nice!"

Mayu pushed at her father to urge him home, and said, in a small voice, "My Mommy's home, too," but apparently the woman didn't hear her.

"Come over to play again, Mayu-chan."

The woman's voice got even more syrupy, and Mayu gave up pushing her father and scampered off into their garden.

"Mayu's been over at your house? I'm sorry she's been a bother."

"Not at all. I'm happy she let me play with her."

The woman twisted her shoulders strangely, tilting her head in a childishly coquettish fashion. Fusao had barely spoken to her before this; the sudden, unexpected gesture confused him. Flustered, he bowed and hurried off after Mayu.

* * * * *

Fusao knew full well that she would find out eventually. But for the time being, he wanted to keep the letter from his mother to the builder a secret from Kiyoko. He knew he had to make his feelings clear to his parents or the situation would get even more out of hand, but he couldn't make up his mind. Seeing old Mr. Tanabe carried off that way, Fusao found it even more difficult to tell his mother—nearly seventy and living alone with an ill husband—that his previous words meant nothing and he didn't want them to live together.

Mr. Tanabe, it turned out, was out of danger but would have to stay in the hospital for the present. It didn't look like he would ever completely recover. Fusao had heard all this from Mr. Ōmori, whom he'd run across, and when he told Kiyoko the news she merely made a few halfhearted, sympathetic remarks.

After much thought one day, Fusao finally decided to contact the builder himself to avoid having him show up when he was out. If that happened, Kiyoko would arrive at the mistaken conclusion that he'd already sent off a reply to his parents, accepting their proposal. Instead of having Mr. Suzuki drop by, he would contact him himself and have him phone to give a rough estimate of the cost. He could then send off a letter to his parents to let them down gently.

Fusao was on his way back home, turning the corner near the Takigawas' house. Glancing up at the pale light seeping out of the entrance window, he was just slipping past the half-opened metal gate when he halted. Something loomed whitely in the darkness of the garden. The shadowy figure murmured, took one, two, three strides forward, halted, changed direction, and took a few more steps.

It was Kiyoko.

"What are you doing?" When he realized it was his wife, his voice stiffened.

"Oh, you're back. Hold on a sec."

She didn't look at him, just held up a hand to stop him. "One ... two ... three ... ," she chanted out the steps in a low voice as she walked toward the cement wall on the east side of the house.

"It would come to about here, I guess. ..."

Turning her body ninety degrees, Kiyoko now faced north

and took a couple of steps toward the hedge that separated their house from the Tanabes'.

"Really, what's going on?" he asked loudly, not so much to ascertain what she was doing as to put a stop to it.

"Mr. Suzuki dropped by this evening," Kiyoko said quietly, raising her arms parallel to the hedge, turning her head from right to left as if siting through her outstretched arms.

"*Damn*. He already came?" His voice, unlike hers, was agitated.

"He said he came to give an estimate for the guest cottage."

She lowered her arms sharply, as if to slap them against her sides, and looked at him for the first time.

"You don't understand . . . I didn't ask him to. . . ."

"Your mother wrote a letter directly to the builder, right?"

"I wasn't happy when he told me about the letter," Fusao explained, "and I was hoping to take care of it before I told you. But I just never got around to it."

"I've known for some time."

"Mr. Suzuki told you?"

"I heard it from Mayu. The day Mr. Tanabe collapsed," Kiyoko answered. Legs together, she stood rooted to the spot. He suddenly remembered Mayu beside him, silently holding his hand as he spoke to the builder through the van window.

"Anyhow, let's go inside," he said. "I've come to a decision and I need to talk with you about it."

She stood there motionless, as if on top of a pillar, her sandals tightly together. He had to get her away from there as soon as he could.

"It's too late for that," she said.

"Why?"

"Because there's nothing you can do."

"But I've made a decision. . . ."

"You should have done that a long time ago."

"There's still time."

Erect, Kiyoko gently shook her head from side to side.

"Why isn't there still time?" His own voice, pitifully hoarse, sounded miles away.

"Because I came to a decision before you."

"What are you talking about? What have you decided?"

"If you built it right up against the wall by the entrance and extended it out about 4 meters, a two-mat space would come out right where the pole is for hanging clothes to dry. The north side would be where that stone is." Kiyoko seemed to relish the words.

"*If* we build it, you mean."

"And then put in a door from the wooden floor section of the foyer that would connect up to the guest cottage."

"No one's building a cottage here, if I can help it."

Kiyoko suddenly fell silent. From the second floor of the Tanabes' house, the compressed voices of miniature people on TV fell down into the dark garden.

"The guest cottage was supposed to be Kōichi's and Mayu's room. . . ." Her words had a warmth to them, as if she were yearning for days long gone. "You forgot all about that."

"I didn't forget. That's why I'm thinking about building on a second story—didn't Mayu tell you?"

"And right here will be the shed I'll live in," she suddenly called out in a crooning voice, cutting him off.

"You think I'm going to let you live in a shed!?" Something hot burst up from within him.

"That's why I'm standing here." Ignoring him, Kiyoko continued to croon.

"You really plan on living here?"

"I've already decided to."

"Well, if that's the way it is, then I'll live there with you."

In the night air came the sound of his wife quietly breathing.

"By the time you figure out what's going on, it's always too late."

A deeply ardent voice he'd never heard before grazed Fusao's ears and disappeared into the depths of the darkened garden.

the lawn

A raccoon was sitting in the third chair.

It was pulled up, nearly flush with the table. Even so, the raccoon could barely peek over the tabletop. They were having a late Sunday lunch, and Michiko was home for a change. Masaki settled himself gingerly into an unsteady chair.

"Come on, Nuta, eat up now."

Michiko pushed over a plate with one oval croquette toward the raccoon. A tiny pair of pink chopsticks were lined up neatly in front of the dish.

The flat little potato croquettes were left over from the day before. Masaki had picked them up in the basement supermarket of the department store near the station just as the place was about to close for the evening. They had spent the night in the refrigerator.

"They might taste better heated up," Masaki ventured. Michiko didn't reply. Instead, she concentrated on lifting a bite of the croquette to the raccoon's mouth with her chopsticks.

"It's yummy, Nuta," she said, dangling the food in front of him, then popped the morsel into her own mouth, gulping it down without chewing.

It would be better if he ate them as they were, Masaki decided, but stood up anyway and reached for the aluminum foil on the shelf. He tore off an extra-long sheet, placed it on his palm, and set two croquettes down. Through the foil, the croquettes had a faint heft to them, the kind of in-between feel you expect from prepared food.

"Maybe the raccoon doesn't need his heated up?" he asked.

"It's *Nuta*," Michiko corrected him instantly.

"But cold croquettes don't taste very good, I guess."

"Nuta-chan—how about some cabbage, with a little sauce?"

Masaki placed the croquettes in the foil inside the toaster oven, hesitating a moment, then set the timer at seven minutes. An image of freshly made croquettes came to mind. A shiny gold crust, fairly popping as they were lifted out of the pan, dripping hot oil. He could almost taste them. Store-bought croquettes were a world apart—no matter how much you heated them up, the insides were always lukewarm. But Michiko had banned frying from her kitchen. Too messy, she told him once, not long after she quit her job.

"I'm going to have to buy you a bib, you're so sloppy. . . ." Michiko picked up the cabbage that had fallen from the chopsticks just in front of the raccoon. She tossed the scrap in the sink as she turned around.

"Don't we have any Worchestershire sauce? Can't have cabbage without spicy sauce on it." He didn't plan to but every time he opened his mouth, Masaki found himself complaining. It was irritating.

"Nuta, he says we need a different kind of sauce. Would you be a darling and get it from underneath the wagon?"

Michiko addressed the raccoon, not him. Masaki was relieved. He knelt down in front of the trolley and pulled out the Worchestershire sauce. Only a splash of the dark liquid remained in the bottom of the bottle.

While he waited for the croquettes to warm up in the oven, Masaki stuffed himself with cabbage. The sauce dribbled down to the bottom of the plate. In college, cabbage had been his mainstay at the school cafeteria. The cabbage was machine sliced, wafer thin. Just before the toaster-oven bell dinged, the telephone rang.

"Nuta—telephone." Michiko spoke to the raccoon, her eyes glancing for a second at the clock on the wall. Before she could get to her feet, Masaki stood up hurriedly and picked up the receiver.

"Is that you, Mr. Masaki?" Masuzawa was on the other end. His voice sounded so clear he must have been calling from nearby. "I was just driving by your neighborhood, and I thought I'd drop by if you're home."

"Where are you?"

"A pay phone in front of a post office. Halfway up a hill. But I've got the little rug rat with me. I took him to see the relatives. I just wanted to have a look at your lawn and then I'll be on my way."

"Your wife's with you?"

"What do you think, I'm driving with a baby on one arm?"

"You I can do without, but I wouldn't mind seeing your wife and baby." Masaki, phone in hand, looked over to read his wife's expression as she sat at the table. She continued to lift up croquettes to the raccoon's mouth, oblivious to her husband.

"Masuzawa and his wife and baby are down by the post office. They'd like to stop by for a minute. What do you think?"

"We don't like that, now, do we, Nuta?" Michiko said peevishly. She leaned forward and pushed her nose into the raccoon's fur.

"He's waiting for an answer. He said they can't stay long." Masaki turned toward the kitchen, his hand clasped tightly over the mouthpiece.

"He's Masaki's friend, so Masaki should decide what to do, Nuta says."

"He's been helping me out so much, after all . . ."

Michiko sat there, spearing another croquette with the pink chopsticks. Masaki took her silence for assent and told Masuzawa to stop by.

It was only a ten-minute walk from the post office to their house, and Masaki had carefully explained the way to get there. Even so, he managed to finish a quick lunch and still there was no sign of Masuzawa. He was driving, so Masuzawa wouldn't want a beer. And the baby, a year or so old, Masaki guessed—what on earth could he offer him? And how far could he count on Michiko to help out? He restlessly paced the room. The phone rang again.

"Hello, my name is Tomita. I was wondering if Michiko is there?"

Masaki had been expecting Masuzawa, helplessly lost and calling for more directions. Instead, the voice on the phone was faintly familiar, slightly accented.

"Oh, Mr. Tomita. I wanted to thank you for all you've done for Michiko. I really appreciate it." Masaki said stiffly, the blood draining out of him.

"You're Michiko's husband, I take it? I should be thanking *you*. I don't know what I'd do without her. Is she in today?"

Masaki had never met Mr. Tomita but had conjured up his own mental image of the man. Middle-aged, well off. Supple fingers with thick black hair growing on the knuckles. Polite but used to getting what he wanted.

"My wife?" Masaki deliberately restated the obvious. He wouldn't mind a bit of his own irritation rubbing off.

"Yes, Michiko." Tomita repeated her name calmly.

"She's here. But we're having guests today."

"I understand. I apologize for calling you on your day off."

Masaki wanted to stall, but Tomita's silence forced him to concede. He called to his wife.

"Mr. Tomita? What does he want?"

With an exaggerated look of surprise, Michiko took the phone from him. He turned his back to her and looked out at the overgrown lawn, his nerves taut. A college friend had introduced Michiko to Tomita, and she began helping out occasionally at the small clothing company he owned. Tomita had called their house several times before. The work, which wasn't steady, had come mostly at the end of the month; this turned into twice a week, and now Michiko was working half of each week there. As she began

to go out to work more, Tomita called less often; today was the
first time in quite a while that Masaki had heard his voice. But
Masaki could always tell when it was Tomita on the phone. His
calls were supposedly work related, but you would never guess
that from Michiko's tone of voice. Even her hands took on an
unexpected softness as they cradled the phone.

"Sorry about the other day!"

Masaki winced at her bubbly opening. In a moment, though,
her tone changed abruptly.

"Me? No, nothing like that . . ." Was Tomita checking to see
she got home all right the other night?

"No, fine, really. Why do you ask?"

What name did Tomita call her by when they were face-to-
face? When they were at the office in front of other people, she
was Mrs. Kiuchi. But what about later, after work?

"I don't mind. Really . . . What? . . . Why? . . ." Michiko's
words were sweet, her phrasing breathless. Standing in front of
the sliding-glass door, Masaki shifted his weight.

"What? She saw it? . . . What? . . . Huh? . . . Sugita did? . . .
But that's odd . . . Right . . . Right . . . Mmm . . . Yes . . . No . . .
Right . . ."

Michiko's simple replies seeped into Masaki as he looked out
at the yard. The next-door neighbors had put out a laundry pole
that stuck out a little over the concrete wall separating their yards,
into his. Masaki stared hard at it. As if she herself noticed how
intimate she was sounding, Michiko suddenly shifted to a brisk
tone.

"What Sugita told me was . . . No, I wouldn't do anything
li—Yes . . . That's right . . . Well, she might think that way, but—
All right . . . Let's do that . . . But—If we don't, my—Oh, stop it,
now . . . don't be silly. . . ."

With Michiko's voice floating, suspended in the air, constrained by his presence, Masaki felt his body turning transparent,
melting into the glass in front of him. He had no sense of where
he was standing. Only the laundry pole above the wall seemed

real. The croquette lunch was far away, a meal from decades past.

Michiko's voice grew hushed. Without turning around, Masaki knew she'd cupped both hands around the receiver. Feeling as if he were about to come face-to-face with something truly frightful, Masaki was about to turn toward her. Just then, the roof of a blue car glided up beyond the wall and jolted to a stop.

"Looks like our guests are here," Masaki said to Michiko, hunched over the phone. Strangely enough, his voice sounded the same as always. Without looking up, Michiko nodded slightly. The car doors slammed shut and the doorbell rang.

Masaki didn't feel right going out to the door with Michiko still on the phone, but he couldn't bring himself to tell her to hang up. It was all he could do to lightly tap her back as he passed by. Her thin shoulders had the unfamiliar feel of an ornament he was touching for the first time. He instantly regretted the contact.

"Man alive! First, the railroad crossing was broken, so I had to back up. Then I must've missed that liquor store you told me about, 'cause I went on forever and couldn't find the right corner to turn at." Masuzawa's cheerful voice boomed just outside the open door. He had on a red polo shirt, and behind him, wearing a green dress, was a woman holding a small child. Masuzawa roughly nodded in her direction. "You've met each other, right?" he asked.

"Remember, you invited me to your wedding." *Hey, I was at your wedding. Forgot already?* Masaki was about to say but changed his mind. Ever since he quit his job and had begun to rely on Masuzawa for translation work, Masaki felt a wall of politeness looming between himself and his friend. The night of Masuzawa's wedding, though, several years before, Masaki was still an easygoing office worker with a steady job.

After the wedding reception, Masaki talked with a few friends from college that he hadn't seen in a while. They sat on a couch near the entrance to the wedding hall and watched the newlyweds say good-bye to the line of guests filing by. The bride and bridegroom, decked out in expensive kimonos, bowed deeply as each guest passed by. Masaki, sitting behind and a little diago-nally from the couple, noticed how each time the bride bowed, her panty line showed clearly beneath her silken kimono. He told his friends, and they all got a kick out of watching. *Here it comes!* they laughed each time the V line of the bride's panties showed up below her tautly stretched buttocks. I always thought women didn't wear anything under their kimono, one friend whispered. Another one who looked well versed in these things countered, No, there's a kind of Japanese-style underwear now that doesn't have any hems or elastic. Well, another one said, in a couple of hours whatever she has on won't be. They sat there for a long while, enjoying the view.

Masaki knew the curve of the bride's behind but had no memory at all of her face. She'd been made up so heavily. The woman in front of him now, holding a small child with thin hair, was plain, with nothing distinctive about her. The child in her arms squirmed around to get a look at Masaki, then not thrilled with what he saw turned slowly back, clutching at his mother. Masaki hadn't a clue how he was supposed to react to this strange little creature.

"Well, uh, why don't you come in?" Masaki awkwardly motioned them inside, his mind never for an instant leaving the image of Michiko still on the phone. He felt awkward and embarrassed, as if the other two were decked out in nice clothes while he alone had on a sopping-wet shirt.

"We just wanted to get a look at your yard and the lawn," Masuzawa said. "I've been wanting to take the tour for some time now. We can get there through here, can't we? Do you mind?"

"Not much of a tour, I'm afraid," Masaki replied. "As you'll see."

Masuzawa nimbly led the way past the crepe myrtle next to the front door to the small patch of lawn.

"We don't take very good care of it, so it's a bit overgrown."

"If you mowed it, though, it'd make a nice little putting green."

"Well, you know me," Masaki said. "Sports aren't my thing."

"How many square meters is it?"

"Seventy-five? Something like that."

Masuzawa took a couple of steps toward the center of the lawn. Masaki stood behind him, shielding the inside of the house from view. Masaki caught a glance of Michiko's back, hunched over the phone in the living room.

"Why don't you put him down?" Masuzawa said to his wife. She nodded and lowered her child to the lawn. The infant stood up on the grass heavily, unsteady for a moment, then plumped backward on his rear end. He stretched out his arms to his mother and began to cry.

"What's the matter, Ken-chan? The grass is so pretty. Let's do walky walky. There you go, upsy daisy!"

Masaki was startled. She'd hardly spoken a word, now this gush of speech. Masuzawa had told him about when his wife was pregnant, how as her stomach swelled up the bottom of her navel pushed to the surface, then ended up looking like a bag turned inside out. What was her navel like now? Masaki mused and glanced at her green dress. Underneath the thin, dark-brown belt round her middle, her stomach rested quietly, unconcerned.

"You can do walky walky, I know you can. Go to Uncle Masaki. Upsy daisy!"

Masuzawa's wife held the child's hands, trying to get him to stand up. Masaki, taken aback by this uncle business, quickly turned to Masuzawa.

"So, he's about a year old now?"

"A year and one month. He's big for his age, but he's a little slow about learning to walk."

"Planning on having any more?"

"Actually, the second one's already on the way."

Masuzawa looked over at his wife on the overgrown lawn, still trying her best to make her son walk. Masaki had just been trying to keep the conversation going; his friend's reply surprised him. Masuzawa might have been discussing a litter of pups, he was so matter-of-fact; at the same time, though, he sounded as if he were letting Masaki in on some erotic secret.

"As long as you're going to have kids, I figure you might as well have them early. When this little one's out of college, I still won't be much more than fifty. Even if he takes a few years to pass the college-entrance exams, he'll still graduate before I retire. If we wait too long for the second one, I'll be retired before he finishes school."

"So, you have it all planned out. . . ."

Masaki felt overwhelmed, as if suddenly much younger than Masuzawa, standing there, his decades ahead all neatly lined up and calculated.

For someone who lived on the third floor of a company apartment building, Masuzawa knew a lot about trees. He pointed to one planted beside the garden wall, a tree whose name Masaki had no idea of, and declared it: "a flowering dogwood with white, no . . . wait, light-pink flowers, right?" Masaki had no way of replying. "Hey, look at that," his friend continued, "I believe that's a laurel." He pulled off a leaf, crumpling it in half, sniffed at the leaf, then let his wife do the same. "I'm not sure about this one, could be a lilac," he said, tapping the thin trunk of another tree. Masaki was amazed. This was not the Masuzawa he knew in college. Masaki tagged along after him; it was hard to tell who was the owner of the garden and who was the guest. If Masaki hadn't been feeling out of sorts, he might have kidded Masuzawa, asking him, *What's the story? Is your company dealing in trees these days?* But it was all he could do to keep from looking depressed.

Masuzawa's eyes roved here and there over the garden for all the world as if he were planning on how to re-landscape it. With a start, Masaki noticed that Masuzawa's gaze rested for a moment on the inside of the house.

"Well, I guess we'd better be running along."

Masuzawa strode over to where his wife was holding her

child's hands, coaxing him to stand up on the lawn. Lightly, he lifted the child up into the air. Masaki peered into the living room at what Masuzawa had been looking at. A flash of white glided past the sliding-glass door and disappeared. Michiko's phone call was finally over.

"Wouldn't it be lovely to have a garden like this?" Masuzawa's wife, her second child hidden away inside her, said quietly as she left; she'd never had a home with a garden. Masuzawa, walking ahead of her with their child in his arms, replied, but Masaki, just behind the woman, couldn't catch it. Letting her husband carry her child, Masuzawa's wife walked, hands clasped behind her. Masaki saw how deeply wrinkled they were. Rough, hot-looking hands. Masaki couldn't shake the image of those hands caressing Masuzawa's body.

Even now that her phone call was over, Michiko wasn't planning on making an appearance it seemed. Masaki wanted to apologize to Masuzawa's wife, who had clearly been at loose ends, but he had no idea what to say. Masaki couldn't lie that she'd gone out for the day; Masuzawa had caught a glimpse of her inside the house. Masaki could well imagine what they'd say to each other as soon as they were safely in their car. Maybe he should call out to Michiko, but if she refused to come outside that would be even worse. Still undecided, Masaki and his guests arrived at the front door.

"Sorry to drop in on you out of the blue like this," Masuzawa said, as they stood just inside the front gate. Suddenly the front door burst open. Michiko stood there, the raccoon in her arms. He had on an infant's light-blue, short-sleeve shirt. Michiko wore a pair of plastic sandals, her toenails painted bright red.

"I must apologize. I had a call from work and couldn't get away," Michiko explained, her voice unnecessarily loud.

"Look, Ken-chan! How cute."

Masuzawa's wife, talkative once more, called out to her child in her husband's arms. The raccoon was just a shade bigger than the child, if you counted the tail.

"This is our little Nuta."

Michiko held out one of the raccoon's forepaws, with its tiny white feet pasted on. Entranced, the child reached out then withdrew his hand and pounded on his father's shoulder.

"It's a friend, Ken-chan. What a wonderful raccoon."

"It's *Nuta!*" Michiko replied sharply, protectively, rubbing her cheek against its head. A look close to panic appeared in Mrs. Masuzawa's eyes, and Masaki hastily added some words of explanation.

"It's our family pet," he said.

"Do you always carry it around like that?" It was impossible to tell if Masuzawa was bothered by the notion.

"We even sleep together," Michiko answered.

Masaki felt Masuzawa's gaze graze him. Their child twisted away from his father's grasp and again reached out for the raccoon. His mother quickly snatched him away and walked out into the street.

Mrs. Masuzawa and Michiko stood beside the car, one with a child in her arms, the other a raccoon. They bowed to each other as if nothing out of the ordinary had taken place.

"Papa, open the car please." Done with her farewells, Mrs. Masuzawa was curt. In one smooth motion Masuzawa reached his hand, his scratched wedding band on, into his pocket to extract a key chain.

Settled into the driver's seat, Masuzawa turned on the ignition and rolled down the window. "Call me Wednesday," he said briskly, looking up at Masaki. "This next job's kind of a sticky one, so I'd better send over the materials to you earlier than usual." He was saying this less it seemed to make sure about the upcoming job than just to have something to say about work.

As the car drove off, Michiko lifted up one paw of the raccoon and waved it. Mother and child were sunk back in their seats and didn't lean out to wave good-bye.

Masaki turned to Michiko. "I don't mind you carrying Nuta around in the house, but I really wish you wouldn't bring him out in front of other people."

"What a dirty little kid that boy was. Nuta's much cuter." Michiko whispered into the raccoon's ears, then, without so much as a glance behind her, trotted back inside the house, her plastic sandals flapping.

Even after the car rounded the corner and disappeared, Masaki didn't feel like going inside. With Michiko, the raccoon, and the black telephone, the house was full enough. While the Masuzawas were here, he had been able to forget about Tomita; now, the man's voice came rushing back at him.

He had no idea what the phone conversation had been all about, but one thing was certain—Michiko was not about to clue him in. If she were to talk, it could only be a premonition of a terrible change in their lives. That's what Masaki feared most and that's why he ran from it, all the time trying his best to convince himself he was better off not knowing.

With a start, Masaki found himself tracing the path taken by his guests as he rounded the crepe myrtle and went into the yard. Just inside the concrete wall was a familiar sight, the tiny bit of lawn laid out before him. When he married Michiko and moved into this house, which her father had built for them, the lawn was just rows of green strips resting on top of the soil. Before long, though, the grass grew and the boundaries between the strips disappeared; the grass grew more quickly around the edges of the yard. Around the borders of the spindly trees, the lawn bore an unpleasant resemblance to scruffy tufts of hair on the back of a neck.

Suddenly, it hit Masaki that Masuzawa was planning to build a house, one that included a garden and lawn. Which explained today's visit. *You call that a lawn?* Masuzawa's wife, sitting beside him in their car, was surely muttering. *It's the first time I met his wife. She's a strange one, don't you think?* Masuzawa replied. *And at her age with that raccoon! What's with that?* his wife said. *She doesn't have any children, that's why,* Masuzawa said. *It's creepy,* his wife added.

"Out for a stroll?"

A face poked up over the top of the cement wall and called to Masaki. The laundry pole was gone.

"Hard to call it a stroll with a garden this size." Masaki breathed a sigh of relief as he looked at the suntanned face of the boy who lived next door. "Guess your summer break's about over?"

"Not yet. We're off until the middle of September," the boy replied.

"That's a nice long vacation."

"Yes, but as soon as it's over, we have exams."

The last thing Masaki wanted at this point was to go back in the house. A chat over the wall with his young neighbor was a much more pleasant prospect.

"What do you have there?"

"Clippers," the boy answered. "To trim the trees."

"Pretty young to be put in charge of the garden, aren't you?"

"Well, they said the branches were making a racket, so I volunteered to take care of it," he said brightly, then lowered his voice. "It makes things go smoother all around if I help out sometimes."

"Hey, I haven't seen that girl around here recently—the one with the long hair."

"Huh?" The boy pulled his chin back in surprise and looked suspiciously at Masaki. "You know about her?"

"I saw you two together a lot, that's all."

"Yeah. It didn't work out."

"You broke up?"

"Yep. 'Bye-bye, baby!'"

Masaki had no idea what had happened, of course, but from the way the boy accompanied his remark with a snappy, two-fingered salute of farewell, breaking up with his girlfriend didn't seem to have left any permanent scars. *Bye-bye, baby,* Masaki mused. If he had given his own farewell salute to Michiko, long ago—before they married—would that have been for the best? The overgrown lawn tickled his ankles.

A phone rang in the boy's house.

"Ah, hah! Another girl, perhaps?"

"I'm on the third one now!" The boy laughed and strode off purposefully to his verandah. He disappeared inside.

With no one left to talk to, Masaki had no choice but to go back into his own house. As he cut across the lawn in a couple of strides, he didn't see Michiko behind the glass door. Instead, he came across a pair of her high heels just inside the entrance, which was still flung wide open. Chocolate-colored leather shoes with delicate, expensive stitching. Masaki carefully shut the door and turned the lock as if to keep her shoes from escaping.

Michiko was sitting in front of the dresser on the opposite side of the house, putting on makeup. Below her low chair, by her feet, lay the raccoon, still dressed in a light-blue shirt. Beneath the hem of the shirt was a pair of matching pants.

"You're going out?" Masaki forced himself to keep calm.

"Mmm . . . Mr. Tomita's got some work for me to do. Something's come up." She narrowed her eyes and spoke to her own reflection in the dresser mirror.

"On a Sunday?"

"His customers' stores are open on Sundays, so why not?"

In her face in the mirror, her thin fingertips spread purplish-grey eye shadow just above her eyelids.

"Some problem with one of their products?"

"Mmm . . . something like that."

Michiko opened a compact, shaped liked an artist's palette, and continued to select makeup colors. A feeling inside Masaki pleaded with him not to ask anything more but the words spilled out.

"Or is it a problem between people?"

"If I don't go there, I won't know that, now, will I?"

As he feared, Michiko roughly snapped her flat compact shut. *You're lying,* Masaki thought. *You talked for that long and you still don't know why he's asking you to come to work?* After the Masuzawas had arrived and Masaki had left her on the phone, what words had she and Tomita exchanged? The very thought made his throat clench. Granted, they might have discussed work, but hovering over Michiko was the lingering scent of a man and a woman and the words they exchange.

Masaki silently reached down and picked up the raccoon from the floor. His neck, body, and legs were all worn and mushed from all the handling he had received.

"When are you going to be home?"

"I'm not even out the door and already you're worried about when I'll be back? Stop it."

"It's not me asking. It's the raccoon."

Masaki held the raccoon so he stood up, paw to his forehead, head tilted to one side.

"What? Nuta's asking me?"

Still putting on makeup in the mirror, Michiko languidly turned toward the raccoon.

"What time will you be back?"

"It might be late, so you go beddy-bye, first, all right?"

"*Bor—ing.*" The raccoon's head dropped, and he shook his shoulders.

"Don't be that way, Nuta!"

"Anyhow, I'll bet it's after midnight."

The raccoon suddenly looked up; one leg in his light-blue pants kicked the air in front of his face violently, two or three times.

"What's wrong, Nuta? If you keep talking silly like that you'll be as impossible as that little boy."

Michiko turned back to the mirror and her eyebrow pencil.

"While you're gone, I just might go back to my home."

The raccoon, with downcast eyes, drooping head, and bunched up shoulders, really did look miserable.

"What are you talking about? *This* is your home."

"No, it isn't. My home is way off past the road. In a cave, deep in the forest where nobody ever goes."

"Don't fib, Nuta. You know we got you in the Ginza."

The raccoon wordlessly shook its hands in protest, so hard

they seemed ready to come off. The next moment, no longer supported, the creature crumpled to the floor.

"Well, it's getting late."

As if brushing something off her body, Michiko stood up. Ignoring the raccoon at her feet, she stepped to the dresser and pulled open the teak doors; they made a faint, dry sound.

* * * * *

Masaki had no idea when Michiko got back home. On nights when she was late, he was used to going to bed before her. But this evening, he had trouble falling asleep. He took a bottle of scotch that he rarely touched down off the shelf, got some ice cubes from the refrigerator, and swallowed the drink back in one gulp, like medicine. Then, he lay down. He switched off the lamp, but a pale shaft of light still shone through a gap in the curtains. Not a streetlight or a neighbor's house but a glow from far away. Feeling the scotch begin to take effect, he got up and drew open the curtains. Below him lay the dewy lawn, his tiny garden, bathed in moonlight. Small trees clustered by the wall. The regular cry of insects settled in his ears.

From the bed he couldn't see the moon. Instead, he caught sight of the raccoon, lying on Michiko's bed, tossed aside as she left.

Hey, raccoon. Mind if I join you?

The raccoon didn't protest as Michiko would have. Or give permission, either. Masaki pushed himself up, leaned far out of bed, and grabbed the raccoon by the tail and pulled it toward him.

Are you a boy or a girl?

Masaki yanked off the light-blue pants, softly kneading between its legs. Just a flat area and the seam where its fur was sewn together. A moment later, he flung the raccoon as hard as he could against the far side of the room. Nuta hit the wall, fell to Michiko's bed, bounced, then lay still as if it had fallen asleep on the spot.

Something made Masaki wake up. The curtain by the bed beside him was open, but the moon was gone. Darkness stole into the room. Out of the gloom, he could make out Michiko's pale shoulders. *She's home,* Masaki relaxed. *Earlier than expected.* He was just reaching over for his watch on the nightstand when he heard a soft thud of something leaping off her bed.

The raccoon.

Lying flat against the floor in the space between the two beds, Nuta raised up slightly and for the very first time walked on all fours, dragging its long tail. Quietly heading for the door.

What's the matter?

Wordlessly, Masaki called out. The raccoon's legs were weak, perhaps—the animal crawled more than walked. Even so, bit by bit, making its way further into the darkness.

Don't go. This is your home.

The raccoon was still just below him, back and shirt still visible; the creature reached the door, and without opening it, disappeared, the tip of its tail the last thing Masaki saw.

"Nuta—don't go."

For an instant, the tail appeared to hesitate but then vanished from sight. From the bed beside him, Michiko, curled up, breathed out softly.

twilight

Something white bulged in the mailbox.

Are we getting two mail deliveries now? Masayo wondered. In one hand, she held a plastic garbage bag filled with empty cans and a used-up ketchup bottle; with her free hand, she pushed open the mailbox lid.

Inside lay a somewhat forbidding copy of the *Neighborhood Association Newsletter*. There were a number of articles, all in the same typeface: dates for a cancer screening for women, a call for blood donations, news about consultations for rehabilitation for the elderly, the date for a neighborhood beautification day. Masayo skipped over these and as always went straight to the black-bordered column on the lower, left-hand side.

"Our Deepest Condolences" it was entitled, the only article in the newsletter that she found had any appeal. The address and name of the deceased were listed, followed by the usual set phrases in parentheses about the deceased's age at time of death and the date of his/her passing. When two people were listed, the black border repeated; in the rare case that three people had passed away, the black border formed a long column with the same polite phrases repeated three times. Seldom did she run across a name she knew, but when the deceased happened to be a child or in their twenties the unknown name would leap out at her. When the person was someone in their seventies or eighties, though, she found herself wanting to say, with a sigh, *Well, that's only to be expected.*

How did the association know all the details about age and date of death? She found the whole matter rather strange because the location of the association's office and the identity of its leader remained a complete mystery. Whenever it was Masayo's turn to take charge of their block, a small old lady would appear from nowhere with a copy of the newsletter and a sheaf of receipts for the association's fees. A few days later, she'd show up again to collect the monies Masayo had received and disappear. Masayo found the simple, one-sided newsletter—a kind of amusement for old people—interesting in how it never failed to print the age of the deceased and the date of death.

When Masayo herself passed away would her name be listed like this in the bottom, left-hand corner? Not the most pleasant thought. More than the thought of dying, what she found repelling was the idea of her name appearing in the newsletter. She pictured the name Yasunaga Masayo typed out on this rough paper, then imagined it changed to Yasunaga *Yoshiko*. She pondered for a moment how she would feel if Yoshiko's name was in the newsletter. *Well, that's to be expected*, she might very well murmur to herself, but inside, she knew she would call out sadly at the name spelled out in this cheap typeface.

The person in the black border in this issue was sixty-nine. An in-between age that made it hard to know how to react, whether one should see the death as natural or lament an early demise.

Just below the obituary column was an irregular line for people's signatures and seals to show they had seen the circular copy of the newsletter. When Masayo saw the name Kiuchi carelessly scrawled there, she was seized by a desire to pass on the whole newsletter to the Odas' across the street as quickly as she could.

She tossed her garbage bag into the receptacle alongside the wall, set the circular on top of the shoe rack at the front door, added her signature to the paper, then cut across the road to put the newsletter in their mailbox.

Over the low, metal front gate, she spotted Mrs. Oda sitting on top of a cement foundation, which nearly covered the whole garden. She was looking quietly down at the ground.

"Mrs. Oda, I brought over the newsletter!" Masayo hesitated to put it in the mailbox without saying anything. Mrs. Oda sat motionless as if she hadn't heard. Unperturbed, Masayo placed the paper in the mailbox; just then, the woman looked up, startled.

". . . Oh . . . thanks . . ." As if Masayo's voice had only now reached her, Mrs. Oda listlessly got to her feet, stepped over the concrete foundation, and walked over.

"I'm sorry to bother you," Masayo said.

"No, I'm sorry, I was thinking about something else. . . ."

Mrs. Oda's complexion was sallow, and she seemed to have aged.

"Aren't you feeling well?" Masayo couldn't keep from asking. It was that time of month, she imagined. How different from the Mrs. Oda she knew, collar of her coat turned up smartly, heels clicking off down the road. It was unusual, too, now that Masayo thought of it, for her to be home in the middle of the day.

"I'm afraid I'm a little worn out. . . ."

"I can imagine it's hard to relax with the carpenters coming in and out all the time."

"No, construction stopped two months ago."

She asserted this with a force that took Masayo by surprise.

The weather had just started to get hot when Mrs. Oda had come over to apologize for all the construction that was about to begin. After that a truck was parked outside every day, with workers pounding down the earth, laying down a wooden frame and pouring a cement foundation from which rebar poles jutted out. For some reason, the construction got to that stage and then came to a halt, and the carpenters came no more. Once, at dinner, Tōru had wondered aloud what was going on with the Odas. They built a foundation, his brother Tsutomu replied, so that means they're going to make a house. Not necessarily, Tōru replied. Well, what then? Tsutomu asked. Maybe they just wanted to make that kind of foundation in their garden. Don't be stupid, they just ran out of money, I'll bet.

Listening to her sons' conversation, Masayo had found her-self inclining her head in doubt.

"Now that you mention it," she said now to Mrs. Oda, "it has been quite a while." *Why did you stop construction?* was the question she really wanted to ask but confined herself to a vague nod.

"At first we planned to build a children's room here. . . . ," Mrs. Oda said quietly, as if following something far off in the distance. Her hair, which was getting long, was pulled back simply and held in place with a rubber band; her exposed face looked dry, as if white powder was about to blow off. "My husband invited his parents to move in without saying a word to me."

"So, the children's room will be the old folks'?"

"No, this room will be for his parents; I wasn't happy about that and told him I'm going to live over there."

She crooked a strangely bent finger in the direction of the small patch of black earth remaining to the north of the foundation.

"You're going to add another room there?"

As a small child does, Mrs. Oda bit her lip and fiercely shook her head.

"That's my spot over there. That'll be fine. That's what I told him." It was as if she intended to play house, sitting with knees primly together on a spread-out sheet. Masayo couldn't read her thoughts but could understand the intensity of her words.

"Is that why they stopped construction? Because you said that?"

"My husband called the builder on his own and had him stop."

"He should have just built the room and let the children move in, shouldn't he?" Masayo said lightly, as it wasn't really her affair. She hoped her words cheered Mrs. Oda up.

"My husband isn't the type to do that."

"But he seems so kind."

"He is—to everybody, and that's why things get out of hand." Her tone turned vehement.

"It must be hard for your husband being a good son."

"If it's hard for him, then he should show it. Instead he shirks his responsibility at the worst possible time, and gets involved with some woman."

"He's seeing someone else?" Masayo asked.

"Of all times to do that, this has got to be the worst."

"That's the way men are. When things get tough, they run to another woman. And when things settle down at home, they do the same."

"And what are women supposed to do?"

Masayo was a bit flustered with the woman's sudden question; she sounded like some young, unmarried woman seeking advice.

"Women just suffer."

"But I don't want to."

Looking down, she kicked at the ground just inside the gate over and over with the tip of her sandal. She had on a cardigan and a thick, checked skirt, but the bare feet in her sandals looked cold.

She fell silent, and Masayo found it awkward to say goodbye. "Why don't you come over to my house?" she said. She wouldn't want her to stay too long, but she felt guilty about ignoring this woman who, though never friendly before, had unexpectedly opened up her troubles to her. Masayo had always thought they lived in two different worlds, she and this young housewife. But now that she had revealed the same worries Masayo herself had once experienced, she felt a growing sense of closeness to the woman.

"No, I couldn't do that," Mrs. Oda looked up, face tensed as if she had just woken up.

"I hope you're not hesitating just because we have an old person in the house."

"No, it's not that. I just have something I have to take care of. Forgive me for all this silly talk."

Her face stiffened, making the tiny wrinkles next to her eyes, dotted deeply with foundation, stand out. Her small, regular features made her lusterless skin seem all the more haggard.

"I left the association newsletter in your mailbox," Masayo reminded her, then went out the front gate. In the end, it seemed, *she* was the one ignored.

When she opened the front door, Masayo heard the clang of a lid on a pot. Yoshiko's lacquer chopsticks were lined up neatly on the kitchen table.

"I thought I'd have some lunch," Yoshiko said, turning around to face Masayo. Yoshiko was standing hesitantly in front of the sink.

"Goodness, Grandmother, we just finished eating. Don't you remember?"

"Oh, is that right? I was hungry so I thought we hadn't eaten yet."

"I grilled some smelt. And you said you liked the radish leaf soup I made."

"Now that you mention it . . ." Yoshiko still looked unconvinced. Nevertheless, smiling wanly, she put her chopsticks away in the holder on the table.

"I don't mind your eating if you're hungry. But if you forget that you've eaten, now that's a problem," Masayo hastily added, and felt a chill slowly creep up her spine. She'd heard stories of old people who'd forget they'd eaten and have one meal after another, but this was the first time this had happened to Yoshiko.

"Would you like me to make some *udon* noodles?" Masayo called out to the small figure retreating from the kitchen.

"It might be cold today, after all," Yoshiko murmured to herself. It was hard to tell whether she'd heard or not.

Yoshiko went into the room where they'd just set out the *kotatsu*, and all was silent.

This was no time to be worrying about other families, Masayo decided. She put the askew rice-cooker lid back on properly and sank down in a chair. Her thoughts turned not for the first time to the long days with Yoshiko, stretching out before her.

* * * * *

Somewhere along the line, Yoshiko had stopped her morning routine of opening the shutters as soon as she got up and her bustling out to get the paper. It might have been around the time she complained that the outside shutter was stuck and couldn't get it open. When Masayo pulled at the shutter, it easily slid open.

When Masayo was out shopping and Yoshiko answered the phone, she'd get the message all garbled. Once she reported that a woman had called asking for Yūzo, which sent a fearful premonition through Masayo. When she asked Yoshiko the woman's name, though, it turned out it was one of her son's girlfriends. Masayo told her solicitously that she needn't worry about answering the phone anymore. So now, even when the phone rang, Yoshiko ignored it. This way there'll be no mistakes, Masayo thought, greatly relieved.

And now, on top of that came this business of forgetting that she'd already eaten, which particularly rattled Masayo. When the two of them were alone in the house during the day, any sound from the kitchen made Masayo jumpy. She didn't mind Yoshiko eating as much as she wanted but not to the point where she got sick. To be honest, though, worries over Yoshiko's health were not her main concern. What she really hated were the scenes that awaited her in the kitchen—Yoshiko ladling out rice, turning her back on Masayo to hide the big bowl of rice in her hands. It was like Yoshiko was possessed. The thought even crossed her mind that she was doing it out of spite. But no matter how many times a day Yoshiko ate, she never seemed to get sick.

Masayo complained about this to Yūzo after he came back late, drunk, but he merely nodded.

"That's what they say happens," he replied.

"You're acting like this has nothing to do with you. It's your own mother we're talking about."

"I know, but there's not much you can do about it."

As he invariably did when the conversation touched a nerve,

he took off his glasses and rubbed his eyes with the back of his finger.

"There'll be even more things to worry about as time goes by," Masayo said. "It'll be dangerous to let her go outside alone."

"That's how it gets at this age," Yūzo said.

Without his glasses, his eyes looked small and sunken; he blinked in the light.

"So that's why I'm bringing it up, because it's a problem."

"But this doesn't mean we're about to put her in an old folks home or anything," Yūzo said.

"Well, there's no use talking about things that are out of the question."

But Masayo imagined, flashing by in the distance, the quiet, empty household they'd have if indeed Yoshiko was in a retirement home.

"Things might be better if she had someone her own age to talk with in the neighborhood," Yūzo said.

"The Odas are adding on a new room and his folks are going to live with them. But they had an argument about it and the construction's on hold."

That's my spot—the image of Mrs. Oda pointing at the black earth hit Masayo vividly. She hadn't seen Mrs. Oda since then and wondered how she was.

"She's not a child, so even if the neighbor's parents move in it doesn't mean they'll be friends right away." Yūzo smiled amusedly, as if remembering something.

"Mrs. Oda looked exhausted," Masayo added, looking at her husband, still smiling, who had his glasses back on. "It seems like her husband's gotten involved with some woman, as well."

"Mr. Oda?"

"Right."

"That's a surprise. But I don't think it's anything to worry about. He's not the type to get carried away."

"I wouldn't be so sure. Unlike someone I know, he may not get carried away, but his wife might take it hard."

"That's why I'm saying it won't get to that point."

"And that's why I'm saying we don't know if it will or not."

The phone rang, splitting the night air. Masayo glanced up at the clock on the wall and stood up. The last train of the night had probably just pulled into the station.

"Hi, it's me. It's kind of late so I'm going to stay over at my friend's place."

As she had expected, it was Tōru's cheerful voice. "What do you think you're doing every night? If you missed the last train, take a cab home."

"Do you have any idea how many bottles of bourbon I could buy for the price of a cab ride? Oh, if a guy named Ohira from my club calls tomorrow morning, tell him I've already left for school, OK?"

"I'll tell him, but tomorrow I want you home at a decent hour."

"All right. Were there any calls for me?"

"A Miss Takigawa called this evening."

"Takigawa?"

"I think that's what she said."

"Oh, you know—Miss Takigawa."

"I have no idea who she is."

"The Takigawas who live on the corner."

"Next to the Odas? But it was a young girl on the phone."

"You know Mrs. Takigawa?—old Mrs. Takigawa—what should I call her?—it's her niece. She's attending a pharmacy school and living with them."

"Why do you know her?"

"I run across her sometimes and say hi. What does it matter?"

In the background Masayo could hear a disturbance and then a muffled sound, like someone singing, engulfing Tōru's voice.

"She's a neighbor, remember, so behave yourself."

"Don't be stupid. She just asked me to get some tickets for her to my college's school festival."

"Well, you should have told me that."

"A thousand pardons. Gotta go!"

Tōru's voice and the background noise were cut off.

He certainly takes after you, she was about to say as she turned around, but Yūzo was nowhere to be seen. The light was on in the bathroom, and she could hear water splashing vigorously.

* * * * *

The two, large soy-sauce bottles she'd bought on sale weighed down her supermarket bag, the handles biting into her fingers. As soon as she turned the corner of the main intersection and entered the road leading to the residential area, the air was still, the cold more concentrated. She hadn't adjusted to the change in seasons yet, and each day's steady drop in temperature made her shiver. The fragrant olives were bursting with flowers a few days ago, their scattered yellow petals like sawdust all around the ground; now the trees stood silently, wrapped in dark green. On the tips of the branches of a persimmon tree, jutting above the hedge, the hard-looking, flat fruit was barely tinged red.

A group of boys from the high school beyond the public-housing complex were approaching, boisterously spilling out over the road. They squeezed around a white car parked beside the road, then spread out again. Following close behind them, a small figure appeared suddenly out of the car's shadow. Masayo found the old lady both comical and a bit pathetic as she walked for all she was worth but still was soon outstripped by the fleet feet of the boys. If Yoshiko went out, which she seldom did now, Masayo thought, that's probably how she'd look. She slipped the shopping bag into her other hand and as she did, thought *My God! It can't be! . . . Or can it? . . . Maybe it is . . .* As these thoughts ran through her mind, the little old lady materialized into Yoshiko.

"Grandmother! Grandmother!"

Masayo trotted over, and the figure slowly came to a halt. She hadn't seen Yoshiko outside the home for some time, and she looked one size smaller, somehow.

"What's the matter? Why did you go out alone?"

"There was a telephone call," Yoshiko replied casually, avoiding Masayo's eyes; she wore the same clothes that she had had on when Masayo left her sitting at the *kotatsu*.

"Who called?"

"I'm not sure exactly, but I think it might be someone from the public-housing project."

"What did they say when they called?"

"They said they had our cat, Tama, and I should come get him."

"It must be some mistake, Grandmother. Tama died almost two years ago."

"But they said he answered when they called his name."

The paper bag in Yoshiko's hand rustled as she clutched at it.

"How did this person know about us? What was his name?" Without realizing it, Masayo's voice grew louder.

"They said they were waiting for me to come over."

"But you don't know the name of the person who called. And besides, you're going the opposite direction, away from the public housing."

Yoshiko, expression unchanged, turned around to look in the direction she'd come from.

"Let's go home. You'll catch a cold dressed like that."

Masayo started to walk in order to urge Yoshiko on, who was muttering to herself. "You don't have to answer the telephone," Masayo began, "and if you have something you need to do, just wait until I get back. And never go out by yourself." Yoshiko, walking beside her, was silent. Masayo was surprised at how slowly Yoshiko walked, something she'd never noticed at home. If I hadn't found her, how far would she have gone? Masayo was less upset than uneasy by this thought.

Yoshiko obediently followed her home. They rounded the corner where the Kiuchis' house was, and Yoshiko went inside their own, which wasn't locked. After puttering about in the kitchen for awhile, she retreated to the room where the *kotatsu* was set up.

Masayo was pouring hot water from the thermos into the teapot when she noticed the paper bag on top of the table—the one Yoshiko had been carrying. From a bakery, the bag looked so wrinkled—as if it had been rung out. Inside were nine, square packs of dried bonito shavings.

For the first time in a long while, both Tsutomu and Tōru were home for dinner. As the three of them ate, Masayo told them what had taken place that afternoon, warning them not to let Yoshiko go out alone. Yoshiko herself, as was her habit now, had eaten dinner at 6:00 and retired at 7:00.

"It's all well and good to tell us that," Tōru shot back sharply, "but the two of us aren't at home all that much, so there's not a lot we can do."

"Like you don't skip school and stay home half the time," Tsutomu said, sipping his soup. He sounded as if he didn't want to be put in the same league as his brother.

"That isn't what I mean," Masayo said. "Of course, I'll be keeping an eye on Grandmother. But in case we have a repeat of what happened today, the only thing to do is search for her outside. So when you're coming home from the station, I just want you to keep an eye out for her to make sure she isn't out walking around by herself. I have to go out shopping sometimes, and I can't watch her every single minute."

"So, you're telling us to watch for her when we're walking around," said Tōru.

"Instead of watching the skirts go by, she means," Tsutomu said, pointing with his chopsticks at his brother.

"Why in the world did you cook this? I can't for the life of me understand how anyone can consider dried radish strips edible." Perhaps trying to dodge his brother's remark, Tōru lifted a piece of dried radish from the mound on his dish, stared at it for a moment, then returned it to the bowl.

"Stop it," Masayo scolded. "Such bad manners."

"Oh!" Tōru called out suddenly. "I did see something last night at the station," he continued. "But it wasn't Grandma."

"Don't startle me like that. What did you see?" Masayo asked, lifting a piece of overcooked, burnt carrot tempura to her plate.

"Mr. Oda was there, at the station. At night."

"So what's the big deal?" Tsutomu asked.

"Dummy. He wasn't alone."

"What, there were five Odas?" Tsutomu asked, unsmiling.

"Gimme a break. The person he was with was this total knockout, a Eurasian looking woman. I couldn't believe it."

"Which station was this?" Masayo stopped eating.

"Our station. The second to last train of the night."

"Was he drunk?"

"He might have had something to drink, but he wasn't drunk."

"So what happened?"

"What do *you* think?" Tōru leaned forward across the table; his arm pushed against a plate, which clinked against the glass salad bowl.

"Who cares, anyway?" Tsutomu said, trying to deflate his worked-up brother.

"What happened?" Masayo said at the same moment, irritated, urging her son on.

"They walked up the steps to the overpass, toward the exit on the opposite side from ours. Before I realized what I was doing, I followed and went out the south exit."

"Get a life," Tsutomu muttered, his mouth full of tempura.

Masayo ignored him, urging Tōru to go on.

"The two of them walked down the deserted streets for a while," Tōru related, "then turned around and headed back toward the station. He tried to avoid being seen, but they walked right by without noticing. Mr. Oda suddenly leaped out into the street to flag down a taxi on its way back to the station. After a bit of arguing with the driver, he bundled the girl into the cab and got in himself. The cab drove under the overpass and sped away."

"Anyway, it looked pretty serious. I could understand it happening at Roppongi or Shinjuku or some place, but getting out of the train with another woman at your own station. Do people really do that?"

Tōru was so excited it was hard to believe he was making this up. "I don't want you doing that anymore, following our neighbors around," Masayo admonished him. But the scene he'd described rose up before her in all its gory details and wouldn't go away. At the very time Mr. Oda was doing this, his wife and two children were asleep at home. Or were they? It was just after midnight, so maybe Mrs. Oda was still awake. Masayo remembered that afternoon and what Mrs. Oda told her about her husband. How her bare feet had looked so cold below the warm-looking, checked skirt. Her husband, on the outside, seemed so gentle, which made it even more unbearable to hear Tōru's description of the man's frantic efforts. Masayo couldn't shake the idea that Mrs. Oda was even now sitting atop that concrete foundation, gleaming dimly in the dark.

"You better make sure *you* never do anything that outrageous." Masayo stood up from the dinner table as if to sweep aside the strange mood that had settled on them as the story drew to a close.

"I think you'd better worry more about Tsutomu than me," Tōru said.

Masayo put the kettle on to boil and returned to the table; she glanced over at Tsutomu. He had grown strangely quiet as Tōru's tale reached its climax, as if some memories had surfaced he was trying to protect his mother from. Masayo suddenly felt uneasy.

* * * * *

Gloomy, rainy weather continued off and on for a couple of days, then the sky turned sharply clear and autumnal. The weather report said a typical high-pressure winter system was settling in, so the mornings and evenings would be cold. As if she had been waiting for this, Yoshiko wet her futon.

Masayo had hung the laundry out to dry on the second-floor, clothes-drying platform and was spreading out the rest on the verandah. Just then she noticed Yoshiko attempting to push her futon out the sliding glass window to air it out.

"It's all right, Grandmother. I'll air it out with this one."

As if she hadn't heard, Yoshiko obstinately continued on unsteady feet to step down to the verandah. Fearing she might fall, Masayo walked over quickly. Yoshiko's body was bony as it rubbed against her. Yoshiko persisted in going to the verandah, and Masayo found Yoshiko's slow, wordless movements exasperating. She lightly brushed her aside and grabbed hold of the futon. A damp, stuffy odor hit her.

"Seems like I was sweating while I was sleeping." A small voice followed Masayo as she stepped out into the garden.

Yellow flowers had started to appear on the sycamore. Masayo began to hang the futon on the clothes pole set up between the tree and the wall, when she was struck by doubt. How could such a withered old body produce so much sweat? And there, clearly visible on the futon, was a splotch where Yoshiko had wet her bed. Masayo touched it, wet all the way through.

"What happened, Grandmother? Didn't you know you had to go?" Masayo kept her voice deliberately low as she called out from the verandah. Yoshiko was crouching down, facing away, trying to stuff the rest of her bed covers away in the closet.

"We'll have to air those out as well. And I wonder if the tatami's been soaked."

Masayo kicked off her sandals to step up into the room, laying a hand on the tatami. It was cold and damp.

"I think it's because I had two cups of tea after dinner last night . . . ," Yoshiko murmured, leaning against a pillar. Her body looked as if it were visibly aging.

Hanging out the second futon to dry, Masayo wondered how far downhill Yoshiko had gone. When she was with her, Masayo didn't feel she herself was that much younger. Masayo was struck depressingly by the notion that she was seeing a reflection of herself in a few years. Anxiously, she felt that inevitably and unknowingly she would start acting just like the old woman.

After hanging out the futon, Masayo remembered Yoshiko's nightgown and underwear. If the futon was this bad, Yoshiko's clothes must be a sopping mess. She cringed at the thought of just throwing them in as they were in the washing machine. Rushing into the house again, Masayo heard the bang of a pot lid falling. "Grandmother!" she yelled out, the blood rushing to her head. The morning sunlight seemed dark and dreary.

Near twilight that day, Masayo, who was shopping near the station, decided, though it might be rushing matters, to buy some disposable adult diapers. If Yoshiko began wetting her bed again, she'd have her wear them at night. As she clutched the awkward package and walked homeward, Masayo remembered how, before Tsutomu was born, Yoshiko had used pieces of old *yukata* and Japanese washcloths, diligently sewing them together to make diapers for her grandchild. Masayo told her she didn't have to make so many, but Yoshiko insisted it was good to have a lot for rainy days. She bought even more cloth and sewed on and on. Human beings can't sew their own diapers, I guess, Masayo thought sadly.

Masayo rummaged in her bag for her key and unlocked the front door, only to find Yoshiko standing erectly in the middle of the entrance.

"Did something happen?" Startled, Masayo instinctively hid the diaper package behind her.

"Mrs. Oda was just here."

"Mrs. Oda from across the street?" Masayo asked in disbelief.

"She asked if you were at home. She seemed to be in a hurry about something."

Yoshiko's voice was unusually clear and sharp. From the look of the sandals Masayo had arranged nicely before she left, now scattered about, she deduced that Yoshiko must have opened the door for Mrs. Oda.

"I wonder what she wanted."

"I told her you were out shopping and would be back soon, and she left. She seemed worried, so maybe you should go over and see."

"I think I will," Masayo replied. She set down her purchases at Yoshiko's feet, then thinking better of it, took them into the kitchen. She put the package of diapers on top of the cupboard and retraced her steps. She urged Yoshiko, who was still standing at the entrance, to go inside because of the cold and then went outdoors. Seeing how tense the visit had left Yoshiko, Masayo was convinced that it had indeed been Mrs. Oda who had stopped by. Tōru's story the other day of Mr. Oda and the woman at the station whirled around in her head, along with a vision of Mrs. Oda's dry, powdery face in the middle of the night.

Masayo cut across the narrow road and rang the front bell several times, but there was no answer. The doorknob twisted open, but the inside of the house was so still it didn't seem anyone was about to answer her calls. She leaned inside and called out. Just then she heard a dull sound coming from behind the house. Thinking she'd take a peek at the back, Masayo skirted the concrete foundation in the garden and ran right into a woman. Mrs. Oda was shining a large flashlight despite the fact that it was still light out.

"Mrs. Yasunaga, you came . . ." Mrs. Oda's face was drawn, her hair gathered in a ponytail, her lips shook slightly.

"What's the matter?" Infected by the woman's behavior, Masayo spoke excitedly.

"It's water, water's coming out . . ."

"Water? Where?"

Masayo was just able to shield her eyes from the glare of the bulky flashlight that was thrust at her.

"At this rate, our house is going to sink."

"There's no way it's going to sink," Masayo said. "Why don't you show me where the water's coming out."

The woman grabbed Masayo's hand, and she squeezed back

hard. Masayo could feel her trembling and felt that she herself would soon start shaking too.

"The well is the problem. They're filling it up without telling me. They never tell me anything."

"Just calm down. There's no well in your house."

"But there *was* one, under the kitchen. I had no idea, but my husband and children knew all about it."

Her throat choked, the woman took short, sharp breaths, her lips trembling as if she were about to cry. A ghastly image hit Masayo of an unknown well deep within the woman's body, suddenly gaping open.

"What about the well?" Masayo said in a dry voice, reproving herself for her fears.

"Water's bubbling up out of the well, and the bottom of our house is soaking wet."

"And you were checking that with your flashlight?"

"Everytime I'm in the kitchen, I hear water below me even though I'm not running any."

Masayo's mind filled with the image of dark water underneath the verandah, lapping at the edges, overflowing the foundation. This must have driven the woman to a nervous breakdown. But at least, Masayo thought with relief, they weren't talking about some bloody body collapsed on the ground.

"I'll take a look. Come with me." Masayo pulled her hand free of the woman's grip, grabbed her by the wrist, and led her around the back of the house. The yard was littered with empty wooden boxes strewn about, a rusty old tricycle on top, a kerosene can. "Where is it?" she asked, urging the woman on. Mrs. Oda followed the square stepping-stones that were subsiding into the moist ground, past what must be the kitchen door, and came to a halt. There was a small square hole, a ventilation hole with iron rods inside bored out of the concrete of the foundation.

"Hand that to me."

Mrs. Oda stood a step away, as if afraid to approach something horrific. Masayo took the heavy, dark-green flashlight from her. She squatted down and stuck the bulky cylinder right up to the opening of the vent hole.

All she saw in the light was a still, blank patch of dark soil with a few bits of wood scraps and small pebbles on it.

"There's no water here at all," Masayo shot back roughly. Anger took hold of her for she had steeled herself for something frightful only to be let down.

"Can't you see it? On the left."

The woman's tense voice flared at her from above. "I can't see it at all," Masayo answered and turned the light to the left. A section of the ground glittered back at her.

"Oh, there it is."

"It's coming out, right? The water," Mrs. Oda said excitedly. Masayo thrust a hand out to the cold ground, putting her face right next to the flashlight, right up against the ventilation hole. In one spot, a kind of blind spot, a depression in the dirt, a bit of water was indeed seeping out. She held her breath to avoid the moldy smell, then let it out, lifting her face. The woman was now squatting beside her.

"Why do you think that's well water?"

"A little while ago, I called my husband at work. He said it must be the well."

Perhaps because she'd convinced Masayo that there was water, the woman's voice relaxed slightly.

"I see. . . . Your husband said that?"

Nodding as she spoke, Masayo looked at her. Where in that pale face of hers would she bury the events of the evening Tōru had witnessed?

"I noticed it around noon," Mrs. Oda said, "and every time I take a look more water seems to be coming out." *The water's not swelling up under the floor but inside you*, Masayo wanted to say, but kept her peace.

"It might be leaking from a pipe."

"No, it's bubbling up. Because there was a well here," Mrs. Oda insisted. Masayo lost the desire to argue.

"Shall we stay here for awhile and watch?" Masayo said, surprising herself. She didn't say it because she was really worried or to comfort Mrs. Oda. Squatting on the ground, Masayo felt an inexplicable calm, a quiet flow swelling up deep within her. Mrs. Oda tucked up her skirt behind her knees and nodded her head just like a child.

". . . But you know," Mrs. Oda said, "don't you think it'll take a long time for the water to fill up this whole space and for the house to start floating?"

Head slightly tilted, she put her hand against the wall and pushed as if to check that the house wasn't bobbing already. Still squatting, she looked up at the high eaves.

"He said the well was really deep . . . ," she murmured weakly.

"Why don't we watch it together until morning?" Masayo asked.

And Masayo really did feel that this was a good idea. She could vaguely picture Yoshiko in their far-off house, having her umpteenth lunch. The disposable diapers on top of the cupboard. The phone in the living room ringing, a call from one of Tōru's girlfriends . . .

"What about your children?" Masayo asked, as if suddenly remembering.

"Kōichi's at his after-school lessons, and Mayu's staying over tonight at her cousin's."

They stopped talking. Under the gathering twilight sky, the two women squatted in silence, facing the wall.

"We'd better save the batteries."

Masayo rested the flashlight on the edge of the vent hole and lightly held the light. Mrs. Oda reached out from the side and gently switched it off.

the visitor

The clock in the square in front of the station showed just past 2:00.

Toshie spied the clock tower in the rotary and breathed a sigh of relief. She'd never been to this station before, and now she knew she was at the right exit.

She handed over her ticket and as instructed turned to the left, walking past the taxi stand. She paused for a moment in front of the three yellow pay phones beside a kiosk, decided she'd come the right way, and continued off down the road.

The air here in the suburbs was clear, but the cold felt different from what she was used to. Cold though it was, the clump of uniformed elementary schoolchildren she saw piling off the bus at the terminus had on short pants. Their legs, bare from the thigh down, looked as if they were covered with white powder that you could write in with your fingernail.

Toshie let the children rush off past her toward the station, bus passes swinging from strings, voices shouting to each other. She looked up at the pedestrian overpass. It's too much for you to climb the stairs, her friend had said, so she was to walk along the bus route, next to the tracks, and cross at the first signal. I don't mind the stairs, she'd replied, but decided that she'd better follow the instructions to the letter or she'd get lost. She cut underneath the stairs.

Bikes were so thick alongside the road that their handles were entwined, and she had to walk at a slant to get around them until she reached the traffic signal. Most people used the overpass to cross the street, it appeared, and though she hadn't gotten far from the station she was alone. She waited for the signal to turn, mentally reviewing once more the directions she'd recited over and over since the night before.

There are quicker ways to get here, her friend had laughed, but I'd better tell you the easiest. Ever since your school days, you've been famous for your hopeless sense of direction.

Toshie felt bad about making so many cars stop just for her and hurried as fast as she could across the street.

Continue in the same direction for a while, then walk along a green, chain-link fence of a parking lot, get to the corner, and turn right. There's no raised curb to walk on, but there's a guardrail, she was told, so be sure to keep inside that. As the land-marks went by one after another, Toshie felt relieved. She was glad she hadn't let her friend insist on meeting her at the station, especially with her bad back. I've come this far without the memo in my handbag, she thought, so who needs it? Her spirits rose, and she forgot the tension she'd felt when she got off the train. No reason I can't just walk on down the road as if this were my neighborhood and I'm out shopping . . .

She passed a corner on the left with a bakery and *soba* noodle shop facing each other; passed in front of a real-estate office, its glass door covered with ads; and just about where she passed the sign for a sushi shop, the road gradually entered a more residential area. The bus takes too long, she was told, "and it was too close to take a cab. It's a convenient location, close to the station, and quiet, with very few cars driving by."

Small, one-story, clapboard homes began appearing behind sparse cedar shrubbery, the mortar wall and metal staircase of an apartment building jutted abruptly out into the street, and small homes appeared with low cinder-block walls topped with iron grating. Quite a few cars were driving past, so she knew she still had a ways to walk.

The road gently curved to the right and began sloping down-ward. *Oh!* she said, stopping still: a black car sped right past her, jeering voices spilling out as they went by. She couldn't make out what they yelled, but the words *Old bag!* were clear. Her heart throbbed and she found it hard to breathe. Even after she calmed down though, those words wouldn't leave her. She felt awful, as if she really had suddenly shriveled up into a miserable old woman. Barely constraining the desire to shrink into the ground where she was, Toshie noticed with a start that the guardrail beside her had disappeared. And she couldn't recall hearing about the road sloping downward. I'm lost after all, she thought helplessly, looking around her. All it took was almost being run down by that speeding car and now I won't be able to find her place, she feared.

A young woman appeared at the bottom of the slope, pulling along her bundled-up child. Toshie approached them and took the memo out with the address from her handbag.

" . . . Hmm . . . I know my own, of course, but I haven't paid too much attention to the other neighborhood *machi* names around here." The young mother inclined her head slowly and passed the memo back.

"What *machi* is your house?"

"The public-housing complex is all Sawai *machi*," the woman said bluntly. She looked back down the slope though the view was blocked.

"That's right," Toshie remembered, "she did say something about a public-housing complex in back."

"I wonder what the name of this *machi* is." The woman casually checked out the light pole nearest her. Below an ad pasted on it was the usual address marker: *1-16 Kita-machi.*

"Maybe I've gone too far . . ."

"Aren't there any landmarks you're looking for?"

"She said it's a quiet road with little traffic. A short side road that ends in a cul-de-sac—"

"If you go around this street, you might find it." The woman was being tugged along by her child who, bent over, was pulling at her; she took a couple of steps away.

"Is there a pay phone anywhere around?"

"There's one in front of that apartment building over there," the woman said, barely turning to speak.

"What happened?" the child's high-pitched voice asked. "Is she lost?"

Hearing this, Toshie felt even more depressed.

She walked down the slope a little, finding the phone booth that was in front of an uninviting-looking building. The time for being stubborn was over. She tossed a ten-yen coin into the slot and thought of how she would scold her friend: What a scary neighborhood you live in. I nearly got run over!

Her breathing calmed down and she waited, but the phone rang on and on, rebuffing her expectations. She must be out, Toshie thought. But how can that be? When they talked on the phone yesterday, they decided she'd come over after 2:00. She put the phone down briefly, picked it up again, and this time carefully dropped the coin in the slot: the same monotonous ringing over and over. Thinking she'd hang up after ten rings, she decided to wait for three more. But this was an unlucky number; fourteen, too, was bad—it contained an unlucky four—so she waited for the fifteenth ring. . . . Maybe the phone call didn't go through. No, it went through all right, there just wasn't anyone to answer. She felt helpless, set adrift in a strange land.

Bad things always seem to happen in threes. Last spring, her grandchild came down with chicken pox and ran a fever. Toshie went out shopping and left her purse somewhere, and her daughter-in-law burned her leg while she was cooking. All in the space of two days.

Toshie went out of the phone booth and started back down the way she had come in the direction of the station. It was her own fault she got lost. The only thing to do was retrace her steps until she came to a place she recognized. The box of cakes she'd brought as a present suddenly felt heavy. Up until the corner with the noodle shop and bakery, everything had gone according to directions.

She walked listlessly, annoyed at the wasted time and effort. In place of the guardrail was a simple white stripe painted on the left-hand side of the road for pedestrians to walk behind. This time she made sure to keep behind the line. Her watch showed it was past 2:30. Maybe she was so late her friend had come out to meet her halfway, she mused. Perhaps they would run across each other on the street.

She saw a white building, a dentist's office, that she hadn't noticed the first time. And she remembered the voice on the phone saying that if she went past the Takahashi Dental Clinic she'd come too far and should turn around. As if illuminated by a spotlight, the map in her head suddenly fell into place. She'd been sure she was supposed to turn left at the third corner past that intersection where the noodle shop and bakery were, but what she should have done was turn left at that first intersection. As she looked again at the penciled memo in her hand, her confidence came back and she turned the corner in front of the noodle shop.

There weren't many cars here, she noticed; her spirits buoyed. Taking a hint from the young mother, she checked the address written on an electric pole just below an ad for a pawn shop; the sign said *Moto-machi 3-chōme*, the address she was looking for. The houses, too, on both sides of the street had a more relaxed feeling to them.

The next corner you turn at doesn't really have any landmarks to watch for, her friend had told her, a bit at a loss. But anyway, that's a four-road intersection, too—oh yes! and there's a thin, red pillar with "fire hydrant" written on it, with an ad for *Bath Clean* or something hanging down. And you'll see square traffic mirrors on either side of the road. If you get there, then the rest is no problem.

A group of high school boys in a variety of uniforms trooped out of a side street into what must be that intersection. Coming closer, she found the red pillar—its top like a bud of a flowering fern—with a round sign with the words "fire hydrant." And sure enough, below the sign was a board with *Bath Clean* on it. One side had come loose, dangling at an angle.

She turned the final corner, and everything was suddenly quiet. Far off, small in the distance, a white car was parked by the roadside. Lush, dark-green hedges and cinder-block walls ran along both sides of the road. Not a soul was to be seen. The clear air was cold, like chilled water. It was hard to believe that the group of boys had just passed by. The neighborhood had that special feeling found in older suburban neighborhoods.

The road was an entrance to a short cul-de-sac, which ended shortly toward the right, so the house she was looking for might be the one behind the wall. She wasn't worried about being lost anymore but anxiously wondered what she would do if her friend wasn't at home. She took a few steps forward as if to crush out these fears.

Narrow alleyways separated the houses. The house right next to her had a white nameplate embedded in the wall with the names Kiuchi Masaki & Michiko. A truck was parked at the end of the narrow cul-de-sac and there was a faint sound of construction work. Just beyond the truck, she could make out a low, wooden building frame with the roof already on.

Toshie crossed and stood in front of the black iron gate of the house on the other corner of the cul-de-sac. The gate felt cold to the touch as she pushed it soundlessly open. She stepped up the single step and reached out for the doorbell beside the black front door. A faint metallic sound echoed inside the house. Clothes rustling, footsteps drawing near. The door unlocking with a click, opening, and a face looking out: *Toshie! You're so late, you must have gotten lost after all, didn't you*—

But nothing moved behind the still door. Each time she rang the bell, its sound sank further back into the silence. So she's not home. . . .

Toshie took a couple of steps back to look around the entrance. The same decorative stone blocks that covered the entrance floor ran halfway up the wall outside; above that on the white wall was an expensive-looking ceramic nameplate with just the name Takigawa on it. So this was clearly Shizuko's house. Just as clearly, no one was coming to the door.

A premonition welled up inside her that she couldn't put her finger on, as if she had come face-to-face with something awful. She'd had this feeling before—as if she were standing on one foot, teetering at the edge of a precipice. She listened carefully to the silent house. An uncanny sensation ran up her spine: Shizuko wasn't gone but transformed. Open the door and there would be a large, *Omoto*-potted plant hidden from view in the shadows; a round half light sticking out from up on the wall; a small window with the vine-pattern bars over it. As soon as it was decided no one was at home, these objects would gaze out, even more intently, at the intruder.

"Mrs. Takigawa."

Unable to stand it anymore, Toshie called out hesitantly.

"Shizuko-san, are you at home?" Her voice was halfhearted, as if she were actually addressing the house.

"That's strange. She promised she'd be here. . . ." Once she'd spoken, she found it natural to speak out loud.

"Maybe I should check the garden," she murmured but hesitated to step right into someone else's yard. Instead, she went to peer in over the wall.

On the road again, she looked to both sides and saw a woman pedaling a bicycle approaching from the direction of the station. Shizuko was nowhere in sight. The house across the way, the one with the nameplate that said Kiuchi, stood still and quiet in the afternoon air.

Toshie continued along the wall, topped with the black-iron grating, when the door of the house on the right at the end of the cul-de-sac suddenly banged open, and an old woman, wearing socks but no shoes, headed straight for her.

"Are you the one who's brought Tama back?"

"Huh? . . ."

The old woman's burst of energy brought Toshie to a standstill. The woman's eyes were yellow and cloudy in her small, concave face.

"Didn't you come to bring Tama back?"

"And Tama would be? . . ."

"But you said you would, right?"

The old woman had on a strange outfit, neither trousers nor old-fashioned *monpe*, which sagged in the rear; she pointedly turned her face slightly away, staring fixedly at Toshie from an angle.

"You think I said that?" Toshie asked.

"Did you already forget that you phoned us? You remember—you said a big, tortoiseshell cat had come—"

"No, the phone call I made was to the Takigawas over here, but . . ."

"What? Tama was visiting the Takigawas?"

"No, Mrs. Takigawa doesn't seem to be at home. . . ."

Grandmother! Grandmother! A high-pitched shout came from the open door and a woman, well-past middle age, rushed out.

"You can't do this. I told you it's dangerous for you to go out by yourself. . . . And look at you, Grandmother, with no shoes on."

The woman took hold of the old woman's arm and bowed apologetically to Toshie.

"Maybe I've got the wrong person." The old woman's eyes suddenly grew weak, her face wilted, bobbing helplessly. As if losing any interest in Toshie, the old woman said to the woman who held onto her that she wanted only to go home.

"Is Tama the name of your family cat?" Toshie, calming down, said, in hopes of comforting the woman.

"It died over two years ago. She took good care of it for so long, and I think old people like her get mixed up sometimes."

"That's quite a long while ago, isn't it? . . ."

"I'm terribly sorry to have caused you any trouble," the woman apologized profusely. From the hint of resignation in her voice, this wasn't the first time it had happened. The woman's expression contained a trace of doubt, too, as if she wondered who Toshie could possibly be visiting in their little cul-de-sac.

The woman took the old lady, her dark-red, woolen socks soundlessly padding, back home. So soon after they were gone, Toshie hesitated to go right over again to look in Shizuko's house; she should have mentioned visiting the Takigawas and finding no one home.

Keeping an eye on the house, Toshie went back out to the main road. Those two women were so different looking, their builds so unalike, she decided that they must be mother-in-law and daughter-in-law. Of the two, the one in socks was closer to her own age, a thought that left an unpleasant aftertaste.

The road in front was still nearly deserted with just two little children approaching from the direction opposite from the station, lugging backpacks on their way home. The silence was irritating. This isn't going to help anything, she suddenly thought, upset. Shizuko wouldn't just leave at this hour, and Toshie grew even more anxious. She strode back to the cul-de-sac, not caring now whether anyone was watching or not, grasped the black fence, leaned forward and gazed between the trees into the house.

A line of cheap flowerpots stood in the center of the narrow space separating the house and the wall. The soil in the pots was hard, the moss on top of what was supposed to be bonsai plants was dry and curled up. The plants looked abandoned. On some, dark, withered strings of grass dangled down, plastered to the sides of the pots. Just beyond was a concrete platform for shoes on which a pair of green plastic sandals had been carelessly thrown. The white lace curtain at the glass door facing the small alley was drawn and motionless.

"Mrs. Takigawa!" Toshie's voice grew higher. Unlike her voice at the entrance, with its lingering trace of formality, now facing the house's belly she called out bluntly.

"Shizuko? Are you there? . . . What's going on? . . . Are you taking a nap?"

She called these out, one by one, craning upward, then settling back each time all the while grasping the iron fence. She
stepped back from the fence to look up at the window on the second floor, where the niece attending pharmacy school was staying. Just then she noticed, way back in the alley, a pale woman
clutching a tray, standing, staring at her. Embarrassed, Toshie
nodded slightly in her direction, and the woman nodded back.
She had apparently come out of the house that was under construction, the one opposite the house that the old lady had disappeared into a few moments earlier. The woman stood motionless
beside the truck, continuing to look in Toshie's direction. Toshie
walked toward her and asked, hesitantly, "Do you know if Mrs.
Takigawa is out?"

"Well, I don't really talk to her all that much. . . ."

The woman dangled the rectangular tray at her side. Her skin
was very light colored.

"She'd invited me over, so I find it hard to believe that she's
not in."

"Maybe she's on her way back."

"But it's almost an hour past the time we were supposed to
meet."

Toshie looked at her wristwatch, and the woman glanced at
her own large, mannish one above the sleeve of her sweater.

"It's very strange. . . ." Toshie said.

"*Is* it now?"

Toshie had said this to herself, but the woman took it seriously, as if she herself was being scolded for something she'd said.

"No, I just mean she's not the type to do that sort of thing. . . ."

"I wonder if something's happened?"

A shadow of fear swept through the woman's sharp features,
and Toshie grew anxious. "Has anything out of the ordinary happened recently?" she asked.

"Did you look in the garden? You can get there through
here."

The woman glanced over at the Takigawas' house, clutching

the tray tightly to her side, and motioned with her eyes. She walked quickly over to the gate, which lay in the shadow of the truck.

"We're having some construction done, so watch your step."

Striding over power tools and bundles of building materials, the woman led Toshie to the wall surrounding her own house. A wooden frame jutted out from the entrance to which it was attached, and in the back of the frame sat two carpenters, teacups in hand, looking out at the women. As they cut across the garden, a little bigger than Shizuko's, Toshie caught a glimpse of the living room, which was a mess, as if they were rearranging things.

There was no wall between the house and the Takigawas', just a skimpy line of shoulder-high trees. The woman slipped between the thick green leaves of a Chinese juniper and the bare branches of a second, skinny tree, and went into her neighbor's yard. "Please go ahead," she said, holding the branches back to make it easier to pass through. Right in front was the wall of Shizuko's house.

"You called out her name, I suppose?"

"Several times."

"Well, all you can do now is see for yourself," the woman said encouragingly, standing motionless by the line of trees.

"But I wonder if it's all right to do this? . . ."

Timidly, Toshie began to walk toward the south side of the house, where the scrawny potted plants were placed. Suddenly, from the top of the platform where the sandals were, something jumped down and startled her. A large white cat ran out to the street, languidly turning its head back to look at her.

"How dreadful!"

Was this the cat that old lady was looking for? And her daughter-in-law pretending she didn't know anything about it . . . But, no—their cat was tortoiseshell color. A chipped rice bowl lay below the shoe platform. Toshie looked back for help, but the woman just stood there, silently holding the thin branches as she looked fixedly in Toshie's direction.

"Pardon me," Toshie said in greeting to the house and pressed her face up against the sliding-glass door. The scene inside was vaguely visible through the folds in the lace curtain. As if to mock Toshie's fears about what she would do if she saw Shizuko's body collapsed inside, the room was in austere Japanese style, a dresser and writing desk, nothing else. It looked unused, less like a place where people lived than an artificially constructed set. The sliding *fusuma* inside was half open, and she could see the end of a sofa in the next room, which was carpeted. Her eyes were drawn to a wide rope—a black belt by the look of it—which lay tossed aside on the tatami next to the open *fusuma*.

Leaving no stone unturned, Toshie rapped her knuckles on the door glass; the sound echoed with no response. She straightened up and looked back. The woman had disappeared from the thin trees. So keen on guiding Toshie, she must have felt her job was finished.

Toshie was too short to reach the bay window in the room with the carpeting. Unless she had a key and could open the house, there was nothing more she could do. Shizuko was almost certainly not at home. The niece who lived with her must still be at school. Well, for the time being, Toshie thought, it's enough to know that nothing catastrophic's taken place. Seeing with her own eyes the empty rooms, Toshie was inclined to give up.

She set off around the side of the house, meaning to return to the lot next door but, free from being observed now, she continued along the wall, passed below what must be the kitchen window, and came out into the back of the house. She didn't care now to check whether Shizuko was at home. Despite a guilty conscience, she suddenly felt like making one complete circuit of the property.

The north side of the Takigawas' land was marked by a thick, dark-green hedge. In the narrow space between it and the wall of the house, a chill hung heavily in the air. Toshie squeezed into the corridor, with barely space for one person. The wall was recessed at one point and on the slightly broader ground was a round concrete cover, followed by a square one. Her eyes were drawn to a tall pile, shoved up against the wall.

Approaching closer, she saw on top of a board three huge, unsteady stacks of books, a multivolume set of children's classics. The titles on top—*Ivan the Fool, Chelkash*—gleamed faintly, evidence that they'd only recently been placed outside. There were dozens and dozens of books in the three tall stacks, and Toshie couldn't believe Shizuko could have carried these out all by herself. Next to the books was a light-blue plastic garbage bag. Even from the outside, you could tell what was filling the bag to the bursting point: all kinds of stuffed toy animals—a dog missing an eye, a bear with its stomach ripped open, a filthy grey rabbit. Next to this was a cardboard box filled with a clump of men's black socks. Tossed on top was an old-fashioned, brass table lamp, its petal-shaped cover cracked. None of the items were dusty or had been rained on; they sat, silent and stolid, as if they'd just been placed there. The scent of Shizuko's hands still clung to them— and to the rubber band around the neck of the garbage bag and the decorative vine wrapped around the stem of the lamp.

I'm going home, Toshie suddenly decided. She had no idea where Shizuko was, but it didn't matter anymore. She couldn't figure out why she'd insisted on investigating someone else's house.

"Take care—," she said quietly to nothing in particular, neither the pile of discards nor her absent friend. She walked back past the hedge and the house, the way she had come in.

The house in back, the apartment building, was set back far from the main street, and the hedge continued on in a line to the next house. Holding onto the wall, grunting with the effort, Toshie found herself at the side of Shizuko's house again. Through the leafless trees, she could see the top of the house next door. A person on all fours on the cold-looking ground, head pressed up to the bottom of the wall, was ceaselessly moving back and forth. It took a moment before Toshie realized that the person was the woman who had guided her, apparently checking around the foundation of her own house.

"Thank you very much," Toshie called out, not wanting to leave without saying good-bye.

The woman looked up, startled.

"She doesn't seem to be home after all. Thank you for your help."

"Was everything all right?" the woman asked in a low voice as she approached. Mud clung to her knees and hands, which she made no move to brush off.

"No one was there. Something must have come up that was more important than seeing me."

"I admire people who can do that—break a promise and leave."

The woman had a bit more color in her face than before.

"It must be pretty hard for you with the carpenters wanting tea and snacks all the time," Toshie said.

"Something has gone wrong with this house, but I can't leave it."

The woman slapped her white, muddy palm against the wall a couple of times.

"But you have such a nice house," Toshie said. "I see you're adding an extension."

"But somehow, it feels like we're destroying it. . . ."

As they walked from the garden to the front gate, a high-pitched power tool roared in front of them. The woman suddenly lifted her thin neck and shouted, but her words were drowned out by the noise.

When Toshie left the alley and went out to the road, the woman was still standing there, erect, next to the truck, looking in her direction.

Good-bye. Toshie mouthed the word and headed off toward the station.

It was getting on toward evening, and more people were on the street now—housewives out shopping, students on their way home from school—hard-leather satchels in hand—a young woman pedaling a bicycle. Cars buzzing past them all.

Toshie was sure now she wouldn't run into Shizuko along the way. She had not been out at all, Toshie began to sense, feeling as if the whole day had been spent in deep conversation with her.

She came to the intersection with the red fire hydrant, the one that looked like a flowering fern, and looked back. Where Shizuko's house was, she no longer had any idea.

As with many Japanese novels, Kuroi Senji's *Gunsei* (translated here as *Life in the Cul-de-Sac*) first appeared in serialization, in this case in monthly installments in the literary journal *Gunzō* from August 1981 to February 1984. A single volume containing the twelve installments was published in April 1984 and won that year's coveted Tanizaki Prize for Literature, an award whose other recipients have included Endō Shūsaku (*Silence*), Ōe Kenzaburō (*The Silent Cry*), and Murakami Haruki (*Hardboiled Wonderland and the End of the World*).

Life in the Cul-de-Sac, considered Kuroi's masterpiece, is written in the distinctly Japanese format called *rensaku shōsetsu* (a novel of linked stories). Typically, a *rensaku* is made up of stories linked by theme or characters; while each chapter can be taken as a separate narrative, together the whole exceeds the sum of the parts. In Kuroi's case this loosely structured type of narrative perfectly fits the project he has in mind with *Life in the Cul-de-Sac*, the depiction of one small neighborhood from a number of different perspectives. One of the direct influences for the novel lies in Kuroi's reading of Sherwood Anderson's 1919 classic *Winesburg, Ohio*, a work that draws a portrait of an entire town by relating the stories of one character after another. Kuroi's first attempt at this sort of narrative of a neighborhood was the 1975 novel *Me no Naka no Machi* (The Town within One's Eyes); his second, and more critically acclaimed, is *Life in the Cul-de-Sac*. Unlike Anderson's work, *Life in the Cul-de-Sac* portrays not a whole town but one small corner of it, yet the lives of the four main families depicted in *Life in the Cul-de-Sac* hint at larger social forces at work in Japan.

The twelve chapters of Kuroi's novel depict the lives of four suburban middle-class Japanese families of the early 1980s—the Odas, the Takigawas, the Kiuchis, and the Yasunagas. Western readers should understand that the setting—the cul-de-sac of the English title—is far different from the image of a spacious suburban cul-de-sac in the United States. The homes in Kuroi's novel are in one of the countless, cramped side streets of suburban Tokyo, neat and well cared for yet cheek-by-jowl with the neighbors.

As one of the few outsiders to the narrative comments in the second chapter (as she passes by the cul-de-sac where the four families live and notices the nameplates on their houses), the names are common enough, and the reader is to suppose—quite rightly—that Kuroi has chosen these families not for anything extraordinary, but quite the opposite, for their entirely typical, ordinary lives. Donald Keene writes of Ariyoshi Sawako's best-selling 1972 novel *Kōkotsu no Hito* (The Twilight Years) that it gives one of the most "convincing . . . picture[s] of what daily life is actually like for most people living in Tokyo today." The same is equally true of Kuroi's novel, which updates this view of typical Tokyo life by a decade. Kuroi himself calls *Life in the Cul-de-Sac* the "drama-less drama" of contemporary life.

Each family is given roughly equal billing in the novel, the chapters alternating viewpoints, with the Oda family the focus of chapters one, five, and nine, the Takigawas in three and eight, the Yasunagas in chapters four, seven, and eleven, and the Kiuchis in chapters six and ten. Viewpoints outside these four families appear in chapters two and twelve as passersby and visitors to the cul-de-sac provide a fresh perspective that makes us, as readers, acutely aware of the way the modern novel, including Kuroi's, allows us voyeuristic access into the private lives of others. To use the vernacular of recent literary theory, in this multiple perspective one might see *Life in the Cul-de-Sac* as an entirely "decentered" narrative, one in which there is no one viewpoint, but multiple perspectives, multiple interpretations.

Still, the Oda family, with which the narrative begins, is first among equals. The Odas were the first family to occupy this little neighborhood, the one family that owned all the land that was later parceled out and sold to provide the homes on which the other families live. The Odas are, in essence, the one "old family" that provides a link to the not-so-distant past when the suburbs of Tokyo were still home to larger, extended farming families in houses more spacious than the cramped quarters of the contemporary nuclear families whose household heads commute in crowded trains to white-collar jobs. In their present configuration, the Odas, a thirtysomething husband and wife with two grade-school children, are at the same time most typical of the present-day nuclear family.

The narrative as a whole is also neatly "bookended" with the image of the well underneath the Odas' home. The first appearance is a hint of earlier, happier times before the onset of the fractured, dysfunctional modern family; the second appearance is an ominous sign of impending crisis. Kuroi's well and its water seeping forth in chapter eleven hint at growing disintegration, even potential madness, in the Japanese family.

In its depiction of the fragility of the nuclear family and a pervading sense of anxiety just below the surface of daily life, Kuroi's work has much in common with that of such Japanese novelists as Shōno Junzō, Shimao Toshio, and Furui Yoshikichi. But what makes *Life in the Cul-de-Sac* unique is the way these strains are played out inside the hearts and minds of four families representing four different stages of life: the Kiuchis, young marrieds with no children; the Odas; the Yasunagas, a couple with two college-age sons; and the Takigawas, an older couple close to retirement. Further, Kuroi's characters confront some of the major social issues of the day in Japan, including rising unemployment, the care of the elderly, the crumbling of parental authority, and the practice known as *tanshin funin* of male

Japanese company employees being sent alone to distant posts.

Taken together, Kuroi's twelve stories of these four families highlight two main issues of concern not just in Japan but in all industrialized countries—the loss of community and the changing roles of women. The novel's original title, *Gunsei*, literally "gregariousness" or "flocking" in the sense of animals grouping, is used in an ironic sense since the feeling of bonding or community is precisely what is disappearing. One critic writes that the image projected by the word "gunsei" is that of "people, each one a little nail in the reconstruction of Japan, faintly twinkling, yet tinged with a kind of metal-fatigue."

Instead of the vaunted Japanese "group ethic," *Life in the Cul-de-Sac* depicts a society of disconnected individuals, of monads cut off from meaningful relationships within their family and with those around them. For most of these characters knowledge of their neighbors comes in whispered speculation and in furtive glimpses through the curtains, while within the home husband and wife, parents and children, talk at cross-purposes. This is a new kind of Japanese "floating world," one that depicts, as one critic sees it, "families adrift."

While we have grown used to viewing Japan through the lens of its now decade-old recession, it is important to remember that when *Life in the Cul-de-Sac* was written, in the early 1980s, Japan was swiftly advancing to a position of economic dominance, the peak of which came in the late 1980s. Kuroi's work thus went against the tide of rising optimism of the time, pointing to a sense of dislocation and strain that was only to fully reveal itself a few years later.

Kuroi's touches of the surreal are particularly effective in underscoring the increasingly shifting, unstable reality he saw around him. Experiencing this blurring and shifting of the fabric of the social order—as marriage, relations between generations, and relations with the community all turn sour—is much like the disorientation one feels when stuck between wakefulness and dream, the real and the unreal. Still, though, the characters all cling to what they have; as Mrs. Oda neatly summarizes it near the end of the novel, "Something has gone wrong with this house, but I can't leave it."

We *do* see instances of genuine concern for others, most significantly in the mutual sympathy between women. This shows up markedly in the final two chapters. In "Twilight," one is struck by how Masayo, turning her back on her senile mother-in-law, her diffident husband, and her wayward son, crouches down beside her neighbor, Mrs. Oda, bringing a small share of comfort to this troubled woman. In the final chapter, "The Visitor," the visitor to the neighborhood, Toshie, never does find out what happened to her friend, Mrs. Takigawa, though she ends up feeling she and her friend had spent the afternoon in a profound, though silent, dialogue. In fact, among the generous cast of characters in Kuroi's novel, it is the women who leave the most lasting impression; if there is any ray of light in this fractured, disintegrating tableau, Kuroi hints that it is found in the empathy between the hard-pressed, stressed-out women in this little corner of Japan.

Life in the Cul-de-Sac demands—and richly rewards—the reader's active involvement. The deeper one reads, the more one discovers a compelling story that is fascinating not just for what it says, but for what it does *not*—the spaces between the episodes that each reader is encouraged to fill in with his or her own imagination.

biographical note

Kuroi Senji is the pen name of Osabe Shunjirō, born in Tokyo on May 28, 1932. His father was an esteemed public prosecutor and later justice of the Japanese Supreme Court. In 1944 Kuroi was evacuated from Tokyo to Nagano Prefecture to escape American air raids. He returned to the capital, where he graduated from high school in 1951, and from Tokyo University in 1955, after which he was hired by Fuji Heavy Industries. He worked until 1970, when he quit to become a full-time writer. With the exception of his wartime evacuation, a few childhood years spent in Nagoya, and a four-year stint working in Gunma Prefecture, Kuroi has lived his entire life in the Tokyo area, mainly along the Chūō Line in the western suburbs depicted in *Life in the Cul-de-Sac*. He remains an active novelist and essayist and is one of the leading literary figures in contemporary Japan.

Kuroi's interest in literature was sparked at an early age. In high school he and some classmates produced a coterie magazine, *Hitode*, which they continued to publish after graduation. In 1949 Kuroi entered a writing contest for students sponsored by the magazine *Keisetsu Jidai*, in which he was awarded second prize and saw a short story of his published for the first time. (His first published work, a poem, had appeared the year before.) A great admirer of the early postwar novelist Noma Hiroshi, in his final year in high school Kuroi wrote to Noma to seek his advice about the best choice of a university major for a budding novelist. Noma, a writer with decided left-wing sympathies, encouraged Kuroi to study economics, contending that "Literature's job now is to investigate humanity within the framework of capitalism." Kuroi took this advice to heart, eschewing the law department for the economics department, where he specialized in Marxist economics. Hired after university by Fuji Heavy Industries, Kuroi worked in the truck and automobile manufacturing sector of the company, continuing his active involvement in literature, particularly with the famous literary journal of which Noma had been a founding member, *Shin Nihon Bungaku,* in which Kuroi published on a regular basis. Kuroi's experience as a long-time employee of a major corporation has given him unique insights into the working world in Japan, a fact that distinguishes him from such contemporaries as Ōe Kenzaburō and Ishihara Shintarō, novelists who became full-time writers right out of college. This point is reflected in the titles of some of these early stories: "Aoi Kōjō" (The Blue Factory), "Tsumetai Kōjō" (The Cold Factory), and "Mechanism No. 1" (his first published story in a national literary journal). Critics see these early stories as allegorical and abstract and note the influence of Abe Kōbō on both Kuroi's early style and approach.

Kuroi began to gain national notoriety in the late 1960s, as he adopted a more realistic style to depict the lives of ordinary white-collar workers, albeit a style still laced with touches of black humor and the surreal. His 1968 short story "Ana to Sora" (A Hole and the Sky) was the first of several stories nominated for the Akutagawa Prize, Japan's most prestigious award for new writers. (In the following two years four of his stories were also nominated; though the award eluded Kuroi, he now serves on the award committee for the Akutagawa.) Kuroi's first collection of short fiction, *Jikan* (Time), was published in 1969 and was awarded the Ministry of Education Fine Arts Prize for new writers. Several of the stories in this collection have become modern classics, and though in them Kuroi continues to focus on the workplace—so much so that at least one of these stories has been included in an anthology of stories in the popular "business novel" genre—his work at this time goes beyond this popular entertainment genre to highlight existentialist questions and a pervasive sense of unease that struck at the core of Japan's modern economic "miracle." In one such story, "Seisangyō Shūkan" (Sacred Production Week), Kuroi depicts a character who, to the consternation of his coworkers, throws himself into his work in a manner unimaginable even to the workaholic ethos of the period; in an ending echoing Kuroi's economics background, the character discloses that it had all been a failed experiment to overcome the alienation between work and life, to answer some basic questions about the connection between self, the family, and one's job.

The title story of this first collection, "Jikan," also introduces a motif Kuroi was to develop in his later fiction, namely the ramifications of the May Day demonstration of 1952 (a demonstration in which he himself participated). For the protagonist in "Jikan," now a businessman, the radical past takes on the form of a haunting figure—a mysterious man in an overcoat—who flits in and out of his life.

Kuroi develops this motif further in one of his most celebrated novels, the 1977 *Gogatsu Junreki* (May Tour). The novel, set in the early 1970s, explores the inner world of one company employee whose friend wants him to be a witness at his trial for involvement in the May Day demonstration. Torn between loyalty toward his friend and a desire to hide his own past, the protagonist, through romantic interest in a young woman in the company, finds himself involved in union-organizing activities in his company, to the extent that he himself is accused of disloyalty to his company, and ends up searching for witnesses to support his own case. The novel explores with great insight the constraints of the white-collar working world and the severe limits to personal freedom and expression inherent in the Japanese corporate world. The final scene is particularly poignant, with the protagonist, now a member of the so-called *madogiwazoku* (literally, those who sit by the window), shunned by his colleagues and consigned, in a world of lifetime employment, to continuing to draw a paycheck yet spending each day in absolute boredom and irrelevance.

Kuroi is generally classified as belonging to the Naikō no Sedai (introspective generation) group of writers who came to prominence in the late 1960s and whose members include Furui Yoshikichi, Abe Akira, and Ogawa Kunio. The term "introspective" was originally a negative appellation by a left-wing critic to describe writers who rejected a more openly political stance toward literature in favor of a less intellectual style depicting the inner lives of ordinary Japanese. Quite soon after this term was coined, however, these writers established themselves as among the literary luminaries in Japan, and continue to be among the most prominent and respected novelists working in Japan today. Of all the writers in this group, it is Kuroi who most clearly bridges the gap between the early postwar, politically engaged writers and later generations.

In addition to his fiction, Kuroi is known as one of the finest essayists working today and is much admired for his eye for the small details of everyday life. Among recent works are a collection of stories set in the Musashino region of western Tokyo, a collection of "short short" stories all laced with generous amounts of fantasy and black humor, and a series of autobiographical novels of his youth. In 1995 he won the prestigious Yomiuri Literary Prize for *Kāten Kōru* (Curtain Call). In 2000 he won a Japan Art Academy Award in recognition of his contribution to literature, and in December 2000 he was appointed a member of the Japan Academy of Arts. In January 2001 Kuroi's novel *Hane to Tsubasa* (Feathers and Wings) was awarded the Mainichi Literary Prize.